THE BORDERLING

THE CHRONICLES OF LASHAI | BOOK FOUR

THE KEEPER CHRONICLES
BOOK 1

JULIEN JAMAR

Pisteuo Publications

CONTENTS

DEDICATION

For my Numinous family,
For their unfailing generosity and limitless support of Lashai.
You are all my favorite Keepers.

ONE

THE MOUNTAINS

Collin stood on a wooden platform looking out over a crowd of everyone he'd grown up with. It took him a moment to figure out what was going on. A large post before him had chains and leather thongs hanging at his eyeline. His legs felt watery as reality rushed in. He was going to be whipped.

He squinted into the crowd. The scaffold felt so high up. It didn't look this tall from down below. Collin saw people who shouldn't be there. Sacha and Jacque stood out in the crowd. Both looked worried. Laurelle was there. No. How could she have been there? She couldn't see this. He couldn't let her.

Someone was reading something about him. They droned on about how he was a criminal. How he'd been disrespectful to an officer of the law or something. He couldn't remember the exact phrase. He couldn't hold any words in his head at the moment.

When he dared to look back at the crowd, he made out Elian's face. Cassai had her head buried in his shirt. Good. He didn't want Cassai to watch either. Why wasn't anyone holding Elle?

A moment before Dershom grasped his forearm and led him to the whipping post, he saw Julius. His uncle stood at the very edge of the crowd. He was poised and tense, like he was about to bolt toward the plat-

form. Collin hoped he wouldn't. The last thing he needed today was for his uncle to die trying to spare him.

Before they bound his hands with leather straps, they stripped off his jacket and shirt. Collin shook even more as the cool air whipped around his bare torso. He heard the words 'forty lashes' and bit his lower lip but didn't cry. He refused to cry.

His hands were lifted, secured and he felt stretched out too tight. He couldn't see what was going on, but heard a swishing sound, and the crowd reacted and —crack —

COLLIN SAT up in his bedroll when he heard the scream. It took him a moment before he realized it had come from him. His back ached and his nightshirt was soaked in sweat.

"It's alright, Collin. You're alright," Jacque mumbled.

Collin saw his hand was completely enveloped in Jacque's long fingers. Jacque was a Lightling. He towered head and shoulders above Collin, but was so kind and passive, Collin never felt small next to him.

"Sorry," Collin said.

"No need for that nonsense. I don't need sleep," Jacque said, turning onto his back and draping his long arm over his face.

"Do you think I woke Josie?"

"She'll be in shortly if you did. It's fine. We all know why. It's no big deal."

Collin pressed his forehead hard against his knees, wishing he could press from his brain the images that woke him at least three times a night. "Thanks for coming with us, Jacque. I'm not sure I'd have gotten this far without you. I'm going to get some air and check on Josie."

Jacque uncovered his face long enough to give his friend a concerned look. "Do you want me to come?"

"No, get some sleep. It may be the only sleep you get tonight."

"Right. Okay. Call out if you need anything, though."

"Yeah, I will." Collin crawled out of the tent and immediately returned for his fleece-lined coat.

Elian had given it to him as a parting gift when he left Lashai to take Josie to the mountains. Collin grinned. Cassai and Elian were now rulers of Lashai. Collin could already see differences in the landscape as Lashai grew accustomed to having a Namarielle on the throne. Grass sprouted in patches of light in the Forest of Fondair. Trees that they thought had died years ago were budding. Saplings pushed through the dirt. He thought of his growing-up years in Plahn and felt hunger pangs at the memory.

He pulled the jacket tight around him. It was too big, Elian was enormous, but Collin was glad of the extra bulk on nights like this. He walked the few steps to Josie's tent. When he pulled the flap back a few inches and peaked in, he saw Josie curled up asleep. Her blonde hair had scattered around her head like a halo. Collin's other companion, Sophie, sat cross-legged on the tent's floor surrounded by blankets. Her bow was in one hand and an arrow tailed with black feathers in the other. Sophie was Kiatri, as was Josie, but the similarities ended there.

Kiatri were known for two things in Lashai: they lived hundreds of years longer than normal mortals, and they were peaceful. It had been a rare exception when they joined the cause against the Fontre and helped the Lashain armies take back the throne of Lashai.

Rarer still was Sophie, a Kiatri who was the fiercest fighter Collin had ever met, except for her uncle, Hollis. Unlike the rest of their kin, who cringed at the thought of fighting, Hollis and Sophie came alive during battles.

"Oh, it's you. Keep it down a bit, won't you?" Sophie grumbled.

"Sorry Soph. She's still okay?"

"She's fine, but really restless. She keeps murmuring

Devilan's name over and over and sobbing in her sleep. It's sad, actually." Sophie pulled her long black hair over one shoulder and laid her bow beside her. "I'm tired. I can't sleep at this elevation."

"We'll be in the mountains by tomorrow night. Hopefully, being home will help."

"The mountains aren't home."

"Surely there's someone or something there you miss."

"I miss Elian and Cassai. I miss Uncle Hollis. They're my home."

Sophie had volunteered to go with Collin to return Josie to the mountains, but Collin never understood why. He suspected guilt played a role in Sophie's sudden, helpful mood. After all, it was she who shot Josie's fiancé, Lord Devilan, assuring his death at the end of the Battle for the Great Castle.

Collin sincerely hoped Josie never found out whose arrow had killed Devilan. That day would be an unhappy one. But they were almost at the mountains. They were almost in the clear.

"Are you cold?" Sophie's question pulled him back to the present.

"I'm fine. The cold air clears my head."

Sophie nodded her understanding. "I heard you cry out. Another dream?"

Collin shuddered and nodded. "The Fontre Draught is evil stuff."

He didn't like to think about the night he almost died at the hands of Devilan's stepfather, the High King, Ffastian. When torturing Collin didn't get the results the King wanted, he gave Collin an evil Fontre medicine which would make him relive every horror in his life until it left him dead. Elian had arrived with an antidote just in time, and Collin hadn't died. He was grateful that, after taking the Draught, the only permanent damage was terrible dreams and four lashes across his back that refused to heal.

"Sorry, Collin."

He shrugged. "It's nothing. Goodnight." He dropped the flap again, to hopefully let Sophie get some rest.

"Goodnight," he heard through the heavy canvas.

He walked a short distance to the Lesser Kai and watched the water rushing along in the moonlight. He wondered if it had always flowed this well, or only since a Namarielle reigned in Lashai once more. He noticed the moon was almost full; it probably would be by tomorrow night. They would pick up the pace tomorrow. He would carry Josie if necessary, to ensure they didn't spend the full moon out in the open.

He ran his fingers through his curly hair and his mind flashed to a wooden platform, a whipping post and the Koninjka named Dershom pulling out his whip. A searing line of pain lit up his back and he ground his teeth together. He wished he was back in the North Country instead of in the mountains. Surely the Lightling's brilliant healers would have something to heal the stripes. They'd done it once before.

"Collin?" Jacque was beside him. Collin hadn't even heard him approach.

"I'm coming back in. I'm trying to stop thinking about…everything."

Jacque rested his elbow lightly on Collin's shoulder. "Don't worry, Armrest. Surely it'll wear off."

Collin took a stuttering breath and the frigid air burned his throat. "I'm sure you're right. Let's get out of the wind. I'm freezing."

COLLIN WOKE the next morning cold and feeling like he'd spent all night wrestling a mountain lion. Jacque's hand hovered near his, as though at some point after he went back to bed his friend had to coax him out of another nightmare.

Sophie's eyebrows rose as he approached. "You look great," she said dryly when he lowered himself slowly to the ground at the fire she'd built.

"Shut up," he grumbled. He sat on the frozen ground and held out his hands to the radiant heat of the fire.

"That's not nice. Maybe next time I'll let you wake to a cold fire ring and nothing to eat."

"There's nothing to eat now," Collin said.

"If you'd leave me alone and let me cook something, there would be."

"How weird is it that we have enough food to take this trek?"

"I know. Before the Fontre raided my village, we were down to one meal per day, and that was plums and goat cheese." Sophie's eyes had gone deep and distant.

Collin nodded. "Same in the Borderlands. We were eating a few boiled greens and some potatoes we'd managed to hide from the Fontre. The only reason we ever had anything was because Elian and Cassai had an unregistered garden, and they gave away as much as they could."

Sophie smiled as she poked the fire. "Crazy. Even before they were king and queen, they were taking care of their people."

Collin nodded again and rubbed his cold hands.

"Good morning." Josie's voice sounded tired and thin, as ragged as her hair and clothes had grown on this journey, Collin thought.

"Good morning, Jo. Come warm up a bit. Sophie says she's making breakfast, but no evidence so far."

Sophie glared and started breaking eggs into a skillet. She gave each egg an extra forceful crack. Collin wondered if she was envisioning his head cracking each time. "I'm making breakfast for Josie and me. Collin can starve."

Josie smiled and sat cross-legged next to Collin. She hugged herself and Collin pulled off his jacket to give her.

"No thank you, I'm alright. Getting warmer now that I'm near the fire." Collin ignored her protest and wrapped the jacket across her shoulders.

"I get breakfast though, don't I, Soph? Why should I suffer for Collin's sins?" Jacque had emerged, his shock of red hair sticking up in odd directions. The beard he'd started growing during the war for Lashai was filling in.

"You may eat, as long as you don't annoy me."

"I'll be a model citizen. I promise. What's that you're... er...cooking?"

The eggs looked brownish and rubbery.

"Ugh! They've burnt again. I wish Sacha was here," Sophie grumbled.

"Here, allow me." Jacque took the spatula and scraped the ruined eggs off the bottom of the pan. The camp smelled of burnt eggs now, but everyone ate without a word of complaint. There were also rolls which had been bagged up for them, but they'd grown increasingly stale since they'd left over two weeks ago. Collin soaked his in weak coffee to soften it enough to bite.

"That was great, Soph. Thanks for letting me have some," Collin said. "We should break camp and get moving. I want to reach the mountains before nightfall. This isn't a good night to be out in the open."

They all pitched in with packing for the daily hike. They'd gotten good at this, Collin thought, as he pulled up the stakes he'd driven into the ground for the tent's ropes. On the first two or three days they'd wasted lots of time trying to figure out who'd already done what and what still needed doing. He assigned the tasks after that, and things went smoother. Initially it felt strange when he gave orders and they all simply obeyed, but he'd gradually grown accustomed to the leadership role they assigned him.

He'd also realized he was used to strong, hardy girls traveling with them. Sophie could lift and pull and haul as well as he or Jacque. Josie had been locked up in a room in the Great Castle for so many years with practically no physical activity except a daily walk with her guard. It took him a few more days to find ways for her to help break camp.

Today, two weeks into the trek, she hauled a bucket of water from the Lesser Kai to douse the fire and she and Sophie folded up the blankets and rolled tents up tightly so they could move.

"What's special about this night as opposed to others when we've been stuck out in the open?" Jacque asked quietly when the girls were out of earshot.

"The moon'll be full tonight. I don't want to encounter a pack of werewolves who haven't tasted human blood in over a month."

"Zeno. I never even thought about werewolves out here. I thought they were a myth." Jacque shivered.

"They're real. Elian and Cassai had lots of trouble with them when they were going through the Forest of Fondair last time. Even in human form they're pretty formidable."

"Just when you think two people can't be any more interesting, you learn they've fought off werewolves." Jacque shook his head and finished folding the last of the tent canvas.

They set out, the three former soldiers carrying the majority of the packs and bedrolls. Josie insisted on taking a backpack from the first day, and Collin had let her increase the weight gradually. He couldn't help feeling that Devilan was watching him even now and disapproving of him making Josie's life difficult in any way.

"How are you today, Jo?" Collin asked in a quiet undertone.

Josie smiled her usual smile and shrugged her pack up on her shoulders. "Devilan's gone. I'm not sure I'll ever have a good day again."

"You will," Collin said. He wondered if he was telling the truth. He couldn't separate the pain of loss from his days either. Maybe it was permanent. Maybe he'd always see his little sister,

Anaya bleeding out on the floor, her throat slit by Devilan's sword, or his Uncle Julius' best friend Phineas' lifeless eyes staring up after Ffastian ordered him killed. "I think... I think it gets better. When I lost my parents, I managed easier than I did after...Naya."

"Who's Naya?" Josie asked. She'd told him stories from her past many times in the previous weeks, but he'd never offered much information about his.

"My little sister. She was...she died right before the war started." Collin bit his lip, praying she wouldn't ask for details. Devilan had slit Anaya's throat in front of him. It was the last blow needed to push the Keepers into starting the war.

"I'm so sorry. She must have been young."

"She was. Not to worry, though, I'm sure she's in a good place now. She's with my parents in Havilah and I'm still here dealing with all this, so..." Collin waved his hand at the dark forest and river, as if they'd done him some personal offense.

But Josie understood. Josie always understood. He was discovering through his friendship with her that not all strength was physical. Josie's emotional and mental fortitude could stand up to any blighter who thought they were tough.

She touched his arm and didn't stop for a while. "I know Devilan killed her, Collin. It's alright. You needn't shield me from the truth. I know what he was."

A muscle twitched in Collin's jaw. "Of course you do. I scream about it in my sleep, don't I?"

Her hand moved down to grasp his fingers. "Never mind. Don't let it consume you. If you do Ffastian wins even though he lost. We can't let him do that."

He squeezed her soft, cool hand. "You're right about too much stuff, you know? It's annoying."

"Sorry. It's a gift, or a curse. It depends on your perspective." She smiled.

"Curse," he assured her.

"What are you two on about? I thought we were in a hurry," Jacque said, dropping back to walk on Collin's other side. "Pick up the pace, Armrest, or we may yet be werewolf food."

"Why do you call him Armrest?" Josie asked.

"Because he's just right for this." Jacque rested his elbow on Collin's shoulder, a gesture Collin had grown accustomed to in the months he'd known Jacque.

They walked in silence for a long while, Sophie in front keeping watch with her bow and arrow ready, and the other three holding onto each other. The sun had begun its early descent behind the mountains when they crossed the shallowest part of the Lesser Kai.

"Wow, that wall is something, isn't it?" Jacque said, pointing out the stone and mortar wall that looked like it had been built very quickly and very poorly.

Sophie's face was a mask. "They built it after the Raid. None of the great masons from the Old Times were available."

"None survived the Raid?" Josie asked.

Sophie rolled her eyes. "None would leave the Troikord. They left us to our own devices because they were too weak and pathetic to venture out. The only ones who came and helped were the Questers from Mount Korin, and they only leave the Kerke on rare occasions."

Collin didn't know much about the Questers except for AJ, Alex and Lukkas. He remembered Cassai singing him and his sister to sleep after their parents died with an old ballad about a dragon and a warrior named Kiatri. She said it was a legend that probably held elements of truth.

"Are the Questers craftsmen?" Jacque asked. They had known Alex and AJ particularly well, but they'd never seen their skills beyond fighting.

"The Questers are everything. Lukkas trains them in all sorts of boring things," Sophie said.

"You're in the line of Questers, aren't you? Did you ever consider going to the Kerke for tryouts?" Josie asked her.

"No, that was Uncle Hollis, who was, in my adopted mother's opinion, the biggest letdown in a thousand generations of Kiatri. Besides, I was a girl. How could I aspire to such glory? I was much better suited to needlework and playing the pianoforte."

Jacque snorted. "Sorry. I meant that to not come out. I thought for a moment you said you were a girl."

"Shut up, Lightling. Or I'll hit you in places that will make you wish you were a girl every time you try to walk for the next week."

Collin couldn't tell if Sophie was joking but thought it best to change the subject. "So, when we get to the gate, do they let us in? Or do we have to check in with someone?"

"They'll sniff and mumble and eventually let us in. Then the Upper Gatesman will call us into his ancient office where we'll have to account for our presence, no doubt. Which is stupid, considering they know exactly where we've been and what we've been doing. Kiatri have so many years on their hands, the higher ups use them to think up more idiotic protocols. Time is for wasting, and they're experts at it."

"Geez," Jacque muttered. "From your description alone I can tell I'm going to love it here."

"You'll hate it. It's the most boring land on the planet."

Josie was so quiet; Collin didn't think about the effect this conversation would have on her until he noticed she'd gone white. Even her lips drained of color and she stared at the wall and gate looking like she was making a great effort not to cry.

"Are you okay, Jo?"

"Oh yes, fine," she said in a small voice. "It's ...when I was here last...when I saw the streets of Dulon for the last time it was...after..."

"Good lord, why don't I ever shut up?" Sophie moaned. "I'm so sorry, Josie."

"I'm alright. Let's get it over with, shall we?"

"Yes! Let the snoring begin." Sophie marched up to the gate and rang the bell, then glared until the small window off to the side opened.

"By the dragon! Sophie? What on earth, girl?" The under-gatesman stared at Sophie like she was an apparition.

"Hello, Guvna. Sorry I forgot to leave a note. I joined the Lashaian Army. We killed a load of Fontre. A lot of us got killed for our trouble as well. We won. There. Now you're all caught up."

But the man she called Guvna didn't seem to hear her words, he was looking up and down her as though drinking her in, and tears poured from his eyes. "My dear, dear girl! I'm so glad you're home!"

TWO

THE TRADE

Collin and his companions stared at Sophie as they heard the heavy gates scrape against the cobblestones on the other side of the wall.

"Um...anything you'd like to tell us, Soph? Who is that man?" Collin asked.

Sophie looked stricken at Guvna's greeting and didn't answer immediately. "I was - I mean, he and his wife took me in as a baby because, well, all my family was killed or gone."

"Really? You never talk about the family who adopted you. Were they cruel to you?" Jacque asked. It seemed too personal a question, but they hadn't had the opportunity to dig into Sophie's stories, and Collin wondered if they'd ever be allowed to again.

"No, of course not. The Kiatri are nothing if not extremely nice." She said the word 'nice' like it was an unforgivable attribute.

The gate opened and Guvna reappeared. He looked at the group again and then gasped. "No, it can't be. Josie?"

Josie flushed and ran to him. "Guvna! How wonderful you look!" she cried as he threw his arms around her.

"Bless my soul, how on earth is this miracle possible? Come in all of you, please. My goodness." Guvna was a blubbering mess as he led them through the gate and closed it behind them.

Sophie approached him when he turned back toward them and he wrapped her in a hug that reminded Collin so much of Julius' treatment of him that it made his chest hurt, missing his uncle.

"I never thought I'd see you again."

"Sorry," Sophie mumbled into his shoulder.

"Not at all, dear girl. I'm so glad you're alright. Let's go speak with the Chief of Gates. He'll be out of his mind with excitement to see you all and to get word from the Inner Kingdom. You say you beat those blaggard Fontre?" As he spoke, he walked them toward a large building surrounded by dismal-looking houses on either side.

"Yes, sir. That is, we restored the Namarielle to the throne. We've got most of the Fontre out of the Inner Kingdom," Collin answered as Sophie had gone quiet. "Alex and Lukkas are returning with a group of survivors, but they're still combing the kingdom to find them all. We wanted to get Josie back to Dulon and settled as quickly as possible."

"Alex and Lukkas? Wonderful news! What of the rest? What is AJ up to?" The group shared a miserable look and Guvna nodded as if he understood. "Of course. Not all survive in a war. We know that. It's alright. Here we are. Let's get in out of the cold. I'll announce you to the Chief of Gates and we'll go from there. Did...did your Uncle Hollis survive?"

Sophie gave her adopted father a smile. "He did. He's got duties at the Great Castle in Lashai."

Guvna nodded. "I'm glad you two were able to reconnect. I truly am, my girl."

"Thank you. I'm sorry I took off. I don't know what I was thinking."

"No need for apologies, dear girl. I'm so happy to see you alive and well. Gretchen will be overjoyed."

"I would love to see her."

Collin saw a side of Sophie he'd never encountered. Grumble as she did about the Kiatri, she looked lighter and happier than he'd ever seen her. It was a nice change, he thought.

They had entered a spacious hall with two desks situated on each side. At one, a woman sat scribbling on a document. She looked up and smiled at the newcomers, then went back to her scribbling. A man sat at the other. He rose and his mouth split into a wide smile as he circled his desk and stuck out a hand to Collin.

Collin looked up at the tall, skinny man and offered his hand as well. "Welcome to all of you!" The man pumped Collin's hand cheerfully and Collin couldn't help but wonder about his age. He looked no older than Collin, but for a Kiatri, a people who lived hundreds of years, he might have been two hundred years old.

"Foster," said Guvna, addressing the greeter. "We wish to see his lordship."

Foster smiled and nodded. "Of course. I will get you in to see him...Josie? By the dragon! It can't be Josie and Sophie?" he yelped.

Guvna grinned. "It is indeed."

Foster embraced the girls in his long arms. Josie and Sophie must have both liked him, because Sophie laughed when he hugged her.

"Hello, Foster. I see you've had a promotion," she said.

"I have," The main straightened himself for her inspection. "I'm under-secretary to the under-gatesman and official head of services in Dulon."

Both girls smiled. "How wonderful! I think you were a chimney-sweep when I was taken." Josie giggled.

"Ugh! You have to remind me of those days? So much soot. I'm still not sure I've scrubbed it out of my fingernails."

"Foster," Guvna cleared his throat.

"Right you are, sir. Sorry. It's been such a long time." Foster grinned at the girls and pulled away. His footfalls echoed off the chipped marble floors. He knocked on a large red door with a golden nameplate on it which read: Chief of Gates. "Your lordship? You have some visitors I believe you'll be very happy to see."

"Ah, let them in then, there's a good lad. Weaver knows I could use some good news for a change. No, no need to shut the door if you're only bringing in visitors." The voice within sounded frazzled. Collin wasn't sure whether this was from the announcement of uninvited guests or dealing with Foster's energy.

Foster bolted back to the group. "He'll see you. I mean, obviously. You could hear him, I'm sure."

Sophie rolled her eyes and mouthed the words, "What did I tell you?" to Collin.

"Thank you, Foster," Collin said, ignoring Sophie.

"My pleasure, indeed. An absolute delight."

As they entered the high doorway, Collin saw a short man dressed in a purple suit standing behind his large, highly polished desk. The Kiatri only showed signs of age after several centuries. This elderly Kiatri's back curved, his fingers clutched a cane, and the wrinkles that creased his face and forehead had Collin guessing in the 900s.

"What the devil?" the old man yelped when he saw Jacque. "What is this now, Foster? You've brought another one to see me? Haven't I suffered enough humiliation?"

"No, sir. No. He's a friendly one, sir. At least I believed him to be. You know, I never asked him. He came with Josie though," Foster stammered, poking his head in the door.

"Never mind, boy. Come in all of you and shut the door, young man." The man jabbed a crooked finger toward Collin.

They all filed in and Collin closed the door as requested. The Chief of Gate's reaction to Jacque left Collin ill at ease.

"Sophie, Josie, how very good to see you both alive and well," the man muttered, waving his hand at the girls as he'd swat away a fly. "Of course, we were worried. Certainly, we were. Lucky thing for you though. Good timing, I suppose."

"Lucky?" Collin interrupted. "Are you sure that's the word for...?"

"Yes, lucky is the word. What did you think I meant, boy?" wheezed the old gatekeeper, hobbling toward them. He clutched a gnarled, wooden cane that looked like it had been taken directly from an ancient tree and polished as it was. It clicked on the marble floor as he approached. "Do you think I don't know what words I mean to use? You've escaped being enslaved, at least for the time being, and I'd call that lucky."

"Enslaved? I thought the Fontre let everyone go." Sophie frowned at the old man with deep distrust.

"Not the Fontre, girl. Our other problem. A new one. Always new problems. Do I get support? Do I get help from the Troikord? No. They sit behind their massive wall and leave us all out here to hang. What do they care?"

Collin stepped forward. Guvna hadn't come with them into the office and Collin wished he had. He'd felt responsible, like the leader of their group, when he rose that morning, but felt more boyish the longer the Chief of Gates glared. "New problem? What's the new problem?"

"The new problem is, people think they're wealthy enough they shouldn't have to work if they don't like it. They want others to do their mopping, sweeping and cooking. Too good for it, they say. Well, I've been doing my own mopping for centuries now, and nobody ever gave me a hand!"

"Your wife and servants do your mopping," Sophie said,

crossing her arms over her chest. "What on earth are you talking about?"

"Don't you take that tone with me, young lady. I know perfectly well my wife can mop! Who do you think you are, coming here and speaking to me of mopping? But we've solved the problem and that's that. Next time, I'll send you in the shipment. That'll sort out your attitude." The man then turned purple as his shirt and he waved his walking stick at Sophie. "I've fixed the problem. I've appeased the wealthy, entitled snots."

"We're so sorry, Chief. Please, don't mind our harshness. We've all been traveling for days and feel quite fatigued. It's made us forget ourselves. Please make yourself comfortable. Tell us all about it. Can we help?" Josie's calm voice smoothed out some of the wrinkles on the man's forehead.

He slumped over with a sigh and his cane clacked all the way back to his chair. As he sank into it, the rest also took seats around the desk. There weren't enough chairs, so Collin stood beside Josie's chair, feeling protective. This was hardly the greeting he felt Josie deserved, coming back after nearly twenty years.

"I don't know if you can help, Josie dear. I don't know if anyone can."

"What seems to be the trouble?"

"The trouble is, we're easy targets, and the Lightlings don't want to put up a fight. They will, mind you. They will fight if they have to, but they don't want to. And we fit into their plans perfectly. We don't fight them."

"The Lightlings attacked you?" Jacque asked, appalled.

"Not attacks, exactly. Demands. Their slave trade has dried up with – well, with that Namarielle girl taking over things. What do you think? They're going to launder their own clothes all of a sudden?"

"Namarielle girl?" Collin repeated. "What in the name of-?"

"They threatened all sorts of things, of course. But there were also rewards for good behavior. This." He patted a crimson bag on the desk with the crest of a jet-black bird embroidered on it.

"Money? They paid you for people?" Understanding dawned on Collin.

"That's Senator Byrd's crest," Jacque said darkly. "I know what happened. They came. They wanted you to turn people over to them. They could hurt you or help you. I know how he works."

"We chose help, of course," whimpered the Chief. "We're still reeling from the visit of the Fontre."

"They left everyone here," Sophie reminded him.

"Doesn't mean it didn't affect us." The Chief sniffed, clearly offended that Sophie would doubt his pain.

"So, you sold them your people and, what? They'll never come back?" Sophie demanded.

"Not exactly. Only they've got this major event every five years. It's mostly fun and games, but there's a sizable auction at the end, for which they need extra

malderones."

Collin's throat tightened at the Lightling word for slaves. "You're giving them people every five years?"

"Only fifty men and women for three decade's work, and then they'll be released. Free citizens of the mountains once more."

"Thirty years?" yelped Sophie.

"What is thirty years to us?" The Chief wasn't asking anyone. His gaze had wandered away toward a portrait on the wall. Collin turned and saw the painting was of a knight battling a dragon.

"Chief, how can you do that? You know what we've suffered at the hands of the Fontre. Now you'll sell us off to the Lightlings?" Sophie demanded.

"Not you, my dear girl. You'll certainly be exempt, and Josie. There was a lottery. Totally impartial. You've no idea what I've gone through. What strain I've suffered at the hands of these wretches. Always with trouble in this city, and the surrounding cities. Everything falls to me. I'm blamed for it all, don't you see? I'm never the good guy. Even when I spare them."

"Spare them? You sold them," Sophie growled. Collin saw her fingers twitch and wondered if she was thinking of the quiver of arrows on her back.

"Thank you for welcoming us into Dulon. I know you've had your share of troubles, sir. I'm sorry about that. Truly." Collin reached a hand toward Sophie, hoping to de-escalate whatever she was planning.

"They left me no choice, my boy, I swear to you. No choice. More pain or ... or this." He grimaced at the bag of coins. "There is one more thing, poor Josie."

Josie looked paler than usual. "What is it, sir?"

The Chief looked at the money bag rather than meet her devastated eyes. "Y...your sister, Miriam, was sold in the lot."

Josie's hand went to her mouth. "No," she whispered.

"Jo." Collin squeezed her shoulder. "Jo, it'll be alright."

"It's only thirty years, my dear," muttered the Chief, getting quieter with each word, as if even he realized what a ludicrous statement that was.

"We'll find her, Jo. I promise you. I'll find her in the north and bring her back to you." Collin made this vow as Josie rose and pressed her face against his chest. Her entire body shook with sobs. Collin rubbed her back. "It's okay. I'm so sorry."

Sophie looked at Collin, doubt etched on every inch of her face. Collin shook his head, hoping she wouldn't say what she was thinking.

"Let's get you home to your family, Jo. What's left of it." Sophie spat this comment at the Chief. But he'd buried his face in his ancient hands and didn't make another motion to anyone as they left his office.

~

As THEY WALKED through the streets, following Josie's lead down many winding passages lined with once cheerful cobb houses, Sophie grabbed Collin's arm and pulled him away from the group.

"What the devil are you playing at, Collin? You can't promise her something like that because she's crying. She believes in you, idiot. You make some brave, heroic, stupid statement to make her feel better, but she thinks you are really going to bring her sister back." Sophie's voice was a low hiss that made Collin's blood cold.

"It wasn't trying to make her feel better. I mean to look for Miriam. I'm going to try and bring her back."

Sophie shook her head and shot Collin a look that shut him up. "Then you're dimwitted as a door knocker. Even if you manage to find one girl in the giant land of the North Country, how can you possibly hope to free her and bring her home? Tell Josie you can't do it. Tell her right now before hope truly sets in and you break her heart beyond repair. She's been through enough."

Collin frowned. "I will find her."

"I will break your arm if you say that again." Sophie gripped his arm hard. Collin felt that if his statement was borne of some ill-placed burst of heroism, Sophie's promise was solid as Mount Korin.

He pulled his arm away. "If I don't make good, I'll let you. I'll break it myself."

"What is wrong with you?" she demanded. The anguish he saw in her eyes softened his response.

"I will do everything in my power as a soldier and a...a

human being, to bring Josie's sister back to her. I promise you, Sophie. It's no idle vow." The gravity in his voice sounded strange to him. He had grown in the last few months in ways he hadn't begun to admit to himself, much less show others.

Sophie's eyes filled with something he'd never seen in them before: respect. "Alright, Collin. We'll see what all your powers can do. But if you can't –"

"You'll break me. I understand."

Sophie shook her head. "I'll help you. If you get in over your head, let me know. I'll help you if I can."

THREE
THE NORTH COUNTRY

The journey back was quicker. The three recent soldiers felt their conditioning as they moved.

They had stayed a few weeks in the Inner Kingdom with Elian and Cassai to give a report on their visit with the Kiatri and rest before they left for school.

Both Elian and Cassai were deeply troubled about the dealings of the North, and Elian spent much of their visit in quiet discussion with Hollis and Cassai. Collin thought they were planning a resolution, but they didn't share their thoughts with him.

Collin grew restless as the time drew nearer for them to leave again. Sophie left ahead of them because she couldn't sit still any longer. Sacha offered to accompany her since he'd secured a job in the kitchen at the Elythium and he wanted an early start. Sophie asked Collin to see her off.

"I wish you would wait with us," Collin told her at the North Gate. "It's only a couple more weeks."

Sophie smiled up at the castle. "All I wanted was to get back here, now all I want to do is go. What do you think's wrong with me?"

Collin shrugged. "I don't think you want an answer to that."

Sacha grinned and chucked him on the shoulder. "We'll see you there, mate."

Jacque, Collin and Collin's uncle Julius set out for Halanah so Collin and Jacque could start Fall term on time. Travel was pleasant this time. The early fall air was crisp but not cold and the trees lining the road were brightening into hues of gold, orange and red. It had been many years since the trees had changed colors. Collin had never seen it.

The Gates of Halanah didn't look the same as they had the first time Collin approached them. He looked from Jacque to Julius and felt sad. Julius would leave him here this time. Collin wouldn't see him for months while he studied at the Elythium.

"You could move here, you know. I'm sure the Light Ones would be happy to have you," Collin said to his uncle.

"We'd love to have you, actually," Jacque assured him.

Julius smiled and nodded toward the giant bell pull. "I think we've discussed this a sufficient amount of times. Ring the bell, Collin."

"Marcus and the others can rebuild Plahn. Why do they need you?"

"Plahn is our home. My home. The Lightlings are lovely to visit, though some of the shine has worn off now we know more about their practices, but still...ring the bell."

"Lady Ella said she was introducing legislation to deal with slavery. Maybe they'll abolish it as a legal practice. Maybe sending Miriam back to her sister will be easier than we think."

"If there's one thing I know about people, it's that they don't give up a life of ease if they can avoid it. Cut off their source of slaves from one place, do they rethink their position? No. They open up a new avenue of flesh and move on. It's like the many-headed monster of mythology, cut off one head, two more grow back. It's the way of humanity. I'll ring the bell." Julius rang and the tall guard appeared, smiling when he recognized them.

"Welcome back to the White City, gentlemen. I sincerely hope you are well. Jacque, how good to see you again."

"We are well, Amicus. Thank you for your kind inquiry." Julius always sounded more formal with Amicus. Collin grinned. He rarely saw his uncle try to fit in like he did in the North Country.

"I trust your journey was pleasant. Allow me to show you to the Hall of Hospitality. You may stay there as long as you like while you get young Collin settled into the Elythium."

"Your hospitality is overwhelming, Amicus. Thank you so much."

"Laurelle was going to meet us here, wasn't she, Jacque?" Collin asked, growing more excited by the moment. It had been several months since he'd seen the girl he loved, and his arms ached to hold her.

"Ah, probably. But she's surely let her schedule fill with shopping and dress-fittings and-"

"Shut up, Jacque."

"Or, that could be her now. Yes, I guess she managed to fit us in." Jacque grinned and pointed to a beautiful girl with honey-colored hair rushing down the street toward them. Dressed in a drapey white gown, tied with gold at the waist - the usual fashion of the North-she looked like an angel.

Collin broke into a smile that hadn't been on his face in the month they'd been apart.

"Collin!" she cried and threw herself at him.

"Elle, my beautiful girl!" Collin wrapped his arms around her waist, lifted her and spun her around, laughing. Then he pulled away enough to kiss her. She kissed him back and they stayed that way until Julius cleared his throat loudly.

Laurelle broke away and ran her hand over his chest, making his skin prickle with gooseflesh. "Goodness, you got taller and... more muscles." Her eyes sparkled.

He bent to kiss her. "Thanks," he murmured an inch from her lips.

She giggled and suddenly seemed aware of the others. "Hello, Julius and Jacque! You both look wonderful." She went to embrace the older man. He hugged her tightly and kissed her head. Collin had noticed a marked change in Julius and Laurelle's friendship since the war. Waiting out Collin's imprisonment in the Great Castle had drawn them close. She hugged Jacque next and almost disappeared for a moment in the tall boy's long arms.

"How's Marc?" Collin asked when they'd all started out again.

"Well, they've figured out a temporary false leg for him. There's lots of new developments, but none mimics the motion of an actual leg. There were scientists here who were working out limb transplants, but it's dried up all of a sudden. They're blaming Lashai, but that's ridiculous. How could it be Elian and Cassai's fault?"

Collin felt queasy. "Um," he looked at Amicus, who walked close by. "I don't know for sure. Maybe we can talk it out later." Laurelle instantly understood his cryptic tone and nodded.

"Of course. I didn't mean to hold you up. Let's get to the Hall of Hospitality. There's some old friends waiting."

They walked with their arms around each other. Collin grinned, remembering this very walk a year ago and how much things had changed since then. Laurelle hadn't shot up several inches as he had. She was no broader in the shoulders, as months of training had done to him, but she was different in other ways.

The war had marked them all with the unique quality of those who've grown older and wiser too quickly. No one is supposed to see and do the things they'd seen and done, and it had made an impression on them, however unwilling they were to acknowledge it.

When they mounted the steps and passed under the giant, pink granite columns of the Hall, he felt another unpleasant swoop in his stomach. It looked different now he knew marble used to build this hall had been mined by slave labor. He wondered if the hall itself was built by slaves as well.

"Are you alright? Your pretty green eyes went dark." Laurelle brushed a stray curl from his forehead.

"Sorry. I'm fine. The darkness is never far off these days."

Laurelle squeezed his waist. It still made him dizzy to be so near her. That was something normal at least.

"Here they are," she exclaimed.

The group of people who had spent so much time with Collin on his first visit to the North was missing one member and the others looked years older. Marc and Sacha's faces both split into huge smiles when he saw them.

"You're back! Finally!" roared Marcole as he hobbled toward them, still leaning on his cane.

"Marc!" Collin closed the distance between them and pulled him into a hug. He was taller than the half-Lightling boy now. It felt weird.

Sacha punched his arm. "Welcome back, Collin."

They pulled Collin into the room he'd shared with his uncle on their last visit. Julius was already there, arguing with Amicus.

"I allowed it last time because I didn't want to insult you, but I must insist you not send slaves to wait on us, my friend. No disrespect, but it goes deeply against our personal beliefs."

"Agreed," Collin said.

Amicus looked upset, but he nodded. "Very well. I will see what can be done to secure you a paid servant. It feels like a waste of funds."

"I will pay whatever wages are required," Julius offered.

"We don't need a servant. We'll look after ourselves while we're here. It's no trouble," Collin said.

Amicus looked even more disturbed by this notion. "We have never failed to serve a visitor entering our lands, especially not an invited guest. Of course I will procure you someone. I simply feel it's making things unnecessarily difficult. Timothy was not adequate for you last time?"

"Timothy was perfect," Collin assured him quickly.

"Then I will see about getting Timothy and pay him a small wage. Will that suit you?"

Julius nodded and offered a conciliatory smile. "It will. Thank you for seeing to it."

"Not at all," said Amicus' voice in a stiff, wounded tone as he glided from the room.

"Well, he seemed cheerful and accommodating," Julius said with a sigh. "I apologize for causing a stir right off. I can't bear another moment of being waited on by someone not being paid."

"No, I'm glad you said something. I didn't know you were going to. That's brilliant," Collin said.

Elle and Marc exchanged a look and they both started talking at the same time. "It'll be fine."

Only Sacha stood in the doorway, his arms crossed, his expression unreadable. "I'll be right back."

Collin looked at his friends. "Is he alright?"

"Sacha is always alright," Jacque said.

"He looked odd though, didn't he?" Elle said.

"Let's go get something to eat. I'm starving," Marc said.

"Please tell me this 'something to eat' includes food that Sacha has been making all morning for our homecoming," Jacque begged.

COLLIN FELT a fluttering excitement as Jacque led him through the giant courtyard of the Elythium. They'd broken off from their group after lunch to see their living quarters and get Collin accustomed to the campus.

"I got us a room together. They usually assign someone your first year, but given our circumstances, they said we didn't have to be separated."

"What circumstances?" Collin asked.

"The circumstances where you have horrible nightmares and start screaming in the middle of the night like a bloody lunatic," Jacque said with a wink.

"Right." Collin felt his face growing hot. "Sorry about that."

"Seriously? It means I won't have to get used to some new idiot who clips his toenails and leaves them on the floor, or turns on the light while I'm sleeping, or any number of annoying habits humans inflict upon their fellow men."

"You'll have to get used to never sleeping because you'll always be calming me down. Big improvement."

"Shut up. That doesn't matter to me. I never sleep anyway. We should be right through here. Yep, says right on the door: Collin of the Borderlands and Jacque. Just Jacque? That's rude. They could at least include my surname."

"Maybe they feel it's actually giving you a bit of honor. Like, no need to add anything else to it. You're Jacque and everyone knows what *that* means." Collin reframed his friend's perception.

Jacque grinned and ruffled Collin's curls. "I'm sure that's what it is."

"Of course it is. You have the key? They didn't give me one."

"I do. Hang on a minute. It's under all the biscuits I nicked from that fantastic tea."

"That did taste like Sacha's doing, didn't it?" Collin said as Jacque continued to dig for the key to their new room.

"Had to have been. I wonder where he disappeared to. Here it is." Jacque produced a small key and pushed it into the keyhole. "Home sweet home. Shall I carry you over the threshold?"

Collin glared. "Not unless you want to lose body parts."

"It's tradition. You really want to monkey with tradition? That bad luck's all on you, my friend. You can't say I didn't offer."

"I won't. In fact, I won't say a word about any of this. Can we go in now?"

It took Collin a fraction of a second too long to read the sparkle of fun in Jacque's eyes before the taller boy had swooped his legs out from under him at the knees. "Welcome home." He half-shouted, half-laughed as he threw Collin onto one of the long, narrow beds.

"I'm gonna kill you, Jacque!" Collin untangled himself from the bedding, which had been folded neatly until he'd been dropped on it.

"Are you? Because, no offense, Armrest, but I'm bigger." Jacque widened his stance and wiggled his finger at Collin, a clear challenge.

Collin launched across the room and hit him low, trying to break his balance. It didn't work. Jacque scooped him up and threw him on the bed again, this time harder than before. There was a loud crack, and the mattress collapsed under Collin and thudded to the floor. Collin smacked the back of his head on the bed frame. He groaned and shut his eyes against the burst of lights and pain competing for attention.

"Oy! Sorry. That was stupid. Are you okay? Are you bleeding? Let me see."

Collin twisted away and tried to aim a kick at his friend, but he was trapped in his broken bed and only managed to hit the other running board. It too broke with a loud snap. "Great," he muttered, secretly pleased that months of training had such an effect.

"Wow. Glad that wasn't my stomach. What were you trying to do?" Looking nervous, Jacque examined the board.

"I don't know. To get you back for cracking my head," Collin said.

"Do you want me to kiss it better?"

"Is this what rooming with you is always going to be like?" Collin moaned.

Jacque beamed. "I mean, probably?"

"Who do we talk to about fixing this mess? Will I have to pay for it?"

"As you don't even have to pay to be here, I doubt you'll have to pay to replace a bed that gave out for no apparent reason."

"No apparent reason? Really?"

Jacque assumed an air of deep innocence. "I don't know what happened, superintendent, it was fine one minute and then, bam broken beyond repair."

Collin shook his aching head and Jacque pulled him out of the bedframe. He took his first real look at their room and couldn't help but smile. There were two tall bookshelves in one corner, two desks and another, unbroken, bed that was as long and narrow as this one.

"Not used to having shorter people here, are they?" he asked, looking at the length of the desk chair and height of the desk.

"I think they've got a pretty diverse mix, but if I may say so, it's a lot easier for a short person to sleep on a bed that's too long, than for a long person to sleep on a bed that's too short."

Collin nodded. "Fair point. Shall we get our trunks and stuff? I left mine with Uncle at the Hall of Hospitality."

Jacque nodded and they left the room, locking the door behind them.

"Well, well, my healthy new minds! How do you fair this afternoon?" A tall man, who obviously worked in some official capacity, was walking toward them, his hands clasped together.

Around his neck hung a name badge on a long leather strip, but his name was written in a language Collin couldn't read.

"Hello, Jenson," Jacque said, clapping the man's shoulder.

"Jacque. I was excited to hear you were with me in Howard Hall. And this must be the Borderling."

"Collin," said the shorter boy, holding out his hand.

Jenson looked at the offered hand, then at Jacque, then he grasped it and kissed it as though he wasn't sure what else should be done.

Collin pulled away. "Ah, you shake it. Sorry. Borderling tradition."

"What a delightful custom. You must teach it to me." Jenson grabbed Collin's shoulders and drew him up to kiss both cheeks. "That's our official greeting."

"Right. Thanks," Collin said, resisting every natural instinct to reach up and wipe off the man's kisses. "Er, we were heading out to get our bags and things."

"I'm sure they'll have them sent over."

"We don't -" Collin began, but Jacque put a hand on his shoulder and squeezed hard to stop him.

"We appreciate the hospitality, but we're heading there anyway to see his uncle and let him know we've got our room sorted," Jacque said.

Collin nodded because he thought Jacque wanted him to.

"Very well, young men. All up to you, of course." Jensen beamed and nodded as he passed.

"Easy on the subversive speeches about slavery, Armrest."

"Why? I know deep down; a lot of these people would agree with us if they knew what we know and consulted their consciences."

"Ah, that's the tricky part. There aren't many Lightlings terribly into consulting their conscience. You know we have a pantheon of gods we worship, and our favorite is Zeno. Can you guess why?"

"No, I hear you say his name a lot."

Jacque grinned. "That's a bad habit. I don't really pray. Zeno is the god of pleasure and ease: two things the Lightlings treasure above most things."

"Who's your favorite god then?"

"I like Samantha."

"What's her specialty?" Collin asked, growing excited since none of the Lightlings had ever discussed their religion with him.

"She's the goddess of humor and mischief."

Collin laughed. "Of course she is."

"You asked."

"Who's the god of taking care of the poor and not enslaving other races for your own comfort?"

"Pretty sure we don't have one for that."

Collin peppered him with questions all the way back to the main entrance to the Elythium, where they were joined by Laurelle, Marc and Sacha.

"What are you two talking about looking so serious?" Laurelle asked, kissing Collin's lips and weaving her fingers between his.

"Lightling gods," Collin said when his breath returned. "It's fascinating. I've never studied religions other than what Elian and Cassai taught me about the Weaver and, of course, what the Fontre forced us to learn during *Hermordes*. So, who's your favorite god or goddess, Elle?"

Laurelle smiled and fiddled with the end of her braid. "My favorites are the Twins."

"The Twins?"

"Hamish and Brennaa. They were born to Nyanna, goddess of the sea, but they rebelled and left the sea one night to find lovers on an island nearby. Nyanna was furious when she found out and banished them to live on land forevermore. They're the god and goddess of misfits and the homeless."

Collin nodded. "I guess that's about right for me. I can't imagine you not fitting in, but I've felt that way all my life."

Laurelle shrugged. "I don't really fit in either. I didn't like studying, so the smart crowd had no use for me. I don't like being cruel to people, so the popular didn't like me either, even though I looked more like them. These misfits were more than willing to have me along though." Laurelle gave the boys she spent most of her life with a loving smile. Sacha pulled her into a hug.

"Yeah, well, one good misfit deserves another, I suppose. You at least always smelled better than the rest of us."

Laurelle pulled away from him, laughing. "I'm extremely glad to hear that. What about you? Who was your favorite, Sacha? I know! It had to be Eleanore, the goddess of cooking."

Sacha grinned and shook his head. "I believe in the Weaver, actually."

Collin looked surprised. "Really? Like, the Fontre Weaver, or the Lashaian Weaver?"

"There's only one Weaver. The Fontre twist Him to make others fear His wrath. The Borderlings made him into a philanthropist because they needed help so badly. I think He is who He is. He doesn't bend and change to suit the whims of mortals."

Jacque nodded. "Deep, Sacha. I guess I should have figured you'd have some philosophical stance."

Sacha grinned. "If I chose a goddess from legend, though…"

"Definitely Eleanore." Elle smiled.

He bent to kiss her cheek. "Absolutely."

"DID YOU GET TEA OR ANYTHING?" Collin asked Julius.

"I did. You'll never guess who brought it," said Julius,

looking slightly embarrassed when the rest of the Lightling companions joined them.

"Who was it?"

Julius nodded toward Sacha. "What? Why?"

Sacha gave them a confused look. "Why, what? I missed something."

"Why did you bring the tea? I thought they were employing Timothy."

"I told them they needn't bother. I'm more than happy to fix tea and carry bags and stuff."

"We're not having you as our servant, Sacha. Not in a million years."

Sacha shrugged. "Too late. I already took the job. Sorry. If I'm not satisfactory you can always complain to Amicus, but then I'll get officially reprimanded and may also lose my job in the Elythium kitchens, so…"

"That's blackmail," Collin muttered.

"Deal with it. You're a war hero and so's your uncle. I'm happy to serve you for a bit. Honored, actually."

This struck Collin deeply. He'd never thought of himself as a war hero while he rotted away in the Great Castle prison and everyone else did the heavy lifting. "I'm not a hero. I only fought in one real battle."

Sacha shook his head. "You were unbreakable. Devilan told us so that night. Said the only way you finally gave him the little bit of useless information or lies was when he was about to murder your friend. That's pretty heroic as far as I'm concerned. You held on and kept us safe until we could reform our army."

Collin swallowed a hard lump. "That's … Devilan said that? I wasn't brave or brilliant or anything. I was blubbering like a baby when he…well, anyway…" He had never told his uncle details of his torture or Phineas' death, knowing it would cause Julius pain. Phineas had been his uncle's closest friend.

"He yelled at Elian while you were changing because Elian

wanted to leave you behind. Devilan said you were ten times tougher than any of us could possibly see and you should be allowed to fight if you wanted. Elian wanted you to be safe."

Collin nodded and tried to steady his emotions. "Great. Okay. Anyone else ready to eat? I'm starving again."

Sacha gave an understanding look and nodded. "Sure. Let's go. We're taking you to that place on Wampler Street, aren't we?"

"Yeah," said Collin grateful to have his diversion accepted without explanation. "That place sounds great."

"Well, good, not great," Jacque amended as he led the way out of the room.

"Coming, Uncle?"

"I think I'll let you get on, actually. I'll be here a couple more days. I'll try it tomorrow."

"Give us a minute?" Collin asked his friends. They nodded and filed out one by one. Laurelle squeezed his hand before she trailed off after them. "Are you okay?" he said when they'd gone.

Julius nodded, but said nothing else. He looked on the verge of collapse.

"Okay, well, get some rest and I'll be back later tonight. I'm spending the night here. The dormitory isn't officially open until tomorrow." Collin left out the part about his broken bed.

"Collin," said Julius. "Did he – was Phineas – did he look okay? Was he tortured badly, or starved or anything?" The haunted look in Julius' eyes was more than Collin could bear.

"He looked as stoic and stubborn as ever. They had mistreated him, but he was strong. He wasn't deformed or anything. They didn't break his limbs or anything like that."

"Were they feeding him?"

"Uncle, do you really need to know this stuff? It'll make you hurt more."

"Please tell me," Julius said in his usual quiet voice.

"I think they fed him some, but not too well. They fed me

too, you know? I was okay in there. I think Devilan was making sure I was at least a little bit taken care of. For Elian's sake if nothing else."

"I didn't understand about Devilan for a long time. I didn't know why you mourned him. Sorry. It sounds like he was your last hope in the end."

"Never mind, Uncle. He wasn't a good man or anything. Nothing you should be sorry about." Collin couldn't handle much more of this conversation. He could only fight down the urge to flee for so long before acting on it. He hoped he'd be dismissed before he bolted.

"I'm sorry. I wish I could have protected you better. I wish I could have protected Phineas or stopped Devilan from killing our little Anaya. I failed you both miserably."

Julius was a tall man, broad shouldered and powerfully built. He was so rarely ruffled by anything; it took all Collin's nerve to stay put and let him be this honest.

"You didn't fail us. The bad stuff was the fault of the Fontre. Your life is your life," Collin echoed something Josie had told him. "No one promised it would be easy. I love you, Uncle."

Julius nodded and wiped his eyes. "Yes. I love you too."

"Do you mind if I go? Are you okay here by yourself?"

The older man took a deep breath and finally smiled. "Sacha's got me all sorted out here." He waved toward a tea tray that looked like it hadn't been touched.

"Okay, so... make a dent in some of that, won't you? Emotional eating makes you feel better. And that's according to Laurelle, so it must be true."

Julius smiled. "You're so grown up you're giving me orders now? I guess it was bound to happen eventually."

"Not orders, suggestions. You look like a wrung out rag at the moment. When was the last time you ate real food?"

Julius shook his head. "Not sure. A while, I suppose."

"Please rest and don't worry. I'll be back soon. I promise."

"I'll be fine."

Collin nodded and left, but he paused past the curtain and peered in at his uncle. He wished he could force him with the power of his will to go to the tea tray and eat or pour himself a cup.

Julius looked at the food and drink for a long moment, then lowered himself onto the bed, buried his head in his hands and sobbed until his whole body shook. Collin bit his lip, at war with himself as to whether he should reenter the room when his uncle didn't know he'd been watching. The deep aching guilt in the pit of his stomach won out and he walked back in.

"Uncle?" he whispered, not wanting to startle the man.

Julius didn't jump, but his shoulders stopped shaking and he wiped his eyes. "I'm fine. I thought you'd gone."

"I wasn't sure you were really fine, so I waited by the door. I'm sorry. I wasn't trying to spy."

Julius shut his eyes. "Right. Not to worry, boy. I'll be alright. Go and enjoy your evening."

"I can't. I'm not leaving you here alone like this. Let's have tea. Let's talk."

Julius looked at the tea tray, then at Collin. He opened his mouth to speak, but instead sighed and moved toward the tray.

A soft tap on the door made them jump. "I hope I'm not disturbing you. I noticed the tea had gone cold. Here's a fresh pot and something hot to have with it." Sacha had returned carrying a pot of tea in one hand and a steaming dish in the other.

The smells filling the room told Collin that Sacha had made them curry. His mouth watered remembering the curry Sacha made in the Inner Kingdom.

"You needn't have bothered, Sacha," said Uncle Julius.

"Are you going to say that every time I do anything for you? Nothing I say will convince you how happy I am to be of service?"

These words must have convinced Julius where nothing else would because he smiled and accepted Sacha fixing his plate and pouring his tea without another word.

"He likes milk but no sugar," Collin said.

"I know," Sacha grinned. "I know how you take yours as well."

"And you like yours with plenty of sugar and very little milk. See? You're not the only one who remembers things," Collin said.

Sacha's grin widened and his cheeks flushed. "Never said I was. Two scoops of curry for you?"

"Three," Collin said.

FOUR

THE LIGHT AND THE DARKNESS

The next three days were filled with meetings for new scholars at the Elythium and dinners with the professors, who Collin had learned were called Omiliti in the Lightling tongue.

Setting up the room in the dormitory to suit Jacque and Collin proved to be the greater challenge. Marc and Laurelle's father, Aeron, had met them both with tears and hugs, and kisses on both cheeks and swore to spare no expense to see Collin's needs met in every possible way. But the reality was, Collin was too short for most furniture built in Halanah.

"We can take him to that second-hand place on Malbrook Lane. They get odd stuff there from time to time," Marc suggested after they'd been to three stores and bought nothing. "Mom's found stuff there for Laurelle and me. Collin's not the only short one in Halanah." Marc elbowed him in a friendly way.

"We'll have it custom built," said Aeron without hesitation.

Collin felt a wrench of guilt. "Please don't do that. It'll cost a fortune and I can put my feet up on a block and study at the desk in the room."

"You will do no such thing." Aeron looked so aghast at this suggestion that Collin and Jacque both started laughing.

"Let's ask at the Elythium," Julius suggested. "They accept students from everywhere. Surely they have alternatives available."

"There's an idea," said Jacque cheerfully.

"I want to do something for him," Aeron said.

Julius looked ready to protest, but seeing the angst in Aeron's eyes, Collin put a hand on Julius' arm to stop him. "I need new moccasins. I've worn mine through and I really liked them. Jacque got them for me last time I was here. I can't remember where from, though."

"Moccasins! I will happily supply them. What else? New tunics? Jacque has a place he likes."

Collin stifled a laugh, taking in Jacque's violent-purple embroidered garment of the day. "Maybe plain ones. I'm not really into fashion."

"He certainly isn't," Jacque sniffed.

In the end, Aeron was satisfied with outfitting Collin with a new wardrobe and three pairs of shoes: moccasins, sandals with straps up to his knees and sturdy boots for journeys back to the Borderlands.

When they returned to the University, Jacque asked a *malderone* if there was any furniture for smaller statured students. She smiled and led them to a storage room two levels below the normal classrooms.

"In here. He can take whatever suits him. No one comes down here and looks any more. That desk over there is really nice. It was commissioned by one of Amistole's star pupils for his best friend."

The girl led them through a room piled high with tottering stacks of furniture. Arms of chairs and legs of desks and tables stuck out in odd places, making Collin carefully watch his steps.

"Amistole? Where have I heard that name? What was the pupil's name?"

"Erik Delastole. I don't know his friend's name, but I think he was a mountain boy. Here it is," called the girl in delight.

"Thank you…er…what's your name?"

"Eskaminelle. Everyone here calls me Eska."

"Thank you, Eska. It's a beautiful desk." Collin leaned down and studied it. He fell in love instantly. It wasn't large or flashy or carved with dryads, but sturdy, simple, made of oak, the perfect height for him, and with three drawers down the side and a shallower one in the middle.

"That'll fit you, Armrest. Is there a chair?" Jacque asked.

"There is. Here, sir." Eska pointed to a comfortable-looking chair made of oak, with padded arms and cushioning on the seat and back.

"Perfect," said Collin.

"I'll carry the desk if you want to grab the chair," Jacque offered.

"No, sir," gasped Eska. "I will get *malderones* to do that. You needn't exert yourself."

"It's my pleasure to exert myself and save you all the trouble," Jacque assured her.

"Yes, agreed. We can manage."

Eska's lip started to tremble and her forehead wrinkled. "If you please, sir, I'll be whipped if I let you do that. If the desk is satisfactory, I would be ever so grateful if you'd let us see to it. If you don't like this one, I can show you others."

Collin shook his head. "Come again? Did you say you'll be whipped?"

"Oh no, not that it need concern you. I'm sorry. I'm not saying you should care about my personal … I meant if you don't like this desk, I'll find you something you can enjoy, sir." The shaking girl took a step back and Collin felt he'd swallowed something sharp.

"No. Of course it matters to me if you're whipped. This desk is wonderful. I love it. We'll go now if it makes you feel better."

"Forgive me, sir. I didn't mean to make you bother about whether I'm feeling alright. Anything you wish is fine."

"Jacque?" Collin said, looking for rescue.

"Right. Have it delivered by tonight, if possible. We'd like to have him all sorted for the start of classes in the morning." Jacque's tone was businesslike, as though he were ordering from a shop in town.

Eske's face relaxed. "Of course, sir. Anything else I can assist you with?"

"We have a few other details we need to see to. We'll let you know if there's anything else." Jacque grabbed Collin's arm and steered him from the room and back up the stairs.

Collin felt steam building inside, starting in his neck and working its way to the top of his head. "What in the-?"

"No. Don't start yet," Jacque warned rushing him faster.

Up another flight of stairs, down a long corridor, Jacque hauled him, rushing faster and faster as though anticipating an explosion in Collin's brain. They reached their room, he flung open the door, shoved Collin in and closed the door behind them.

"Okay, now."

Collin exploded with a string of curses that would have made Julius furious. "They beat the *malderones* if we do stuff ourselves? What kind of place is this? They say they're enlightened and go off on me about not liking the Fontre last time? What right have they to enslave another race to begin with, much less whip some poor little girl who's trying to help people?"

Jacque stood against the door, arms crossed over his chest, looking calm as ever. Occasionally during Collin's roaring Jacque would nod silently and let him continue.

"Where do they get off acting better than everyone else all the time and then treating other people like they're property?"

43

His anger had fizzled and he felt deflated. Jacque was still silent and Collin wondered if his friend thought he wasn't finished. "I'm done."

"Agreed."

"Seriously?"

"What should I say, Collin? That I hate the system how it is? I do. I don't believe we should have slaves. Do you want me to rant with you? Because I'm all for it, but you seem to have a good thread going, didn't see a reason to jump in."

"I know."

"Good. Ready to go meet the others or are you staging a hostile breakout in the *malderones'* corridor? If you do, by the way, I'm in."

Collin finally looked at Jacque's cheerful face and couldn't stay angry. "Do you ever get tired of agreeing and going along with everything I say?"

Jacque shrugged. "I told you the day we met, you're a beast, and whatever you're doing, I'm with you."

Collin grinned and felt the knot in his chest begin to loosen. "I wish I was more like you and less like a kettle about to boil over every second."

"Meh, the world needs a few boiling kettles, we can't make tea without them." Jacque winked and opened their door. "And tea sounds really good right now."

"It really does. Or a hostile breakout in the *malderone* corridor…one or the other."

JULIUS WAS LEAVING the next morning and Collin woke up too early but couldn't fall back to sleep. His uncle lay in the bed beside him, his snoring erratic, as though he too wasn't fully relaxed even in unconsciousness.

Collin turned to one side, then the other, trying to get comfortable on the bed. He'd never thought a bed could be too soft, but after so many months of sleeping on forest floors, hard cots and the stone floors of a dungeon, the bed was more than he could bear.

In the depths of his mind, he felt unsettled. He'd thought coming back here would feel like coming back to the place he'd loved before. Now it felt more foreign than when he'd first walked through the gates over a year ago.

"Can't sleep?" Julius said, startling him. He hadn't noticed the snoring had stopped.

"Does Halanah seem different to you this time?" Collin asked.

"A bit. Less strange because I've been here and knew what to expect, but not as exciting, because I knew what to expect."

"Maybe that's it. I feel I can't calm down and be at peace, you know? This bed is too soft."

Julius chuckled. "The bed is ridiculously soft. Who did they make this for? A rajah?"

There was a long silence before Collin turned onto his back. "What if war has ruined me for normal life? Someone dropped a pitcher in the kitchen yesterday while Sacha and I were in there, and I swear I reached for my sword. It wasn't there, of course, but still."

Julius patted his arm. "You'll be alright, Collin. It can take years to feel totally settled again, and you have plenty of time. Learn all you can here. Enjoy it. Then come home, won't you? It'll be much too quiet there without you."

Without anyone, Collin thought into the darkness. Anaya was gone and more than half their villagers had been killed or terribly wounded in the war. "I'll come home as soon as possible, I promise. We'll rebuild the house and maybe even try another garden."

"Elian has promised livestock to those who fought in the war and some rebuilding money and materials. The Weaver bless that boy."

"Boy?" It was still weird to Collin that Julius thought of Elian as a boy.

"Young man – whatever. You all seem like boys to me. Not as much now. You've changed a lot this last year."

"Knock knock," Sacha murmured from outside their curtain door.

Collin got up and pulled back the curtain. Sacha held up a tea tray laden with scones and a full tea service. The Fontre boy smiled at Collin, his black curls sticking out beneath a white rag tied around his head.

"How could you have known we were already up?"

"It's my job to know," he said.

"It definitely isn't," Collin said.

"I couldn't sleep and I kinda figured you couldn't either. I thought if I came up with the tray and didn't hear anything you'd never know the difference, but if you were, I'd look like a super good servant and get a better review." He wiggled his eyebrows and moved past Collin.

"Sacha, you are by far, the most fantastic servant I've ever had," Julius said in a tired voice.

Sacha grinned as he stirred milk into Julius' tea. "Don't get up. I can bring it to you. Blueberry scone, or pinkberry?"

"Pinkberry. Thank you."

"Collin?"

"Same. Thanks, mate."

"Wish you weren't leaving today, Julius." Sacha handed him his tea.

"As do I, dear boy, but it's time. I have work to do, and so do the two of you. I'm leaving and letting you get on with it."

FIVE
THE OMILITI

Collin had butterflies in his stomach as he headed to his first class. He hadn't attended any formal classes since he'd gone to the tiny grammar school in Plahn. The rooms of the Elythium were small and filled with cushions for the students to repose against while the Omilitus discussed great works of literature, philosophy or mathematics.

Collin hadn't been sure exactly what he wanted to study, so he'd signed up for whatever Jacque was taking. The only class he had separately from Jacque was Philosophy of Social Justice, which he thought would be fascinating taught by someone who supported a society built on slave labor.

He walked into the class and saw the professor was tall as all Lightlings were, but older than most he saw milling about the school or in the street markets.

The Omilitus looked up but said nothing as Collin found a seat.

Collin settled on a pile of cushions by a window which overlooked the lake, and grinned. He'd dreamed of this moment since Elian taught him about the Light Ones ten years ago. A strange sadness followed his euphoria. So much had happened since his boyhood hours spent in the sheep pasture, reading aloud to Elian.

"Let's get settled and situated," the Omilitus said quietly as students continued to find seats. He looked down at a scroll he'd been perusing. "I hope you're all bright and prepared to begin a new year. I'm Omilitus Hamil. I've been teaching at the Elythium since I was only a few years older than you are.

"Taking this class is a privilege. If you all remember that, we'll get along nicely. If you forget it, we'll think of ways to refresh your memory. I see there are new faces and races this term." He looked up from his scroll as two boys close to Collin's age walked through the arched doorway.

Collin barely suppressed a gasp. The boys were Fontre.

"Find somewhere to sit, if you will. I've already begun my lecture," said Om Hamil. "Of course you will recognize our brothers from the South. Fontre are, of course, welcome here, in spite of recent events." The sour look on his face left Collin in little doubt what his new professor thought of those events. Collin's heart rate picked up as the two boys settled into cushions next to him.

One winked. "Good morning, Collin," he murmured. Hearing his own name from this hostile stranger erased all reasonable thought from Collin's brain. His jaw tightened and he started to reply but was cut off by the professor.

"And, of course, we have a student from the Borderlands," said Om Hamil. "I presume you won't let any petty prejudice interfere with your pursuit of enlightenment." This was aimed directly at Collin.

"No, sir," Collin said. He sounded angry, but he hadn't meant it to come out that way.

"Keep your tone respectful, boy. Dietrich, perhaps you could open to the first chapter of your textbook and read the Monseigneur's Manifesto. Based, of course, on the great Monseigneur Compton."

The Fontre who'd addressed Collin opened his book and began to read. Collin had read the Manifesto the night before and had many questions he'd written down to ask in class, but now his brain felt it was on fire. He knew there were still a few Fontre left in the North Country, but not young warriors. Not here at the Elythium.

"Thank you, Dietrich. Class, let us discuss."

The class came alive. Everyone had thoughts. Collin didn't hear anything. Students droned on around him for a long while.

At last, his mind stilled, and he looked at the professor. "How does this leave you ethically with slaves?"

The chatter died and the Omilitus followed everyone's gaze to Collin. "I didn't hear your question."

"The Manifesto goes on and on about equality and justice. I wondered how you feel this applies to the slaves who work for you all."

"Are you indeed wondering that? It sounds oddly like a statement, boy. No one may make a statement in this class. There are no slaves in Halanah. Slavery is, of course, illegal here. Perhaps you've been misinformed."

"*Malderones* then," Collin persisted. He heard a few of the girls gasp in surprise. "You call them *malderones,* but it amounts to the same thing, doesn't it? They aren't paid for their work."

The man raised one eyebrow. His chest puffed up and he made his way through the crowd to Collin's corner.

"It's Carl, isn't it?" he asked.

"Collin."

"Hm..." He looked annoyed that Collin dare correct him. "So, Collin. You lived in the Eastern Borderlands, correct? What was the main trade there? Goats?"

The class snickered.

Collin had his temper under control now and didn't rise to the jibe. "Plahn did no major outside trading, but I worked at a print shop."

"A print shop? I see. Well, Collin of the print shop, it might surprise you to find a bigger, broader world out here in the more civilized regions of society. We have those who work for us, like *malderones*, who are paid, as far as I can tell, a more than fair wage for their labors."

"None that I've met were paid wages," Collin argued. Om. Hamil's neck turned red. The color slowly crept up to his jawline and finally his cheeks.

"Of course, I'm not in the habit of regularly conversing with *malderones* about their wages, but I would advise you to watch your assumptions. We will give you a few days to acquaint yourself properly with the lifestyle you are generously offered here at the Elythium. If you find it's not to your liking, I recommend you move on to a place more suited to your state of mind." His voice was perfectly calm, but Collin noticed his face burned crimson all the way up to his hairline.

"Of course, sir," he said, matching Hamil's calm.

"Very good. I believe we shall dismiss on that note. Memorize the Manifesto for further discussion." He was all business again.

Collin realized he'd forgotten to breathe while the professor glowered down his crooked nose. Now that the man was strolling away, he pulled in a few deep breaths before packing his copy of Monseigneur's Memoirs. He'd pushed himself from the floor when he found the two Fontre boys blocking his way.

"A print shop, eh? I heard about a printer from Plahn a few months back. Maybe you knew him? Phineas, I think was his name?"

Collin glared at Dietrich. "Let me pass."

"You don't remember him? Interesting. I'm pretty sure he mentioned something about you...or maybe screamed it, more like. Wasn't Collin the name he screamed, Thom?"

The other boy grinned. "Sounds right. His brain was pretty

muddled at the time, I remember. I believe I was pulling his thumbnail out."

"Good thing you came here, then. You'd have found yourself in a nasty fight had you not escaped to the North. Living here is, no doubt, the cushy life you crave," Collin said.

Dietrich took another step toward him. "We were sent here. We certainly weren't afraid of your ragtag army, or any kind of fighting."

"Of course you weren't. To be fair, my ragtag army did kill most of you and imprison the rest. So, I'm saying, your lucky moment. Now, if you'll excuse me, I have another lecture." Thom pushed him toward the corner, but Collin laughed in his face. "Do you seriously think you're scary here amongst the pillows? Do you know what happened to me after you boys fled town? I was imprisoned; tortured by Lord Devilan himself and then—to round things off —your High King had a go at me. If you think you're intimidating after all that, I assure you, you aren't. Have a nice morning, boys. I'll see you around the student gardens."

That final blow must have landed, for neither boy moved as Collin pushed by. He knew he should be afraid. Last year he certainly would have been. Instead he was furious. How could anyone at this school who claimed to be "enlightened" teach such a class?

"Hey, Armrest," chirped Jacque catching up to Collin from another hallway.

"Hey, Jacque."

"Are you shaking?"

"It's nothing. Well, not nothing. There are Fontre here. Did you know that?"

Jacque's eyebrows shot up. "There've never been Fontre here except Sacha and Kirkus. Are you sure?"

"They were in my first lecture. By the way, I'm pretty sure Om Hamil hates me."

"What are they playing at? They've never been openly coop-erative with the Fontre." Jacque seethed all the way to their next lecture.

Collin tried to shake off the feeling that something was going badly wrong. He'd thought university life would be books and lectures, and maybe the occasional party he could take Laurelle to. Now he felt a sense of sinking dread in his abdomen. "It's fine. I knew all the Fontre weren't cleared out of here. I guess I wasn't expecting to take classes with them."

"I certainly don't want to take classes with them. If they're in this lecture, we're leaving, deal?" Jacque peered around the corner into the classroom.

"Sure."

"Moot point. They're not in this class." The Omilitus in Foreign Studies was a man no taller than Collin who looked about 20. He had a soft voice and manner that reminded Collin of the kind teacher at his grammar school back in Plahn.

"I'm Omilitus Finnel. I'm sure you've noticed I'm not from around here."

Collin looked at Jacque in surprise. A Kiatri.

"Thank you for your promptness. I think you'll find our studies of neighbors from other regions fascinating. I'll rely on some of you for correct information. I've never lived in the Borderlands, but I visited many times in my youth."

A girl from the north raised her hand. "Sir, do you mean you're not a youth now?" A girl beside her giggled. But Finnel only smiled a patient smile.

"I'm slightly older than I look, Carrie. I've visited many places in my 143 years." There were a couple of quiet gasps at this. A couple of Lightling girls looked disappointed. Collin wondered if the girls were hoping they'd have a chance at a rela-tionship with the youthful teacher. "If I'm very lucky, perhaps I shall live a little longer and enjoy more travel."

"I'd steer clear of the Borderlands if your goal is longevity," the girl named Carrie said. "They were on fire at our last report, weren't they?"

Collin frowned, but dared not speak. He'd been in enough shouting matches for one morning.

"I heard that unfortunate report. Only a few towns were affected, from what I gathered. It was still a great tragedy. The first to burn was the home village of one of our new students. Collin, were you affected by the accident?"

Collin cut his eyes toward Jacque who was openly glaring at Carrie. "It wasn't an accident, sir. I believe you've been misinformed."

"You burned your town on purpose, you mean?" Carrie asked in a tone that told him no matter what he said, he'd be mocked for it.

"Of course they didn't burn it down. How dim are you?" Jacque croaked. Collin elbowed him in the ribs. Something in Finnel's eyes warned Collin that bringing up the war was a bad idea. Jacque looked at him and he shook his head and mouthed, "Don't."

"It was a tragedy and it affected me, but I wasn't there at the time." Collin pulled out the class textbook and opened it so he could avoid the stares of his classmates.

"I'm glad to hear it, Collin. I'm sorry about your loss. Plahn was a beautiful town when I visited, and full of resilient people. I'm sure they'll restore it to its former glory in no time. Now then, class, open to chapter one, and let's begin our journey of the Worlds beyond the North in the beautiful mountains of the Kiatri Realm." Om Finnel's voice, while still soft, held a finality that told the class the discussion was over.

Collin gratefully flipped to the first chapter and let Finnel's voice calm his frazzled nerves. The lecture was fascinating, but Collin retained no more of it than he had Omilitus Hamil's talk. While vastly different in their approaches, both teachers seemed tense, and Collin was aching to discover what force held them back from speaking ill of the Fontre.

"Surely the Fontre don't hold any power here," Laurelle said when he shared his concerns over a sandwich in the garden that afternoon.

"No, not real power. Not like it was in Lashai. Still, something's up. I can tell by the way they all acted around those two Fontre who were in my first lecture. They weren't nervous around them; they want to be liked by them."

"Maybe the Fontre boys are popular here at the school. Wouldn't be the first time Northlings sided with someone because they liked the color of their shoes. Anyway, can I change the subject now?" Laurelle tucked her silky hair behind her ear and started rummaging through the bag she'd packed the sandwiches in.

Collin watched her and smiled. She seemed slightly older than the day they'd met, but otherwise she was unchanged by the war. He envied her ability to blend back into normal life without missing so much as a hair appointment.

He bent over and kissed her head. "Talk about anything you want."

"This." She emerged smiling from her bag and handed him a sheet of beautifully painted parchment. "Read it."

"Come one and all to *Helios Carnivalle*. Celebrate with your families and enjoy the biggest festival in five years. Eat delicious food. Consult the great oracle of Pythia. Watch matches of magnificent strength and skill. Attend the largest auction of *Malderi*. Three-day event begins at sundown on the 24th."

Each tantalizing event was printed in unique lettering.

"I can't wait! It's three weeks away. Will you take me? It's great fun!"

Collin smiled at her enthusiasm. "Of course I'll take you if you want to go. Where is Helios?"

"That's not a place, she's the goddess of the Sun. It's in Deliniphia. A day's drive if we take Papa's wagon."

"Sounds fun...I guess. What is it?" Collin couldn't contain this question any longer.

"Carnivalle! There are rides and foods from everywhere and this magnificent circus! You won't believe what they train animals to do. It's the best show of the year and I'm finally old enough to go!"

"Your parents haven't taken you?"

A shadow fell on the girl's golden features, "You know how they are. Family values and old-fashioned traditions. They think stuff like this is terrible. I think it's mostly because they still think I'm a baby. Nihl went last time and he was only twelve. He said it was brilliant." Her voice cracked a little when she said his name and both were silent for a minute waiting for the emotions to pass.

"If you want to go, I'll take you. If you can fight in a war, surely you can handle a bit too much rich food at Carnivalle." Collin squeezed her hand. The crease between her eyes deepened and she looked away from him. "It's okay, Elle."

"Sorry. I know he was...I know what we were doing was dangerous. I don't know why I thought we might all come home. Now Marc has that horrible cane and Nihl's gone and I'm...I wish it never happened."

"We all wish it didn't have to happen."

"But did it? Some of the senators were still in talks with the Fontre. They said war could have been avoided if others had been willing to communicate better."

Collin felt like she'd punched him. His back gave him the first twinge of pain he'd had in a long while. "What does that mean?"

"Nothing. I'm not saying anything bad against you or anything. Never mind. Sorry I mentioned it."

"It's fine. Okay. Let's...let's talk later. I have to get going anyway. There's a book I need from a library across campus. I'll see you later." He leaned over and kissed her. Her lips weren't sweet and soft as they usually were. Despite this, when he pulled away, she smiled. "I'll see you later then."

"Dinner tomorrow night, right?"

She nodded, blew him a kiss and walked away.

SIX
THE CHANGES

Collin woke for the third time in the first week in a cold sweat. Jacque sat on the floor next to Collin's bed, his red head lying on the mattress, his hand near Collin's.

"Jacque," Collin muttered, trying to take deep breaths and get his heart to stop pounding. Suddenly the light cover over him was much too hot to bear.

"Mf, hugglemuck."

"What? Wake up." Collin rolled over to sit on the side of his bed and smacked Jacque on the shoulder.

Jacque bolted up and his hand went to his side as if drawing a sword. "Get away from me. I'll gut you!"

"Jacque, it's me," Collin got to his feet. He grabbed his friend's arm. "It's me."

Jacque's eyes focused on Collin at last. "Zeno. Are you alright? My neck hurts. What a stupid sleeping arrangement." Jacque rubbed his neck.

"I must've woken you in the night. You were sitting by my bed and fell asleep."

"That makes sense. Yeah. You were screaming again. The stuff no one tells you about soldiering, eh?"

"Huh, yeah. Elian always made it sound so fun," Collin scoffed.

Jacque was walking slowly through the room now, pulling on his pants and tunic. "Elian talked about being a soldier when you knew him before?"

Collin laughed. "No, absolutely never. He wouldn't say a word about any of it, actually. He hated his previous life so much."

Jacque threw Collin a tunic from their trunk. "Get dressed, mate. Let's get some breakfast. Sacha's been baking lately and there's nothing a pastry can't fix."

Collin felt almost cheerful for the first time that week.

He and Jacque went through the back door into the kitchen, the door Kirkus had led him through the day Collin met Sacha. It was against the rules for students to be in the kitchen, but Jacque didn't seem to have much use for rules.

"Oy, Sacha!" Jacque chirped.

Sacha had his usual white bandana wrapped around his black curls and wore a large canvas apron. Two *malderone* girls stood next to him, the same two Collin had seen last year. One Lightling boy stood on the other side of the table following Sacha's orders. The Fontre boy wore the usual expression of deep concentration Collin had come to associate with Sacha cooking. His face broke into a grin when he saw his two friends.

"Hey, you gotta stop coming in the back way. You're going to get me in trouble. Hey! Fold those egg whites gently, Teylus. I spent ten minutes whipping them up!" he barked at the Lightling boy.

"Come eat breakfast with us. I like hearing about the emulsification of each separate ingredient while I try to enjoy a meal. Helps digestion," Jacque said, tossing Collin an apple from the giant bowl in the middle of the counter.

"Those are for tonight's dinner, Jacque." Sacha groaned. "Give me a minute and I'll come with you. I've gotta show Brenna how to get the suet pudding going."

Jacque made a face and rolled his eyes at Collin. "Fine. But we're not saving you any porridge."

"Grate the suet into this bowl and set it in the cold room. It can't melt before the right time or the whole thing'll be ruined, alright?" Sacha said to Brenna, sounding harassed.

Brenna's eyes sparkled. "Yes, sir, Sacha. I'll get it cold right away."

"You two are seriously throwing off my routine," Sacha said as he pulled the apron over his head.

"Sorry we like your company. We don't mean for our friendship to get in the way of your routine," Jacque said. He gave Sacha a wounded face that looked so ridiculous, Sacha punched him.

"Seriously, I can't talk him into coming in at the proper door," Collin muttered. He felt a weird fluttery feeling in his stomach when he saw two Omiliti eyeing them with sour expressions.

"Isn't that Omilitus Hamil?" Jacque asked.

"That's him," Collin said. He set his tray down and wished Jacque would do the same.

"Right. I wanted to have a word with him, actually. I'll be back."

"Jacque, don't. Let it go, mate. Eat your porridge, okay?"

Jacque glowered across the room, and then seemed to consider Collin's words. "Fine." His wooden tray clattered against the table and several people jumped and looked in their direction. Jacque winked at Omilitus Hamil, who scowled back.

Collin took too large a gulp of his scalding hot coffee. His next words came out strained and high pitched. "We've got Sacha with us too. Let's not cause problems that might jeopardize his job here, okay? That's a poor way to repay him for making us this delicious porridge."

Jacque sank into his seat.

"What happened?" Sacha asked. He craned his neck to see Hamil.

"Nothing. Please stop looking. We'll tell you later. Let's say, I didn't exactly expect the welcome I've had here. I thought they wanted me to come."

Sacha shrugged. "Maybe some do. Hamil's always been a bit of a ..." Jacque nudged him as the man in question approached their table.

"Good morning, gentlemen," he said, wearing the same sour expression.

Collin nodded in what he hoped was a polite way and took another spoonful of breakfast.

"Good morning, sir," Jacque muttered.

"You're one of Raul's boys, aren't you? Nihl, isn't it?"

Collin's eyes shot to Jacque who rose from the table. "Jacque," he said loudly.

Hamil narrowed his eyes at the Lightling boy. "That's right. Nihl never came back from that bloodbath of a war you started." He looked at Collin. "Did he?"

Collin felt his face flush. He frowned. "You should leave."

"Hazard of war, of course. Thankfully, our Senate saw the dangers and steered clear. Anyway, I hope they'll be no more disturbances in my class or elsewhere on campus. I won't abide petty prejudices in my lecture hall." He strode away with a wave of his hand, not as if he was bidding the boys farewell, but as if he was dismissing them from his morning.

Jacque trembled as he sat down.

"He was out of order, Jacque. I'm so sorry. Are you alright?"

"I'm good." Jacque shoved in a large mouthful of porridge and then jumped to his feet again. "I've got stuff to grab from the room before my first lecture."

"Alright. Well then, I guess I'll see you next hour?"

"Yes. See you."

"I have to get back to the kitchen," Sacha said. "Are you okay, Collin? Your face is all white."

"Fine," answered Collin. Though he was no finer than Jacque was. Sacha chucked his shoulder as he walked off with his tray. Collin sighed and calculated how long it would take Jacque to get to their room, punch whatever he wanted to punch and get off to class. Collin had left his books on his bed, but he didn't want to run into his friend when he needed to be alone.

He was deep in these unpleasant thoughts when he heard something smash behind him. He jumped to his feet and swiveled around.

His heart pounded fast. The Fontre boys had entered the hall. They'd seen Sacha and come straight at him. Collin saw that Sacha's tray had dropped and his bowl was now scattered shards.

"Look at the mess you've made, Sacha," said Dietrich. "But you work in the kitchen, don't you? I suppose they won't mind scrubbing up after you."

Collin wasn't aware that he'd moved, didn't realize he'd left his table, but suddenly he was standing right next to Sacha's shoulder. Sacha looked calm, but serious.

"It's no matter. I'll clean it up," Sacha said.

The two Fontre took another step toward Sacha and Collin. "At least you have your little Borderling to protect you."

Collin laughed. "Protect him? The man who took out more Fontre soldiers in one night than most killed in the entire war?"

"Stop, Collin." The warning in Sacha's voice surprised Collin.

Dietrich's face drained of all color in his fury. "You did fight with them then? They told me you and your father had turned traitor. I knew you were never a real Fontre, but I didn't think you'd stoop to that."

"I didn't realize you'd taken to thinking. It doesn't suit you. Don't you have anything to add, Leon? I need to get back to work."

The other Fontre boy's eyebrows knit together.

Collin opened his mouth to speak, but Sacha grabbed his arm and yanked him away. "Don't start anything with them, Collin."

"I'm not afraid," he protested.

"They're being protected by people you should be afraid of."

"People here are protecting them? Why?"

"The Senate is protecting them. In fact, I'm pretty sure they planted them here to make sure no one speaks well of what happened in Lashai." Sacha glanced over his shoulder.

"They didn't follow us," Collin assured him.

"Good."

"What changed everything here? *They* invited me to join the Elythium. I thought they at least sort of supported the cause."

"The war changed things, remember? Under the Fontre, Lashai supplied them things they got used to having. Now that the granite mines are being run differently, the price of granite has skyrocketed. There are no more slaves coming in and...and I heard there's a really prominent senator who can't get the organ needed to save his wife's life."

"Did they know how barbaric those enterprises were? That they were cutting up prisoners against their will?" Collin shuddered. He felt cold, like he was back in the dungeon. Ffastian loomed over him again, talking of how much money Collin's insides were worth.

Sacha shook his head and kept walking. This time Collin followed him voluntarily. "They don't want to know."

SEVEN
THE BROOM CUPBOARD

"Did you see this? Elle wants me to take her." Collin and Jacque were sitting in their tiny room and the light had begun to slant all the shadows the full length of the room. The flier Laurelle had handed him the day before fell from his book bag as he pulled out *The Rise and Fall of the Dukain Empire* he needed to read.

Jacque frowned as he scanned the flier. "I don't think you should go to this. I definitely don't think you should take Laurelle."

A group of older students passed outside their window, laughing and talking about their day. Collin wished he felt as light and cheerful.

"Why? She says it's fun. There's vendors and food and stuff."

"There's vendors alright. Do you know what auction of the finest *malderi* means?"

The word sounded familiar to Collin and he was frustrated for not remembering. "I don't know. Livestock?"

"Slaves."

"Oh right, I figured if it was slaves they would call them *malderones*. Why *Malderi?*"

"Some stupid new word they've made up."

"But why? Why call them *malderones* at all?"

"If they called them Riverfolk, or Kiatri captives or anything that reminds them these people had lives, and histories and heritage, they would see how despicable it is. They claim their original ancestors migrated from *Maldera*, one of the little Islands in the Southern Seas. They say when they were brought here, they enjoyed working for the Lightlings because of the beautiful cities they had and the opportunities they afforded them."

"Oh." Collin couldn't think of anything else to say. He didn't want to be too harsh about Jacque's people.

Jacque looked upset. "I believed it for years. We had two *malderones*...don't know if I ever told you that." Collin felt the swoop in his stomach he'd come to associate with unpleasant surprises. Collin shook his head. "Aster and Amilie. I have no idea if those were their given names. We usually rename them with something we can pronounce. My dad brought them home years ago for my mum. I'm sorry, mate. I honestly had no idea."

Collin shrugged. "It's not your fault."

"My parents are having a rough time right now, for obvious reasons. They miss Nihl and they're furious with me for leaving in the first place. To make matters worse, when I got home I...I smuggled Aster and Amilie out in the middle of the night. I had to. I couldn't live with it."

"What did they do?"

Jacque leaned his head against the wall. He looked up at the ceiling and Collin saw his Adam's apple bounce when he swallowed. "They said I wasn't their son anymore. They wouldn't pay for me to be at the University this year and that...that they wished Nihl had come back instead of me."

Collin had never seen Jacque cry. He could tell even now he was trying to recover, trying to think of some way to pretend it was a joke. "Jacque, that's awful. It's my fault. I should never have taken you. I should have said no the moment Nihl told me your parents didn't want you to go."

Jacque cocked his head toward Collin and managed a smile. "You could have said no all you wanted, Armrest. You couldn't have stopped us going. We were ready to do something real. Something that wasn't...this." Jacque threw his hands up indicating the room, the kids outside laughing and drinking, the beautiful façade that was the Lightling world. "Imagine doing this for all of your life instead of what we did."

Collin looked around and grinned. "I don't know. I might like doing this for a while. It's kind of nice not having swords swinging in your direction all the time, torture, the food...All of this is fine."

"Nihl hated it. He was sick of the games and vapid girls. He wanted to make a difference and he did. My parents don't see it, but that doesn't matter. They can burn in Sheol for all I care." Jacque curled his long frame toward the wall.

Collin bit the inside of his cheek and wondered if he should say anything else: if he *could* say anything that would make Jacque take back the terrible thing he'd said. "Are you going to bed already? It's barely six and we haven't had dinner."

"You go. I have a paper to work on."

"You have a paper to work on the second day of lectures?" Collin scoffed, hoping to lighten Jacque up again.

"Hark who's talking! How many books did you check out of the library this afternoon?"

"These are for my Regional Studies class. I wanted to brush up on the history of Dukai. Finnel says we'll start there next week. Did you know they used to be more advanced than the cities here? Right before they collapsed they were at the height of Lashaian civilization."

Jacque stretched his arms and opened his mouth in a wide, ostentatious yawn. "Didn't you say you were going to dinner?"

"Fine. I'll bring you back food."

"Oy, hold up a minute, I forgot I wanted to give you something." Jacque seemed to perk up as he reached into his desk drawer and withdrew a small leather pouch. "I don't know if it'll work. But I thought you should have this if anyone should."

Collin opened the soft leather and turned it over, catching a pure, silver ring in his palm. "I don't know what to say." His throat felt like he'd swallowed something much too large when he realized the ring had belonged to Nihl. It was one of the matched set that pulled one brother to the other's side in an instant.

Jacque laughed, but not his usual laugh. It sounded deeper and older and less cheerful. "It's probably a bit big for any of your fingers. Maybe try your thumb?"

Collin slipped the ring on and off his fingers until he got to his middle finger, which was thick enough to hold the ring in place. "It fits fine."

"Enjoy supper." Jacque pulled a book over and settled in to read.

Collin stared at the shiny ring on Jacque's finger for a second and then at the one on his own hand. "Did Amilie and Aster get away safely?"

Jacque glanced at him and then back at the book. "No."

COLLIN FELT like a rag wrung out one too many times as he went into the dining hall for supper.

Supper was chicken in the most flavorful sauce Collin had ever eaten. Sacha had served it alongside noodles, salad and a dessert made of apples and buttery crust. Collin noticed as he ate his meal that the two girls Sacha worked with in the kitchen kept passing his table and looking at him. Finally, Brenna gathered enough courage to approach him.

"Sir, you're...you're Sacha's friend?" she asked, almost in a whisper. Her voice trembled when she spoke. Her hands were clasped tightly in front as if, if they separated, she might not be able to speak her mind.

"Yes. You don't need to call me sir. Would you both like to sit for a minute? Is that allowed?" Collin knew the girls had very strict rules and didn't want to get them in trouble.

The girls smiled at each other. "We need to ask you something, but not here. Can we talk somewhere secret?"

Collin glanced around. "No one's nearby. Can't you tell me?"

Both shook their heads and they hurried away like mice who've been discovered in the biscuit bin.

"Okay, wait," Collin called out to stop them. They paused but looked poised to bolt as gathered his bag and picked up his tray of food. "I'm coming."

Collin felt several glances follow him as he left. It wasn't normal for slaves to be in the dining hall, much less speak to a student. Oh well, he thought, they all think I'm a lunatic anyway after Omilitus Hamil and those two Fontre blokes.

The girls hurried down a darkened hall which led to the kitchen. They passed the door and paused at a broom cupboard. "In here."

"I...uh...seriously?" Collin stammered. He put his tray of uneaten dinner on the floor and ducked into the dark room the two girls had crammed into. "Right. Well, no one else will bother us, because no one else will fit. Right?" He chuckled at his joke but neither girl cracked a smile.

"We've heard what you are like, from Sacha and others. We have ..." The girl looked close to tears, but she bit her lip like she couldn't continue. She cast a helpless glance at her companion, who nodded.

"Yes. We wanted to ask you for a...for something."

"A favor?" Collin supplied.

Her face brightened. "That is it. Yes! A favor, sir. We are in trouble and we are wanting a favor."

"Okay. First things first, though. What is your name? I know you're Brenna, I know you work with Sacha, but we've never been introduced." Collin nodded to the girl he didn't know.

The girl who'd been near tears widened her eyes even more and giant tears spilled from them. "Please sir, you needn't worry over something so beneath you. It is too big a thing we ask already."

"Please, stop calling me sir. I'm Collin," Collin extended his hand as far as possible in the space they occupied. "Please tell me your name and how I can help."

"It's okay," Brenna encouraged her, "he's kind. We'll tell him and maybe it'll be alright. I'm sure he's safe. Her name is Ayla."

"Thank you."

His thanks seemed to send Ayla into a similar state of mind for she strained, trying not to tear up. "I don't know how to tell you this, sir... Col-Collin. Sorry. We c-came from the border of the Northlands, you know? We lived there years ago. We were taken and...and we've worked for many masters, sir. It's been difficult, but we're together and it's more bearable that way."

"But now..." began Ayla, but she burst into tears again and Brenna put a hand on her shoulder. "But now Brenna is to be traded, sir. He's not a nice person at all, sir. He...he has a terrible rep...rep...something."

"Reputation?"

"Yes, sir. Thank you, Collin."

"No problem," Collin assured her. "It's really no problem. When is this happening and how can I help?"

"In days. A few days, sir. It's too...it's wrong to take her. We've always been together," Ayla repeated as if Collin might not understand if she didn't emphasize this point.

"I'm so sorry."

"I don't know how you can help. We've heard things about you. Good things. Like, you care about people others don't.

Malderones, you know? We thought if anyone could help, you could."

Collin felt his pulse quicken. "What about Sacha? Have you spoken to him?"

The two looked at each other. "Sacha cares for us, sir. He is already unsteady in the kitchen with the new master. If he does something and they find out he'll be in terrible trouble."

So will I, thought Collin with a sigh. "Meet me here tomorrow morning. Let me think about it overnight, okay? I'll think of something. Will they take you before then?"

Brenna shook her head and her lip still trembled as she spoke. "He says I have a few more days. I'm supposed to be preparing a wardrobe. He gave me ... f-fabrics for sewing."

Collin frowned. "Who is it? Who's taking you?"

"Senator Byrd, sir. Do you know him?"

"Not really. But I've definitely heard of him. Alright. Tomorrow morning. Bring a bag with a change of clothes." Collin had begun forming a ridiculously risky plan even now.

"Thank you."

"Get back before they notice you're gone, or we won't get a chance, okay?"

Both nodded and Collin stepped backward out of the cupboard so they could spill out and scurry back to the kitchen. He worried the new cook would notice the girls' crying and punish them, but he couldn't be seen with them or he might destroy the fragments of a plan he was formulating.

As they disappeared through the kitchen door, Collin saw Laurelle standing at the entrance to the hallway, staring at him. She held a basket and looked even prettier than usual, even with narrowed eyes.

"Hey, Elle," Collin said, wondering why her chest rose and fell so noticeably.

"Hello. Hope I'm not interrupting anything," she snipped off the end of several words and Collin's brain began to work over-time to figure out what he'd done wrong.

Collin shook his head. "No, that's nothing. I mean it's defi-nitely something, but I can't talk about it." Every word he said seemed to be making things worse. As he drew closer to her, he saw her neck was bright red and the color was creeping up her face. "Elle?"

"Really? You can't tell me, but it's something?"

"No...not like that. Come here. Let's go somewhere else."

"Is that your dinner tray?" she asked, a little distracted from whatever turmoil her thoughts were in.

"Oh. Yeah, I forgot I left it. Um...I wish I could've eaten. It was so good," he muttered more to himself than to her as he went back the length of the hallway to retrieve his food.

"You can certainly eat it. Don't let me interfere with good food."

"Elle, please let me put this tray where it goes. I see you're upset, but everything is easily explained. Give me one second." He started to panic. She nodded, but her jaw was stiff and he saw ice in her normally warm eyes.

He dropped his tray off at the table stacked high with dirty dishes and discarded food. She waited impatiently at the entry to the dining hall. He opened the door and she led the way into the courtyard.

"They came to me and needed to talk about something. They need help. That's all it was."

Laurelle said nothing for a moment that seemed like an hour. "Mm-hm," was all she said when she finally made a sound.

"If we can go somewhere less crowded, I can tell you every-thing. I really didn't do anything, I swear I didn't," he continued.

"Let's go to the Basement Room."

"What's the Basement Room?"

"It's where we took you for our *Katevo*, the night before we left."

Katevo was the Lightling tradition for sending someone off to school, or war – a coming-of-age ritual.

"Okay. That's a good spot." Collin followed her and wondered if he should keep trying to explain. She seemed to be cooling off by the time they reached the staircase. Collin remembered with a smile how Sacha had practically carried him down that night.

She had to wiggle the doorknob several times before it gave, and they could enter. "I don't know why they don't fix this doorknob. It's so obnoxious," she huffed.

The room smelled of mold and dust. "Wow. I wonder how long it's been since anyone came down here. So…what's in the basket?"

Laurelle handed it to him, her expression still full of pain. "You've made quite an impression your first week."

"Have I? Why do you say that?"

"Everyone's talking about you and the stuff you say."

"Stuff? Like, to Hamil?"

"To everyone. Your uncle wouldn't accept Timothy as a *malderone*, he had to be paid while Julius stayed. You keep talking nonsense and asking questions in your lectures. I heard you even started a fight with some Fontre boys who are taking courses at the Elythium."

"You heard…what? I started a fight with them? Who said that?"

"It doesn't matter who said it. It matters that you've been here one week, and everyone is talking about you," she said. "Now two slave girls come out of a closet after you've taken them in there. Are you crazy?"

"I didn't take them there. They took me." Collin could tell instantly this was the wrong thing to say. "That came out

71

wrong. They needed my help. One is about to be traded to some horrible bloke and they thought I might be able to stop it."

Laurelle closed her eyes and walked away from him to find a pillow to sit on. "They thought *you* could help. Why you? Why haven't they asked someone they know? Some friend of theirs or something?"

"I don't know. They said they knew I cared about the *malderones* and thought I might have an idea."

"See? This is what I mean. Why does everyone already know you're the one to come to? Do you know the kind of trouble all of us could be in if it gets out we're helping *malderones* do things they shouldn't? You could be arrested, or worse. You could get Sacha in trouble. They already think badly of Jacque too. Did you know that?"

"Who thinks badly of Jacque?"

"A lot of people."

Collin's eyebrows collided. "When you say 'they think badly', I'm assuming you mean they think we want to free slaves. Right? That's what you mean is bad?"

"Of course that's bad, you idiot! You can't go around freeing *malderones*! Do you know what Jacque tried when he came back here? He tried freeing his own parents' *malderones*. They've been in that family almost since they were born and he tried to smuggle them out to their own families. How can you think that's okay? I know you think them good people who don't deserve their lot, and I love you for that. I love that you want to learn their names and do all these sweet things to make them feel better, but don't you see what this leads to? You're breaking the law. And Jacque is breaking it with you. He would have been in enormous trouble, but he wasn't successful and his father wouldn't tell the authorities any details." Laurelle seemed to have run out of words for the moment, so she simply sat and stared at him with an expectant expression.

"Elle, I can't...there are laws that are rubbish. You know that, right?"

"Of course I know that. Don't talk to me like I'm a stupid little girl."

"What? I'm the one always saying you aren't stupid. What is this? What are you trying to get at?"

Tears ran down her beautiful cheeks. She was so pretty it made Collin's chest ache. "I don't know."

"I'm sorry. What can I do?"

She shook her head. "You're too...good. You know? You care so much about things and I'm glad you do. But it's so exhausting. I've already fought one war with you. I want peace now. I want to be an ordinary person. I want to live in a pretty little house and have nice things. You want to...fix the whole world."

Collin's throat was starting to burn with emotions he was trying to tamp down. "I don't need to fix the world, Elle. I'll call it off, alright? Please don't do what you're thinking of doing right now."

"I...I want you to know...I'm not sorry I went with you to Lashai. I'm glad to have done something that brave and worthwhile. But, I can't be that always. I wish I could. I ... I really love you." Her voice broke, but she didn't stop looking at him with that horrible finality in her eyes. She was done.

Collin felt too hot and then too cold. He was shaking and he didn't know what to do. "I r-really love you too."

"I'm going now. I'm so sorry." She left the basket in his hands and fled, letting the door slam behind her in her rush to escape.

EIGHT
THE RESCUE

Collin had almost no memory of walking back to the Elythium that night. Everything felt wrong. Why were the stars so bright? Shouldn't the children stop laughing? Was the fountain supposed to splash so cheerfully? He kept taking steps until he was somehow at his own door.

He opened the door and saw Jacque lying on his bed, a book open in front of him, but he was staring out the window instead of reading.

"Hey, Armrest, are you...hey! What's wrong?"

Collin wiped his face. He hadn't noticed he'd started crying again. "Elle's done with me. She's...she wants to be ordinary and I'm not ordinary enough." More tears. That was getting annoying. He dropped the basket on his bed and stared at it.

"Seriously? What? What does that mean? You're not ordinary? That makes no sense."

"It's my fault. It really is. I've done nothing but cause trouble since the moment we met."

"Did she say that?" Jacque demanded.

"Of course not. She was sweet and perfect. She always is. It's fine. I'm alright."

"What's in the basket?"

"I don't know. I think we were supposed to have a picnic." Collin finally pulled the checkered napkin off the contents. A loaf of homemade bread, a wedge of cheese, two apples and a bottle of wine nestled inside.

Collin felt his breath catch in his throat. His mind's eye pictured Laurelle carefully packing this little feast for them, then finding him with Ayla and Brenna in that cramped broom cupboard.

"Do you want to do something really stupid with me?"

Jacque's eyebrows shot up. "Sure. I always want to do something stupid with you. May I ask how long we'll be in prison for said stupid thing?"

Collin laughed. "We could actually get killed for it. I suppose. I want to get a couple of slave girls away before one is sold to Senator Byrd."

"Yep. That's as stupid as it gets." Jacque snatched the bread and took a bite straight from the end of the loaf. "What time?"

THROUGH HIS WINDOW, Collin could see Sacha sleeping. It was dark in his room, but the moon was half-full and it cast everything in an eerie bluish light. He tapped the window and the Fontre boy lurched to his feet, his sword drawn before he'd seen the source of the noise.

Collin jumped, even though he was nowhere near Sacha's sword. He took a deep breath and tried to calm his pounding heart.

"Did he wake up?" Jacque whispered from the other side of the window.

"He woke up alright. If I'd been standing next to his bed, I'm pretty sure I'd be dead right now."

Sacha looked around for whatever had woken him and finally

glanced at the window. Collin gave him a sheepish wave and Sacha rolled his eyes, threw his sword on his bed and came to the window. He lifted it enough to talk to the boys outside. "What?" he demanded.

"Sorry, mate. We need help with something." Jacque poked his head round so Sacha could see him but didn't get within arm's reach.

"And it couldn't wait until morning?" Sacha growled.

"No. We want to get Brenna and Ayla freed before Brenna gets traded to that senator who wants her."

Sacha rubbed his forehead and then sighed a deep sigh. "Alright. Let me get dressed. I almost killed you just now, by the way."

"I'm aware," said Collin.

Sacha moved around his room, pulling on his tunic and brown pants. Instead of leaving through the door, Sacha came back to the window, eased it up a bit more and handed Collin his sword.

"Hold this. I'm coming out this way," he whispered.

Collin took the sword and stepped back so his friend could get out. "Why don't you leave out the front? Your father isn't here to get onto you or anything."

"Trust me, Copolo is meaner than ten of my da. If he hears anything, I'm dead."

The three boys sneaked through the black streets.

"Let's go to the bathhouse. There's never anyone there at this time of night," Jacque suggested.

"Brilliant. Let's do that. And hurry. I have to be back for my morning shift in less than five hours." Sacha led the way and neither boy noticed Collin's discomfort.

They reached the bathhouse and started stripping. Collin rolled his eyes and did the same. Jacque dove in and swam two laps before he came back to the boys. Collin guessed he had missed coming down here.

He dove into the warm water and swam back to the wall almost immediately. He didn't get in water often. It felt good, like the weight of his troubles was lifting away with the dirt on his body.

"Better?" Collin asked as Jacque finally swam to them.

Jacque grabbed a bar of soap from a little box in the side of the pool. He lathered it up and rubbed it all over himself, turning his pink skin white with bubbles. "Yes. I should come here more. I always forget how nice it is."

"So, how are we saving the girls?" Sacha cut to the chase.

"And how are we not getting arrested. I feel like that's a crucial, yet rarely discussed, point," Jacque asked. He handed the soap to Collin.

Collin took the slippery bar and rubbed it around his hands. It kept squirting away from him. He finally gave up and passed it Sacha, who plunked it back in the box without using it.

"Okay, they say they've still got a couple of days, right?" Collin asked Sacha, "But, I want to get them out tomorrow morning. They're on early shift, right?"

"Yes. I should've figured we weren't only risking my life, but also leaving me short-handed for breakfast."

"Sorry, Sacha. If you don't want to risk this, it's fine. We'll figure out a plan that doesn't involve you," Collin offered.

Sacha glared. "I've known Brenna since we were ten years old. Of course I'm going to help you get them out. What do you want me to do?"

"Cover them up with garbage," said Collin. He immediately backed up. Sacha bowed up as if to punch him. "I'm open to other suggestions. This is all I can think of to get them out unseen."

Jacque looked thoughtful. "That could work. The pig farmer at the edge of the city lives in the perfect spot to smuggle them out."

Understanding dawned on Sacha. "So, we cover them in

blankets, shovel scraps over them and take the wagon to Stanson's? What will we do when Stanson dumps the cart, and two girls fall out?"

"I'm going with them. I'll fight him or something. I'll make sure they get out," Collin answered.

"Also, I think the driver is going to call in sick tomorrow, leaving a driver opening available," said Jacque. Collin grinned and nodded.

"What do I tell Copolo when he realizes two of his workers aren't coming in?" Sacha asked.

"They're sick?" Collin suggested.

"They're late?"

Sacha's lips pressed in, like he was holding back words that might get him in trouble. "He's smart, and he knows Brenna is being sold. He's been working her like a dog lately. He'll be furious and investigate immediately. I wouldn't be surprised if he's got people watching them to make sure they don't bolt."

Collin shrugged. "Tell him you don't know. You haven't seen or heard from them."

"I'm a lousy liar. But I'll give it a shot."

"Thanks, Sacha. We'll be back as soon as we can. Hopefully we can cover it up pretty well."

"What are you going to do to Stanson?"

Collin pulled himself out of the bath and grabbed a towel. "Fight him."

Sacha frowned. "He's a good person. Don't hurt him."

"If he's a good person, I won't have to." Collin said. "I've got one more thing to do before sunrise. I'll be back in a while."

Jacque looked at him. "What do you have to do?"

"Ask a favor of someone. I'll see you soon." Collin grabbed his clothes and left the pool before his friend could ask any more questions.

~

LAURELLE AND MARC'S street was lit by tall street lamps at every other yard. Collin wished they weren't so bright. He didn't want attention. As late as it was, a few windows were still lit in the houses leading to Laurelle's.

He padded through their yard and sneaked around the back, where he knew Laurelle's window was. Her curtains were open, and she was curled up on her bed talking with Marc. Marc sat on the end, fiddling with his cane. Collin tapped on the glass.

Marc jumped and looked at the window. Collin was grateful there was no sword nearby.

Laurelle looked at Collin like he was a ghost. "What on earth?"

"I'm sorry. I'm so sorry," Collin said as she opened the window.

"Please go. I really need some time…"

"No, I know. I promise, I'll leave you alone after tonight. I need something and I don't know who else I could possibly ask. You're the only girl I know here."

Laurelle sighed and cast her brother a look. Marc's jaw was clenched. He glared at Collin. "What do you need?" she asked.

"Dresses. Two if you can spare them. I'll pay you back some day, if I can, but you won't get them back."

"Seriously?" Marc asked pulling himself off her bed and hobbling to the window.

"I know," said Collin. "It's ridiculous. You don't have to give them to me. I'll figure something else out if I can."

"It's for something noble, isn't it? One of your silly crusade things." Laurelle looked tired, and not the usual kind. Collin thought she looked weary all the way to her bones. Weary of him, he thought, and of his silly crusades.

"I shouldn't have come. I'm sorry. I'll figure out something else. Get some rest, okay?"

"She was trying to do that when you showed up at her window. You've got some real nerve, Collin," Marc fumed.

Tears pooled in Laurelle's honey-colored eyes. "I'll do it. You can have whatever you need." She went to her closet. "What kind of dresses? Do they need evening things, like for a party, or day to day?"

"Day to day."

She nodded and pulled out a blue tunic and a red one, both of which Collin thought were probably beautiful on her. "Here are a couple of scarves they can use to hide their hair. I assume the purpose is to hide?" she asked, but wasn't really asking. "What about shoes?"

"They could probably use those as well."

"Okay. These moccasins are really sturdy. They'll last a while if they care for them." She pulled two pairs of soft leather moccasins from a shelf.

"You're a wonderful person, Elle. Much too good for me. Again, I'm sorry to bother you. I hope you get a good night's rest."

"It doesn't matter, Collin. Good luck with whatever you're doing. I hope you don't get caught and that … that whoever you're helping is safe."

He gave her a sad smile, nodded to Marc, and ducked out into the street again. He felt an enormous weight in his chest as he walked away. The dresses smelled like her. He took a deep breath and broke into a run.

THERE WASN'T time to go to bed and Collin felt heavy with the sleepless night as they sat outside the kitchen waiting for Brenna and Ayla to arrive.

Sacha made them all coffee, but he didn't dare use ingredients from the kitchen to make it sweet and creamy as he'd made for Collin before. It was black and bitter and strong. Collin sipped it, wondering how people got addicted to the stuff.

"Ah, the nectar of the gods," Jacque gushed as he took a deep pull of his cup.

"Which gods? Remind me to avoid them," Collin muttered. Jacque laughed but sobered up quickly when they saw two small figures shuffling up the street, black silhouettes in the purple dawn. "They're coming. Get out of sight. Crap. Sacha was right. There's two men following them. Look." Two other black outlines, much taller than the girls followed them down the street, too far away to be noticed by them.

He and Jacque ducked out of sight and waited for the girls.

Ayla and Brenna came through the doorway, but neither man came with them. Collin breathed for the first time since he'd spotted them.

"Ayla," he whispered. "Don't scream, it's me," he said quickly, hoping to stop her natural reaction. She gasped but Collin put a hand over her mouth to muffle the sound. "It's Collin. We talked yesterday and we have a plan. Please don't scream." He felt her relax and pulled his hand away.

"Collin, sir, who is that?" she pointed to Jacque.

"That's Jacque. He's my best mate, and he's your driver. It's going to be okay. We're getting you out of here today."

Both girls' eyes widened and they exchanged looks of disbelief. "How?" asked Brenna.

Sacha poked his head out of the kitchen. "Very quietly and quickly. Come on."

"Sacha? No, you cannot. We told you not to ask him," Brenna moaned.

"Sorry. We'll do our best to keep him out of trouble. We have to move now." Collin explained the plan as fast as he could while they pulled the girls into the cart that usually carried out the trash. The two grinned in excitement and lay flat against Collin while Jacque and Sacha laid burlap sacks over them.

"Can you breathe?" Jacque asked. "We'll avoid piling too much on top of your heads, okay?"

Collin braced himself as he felt the first shovelful of old vegetables drop onto his legs. Brenna let out a quiet little squeak and Collin groped through the darkness for her hand. "Hold my hand. It's going to be okay. If you can manage to keep still and quiet, we might be able to get you out of this mess and back to your family," he whispered so close to her ear he could taste her hair —like coconuts.

"I'll try," she whimpered.

"You can do it. Squeeze my hand when you wish you could scream."

More shovelfuls were dropped on them. Brenna's grip was surprisingly strong for such a tiny girl.

Finally they felt Jacque mount the driver's seat and the cart lurched forward. Collin closed his eyes, although it was pitch black under their blanket of sacks, and prayed they could slip away unnoticed.

Brenna was squeezing his hand very hard when the cart came to a halt. Muffled voices were asking Jacque questions. Collin strained to hear them, but eventually they started moving again. It was a long, dark journey. Collin wondered what was happening with Sacha. He wondered if his friend was in trouble for the girls not showing up. What if, even now, the senator's men were searching for them?

Collin found a way to shift that made breathing easier. "Hey," he whispered to the girls. "If you turn on your sides, there's more air."

Brenna twisted around so she was facing him.

"What are you doing back there? Everything okay?" Jacque called down.

"Trying to find a better position for breathing," Collin shouted through the pile of garbage.

"Okay, we're coming into a town. Stay as still and quiet as you can."

"How much farther?" Collin asked.

"We have to go all the way through this town to the outskirts. It's still a while. Sorry."

The smell of rotting food grew stronger and stronger. At first, Collin held his breath, but eventually, he had to breathe the air available. He could barely make out the outline of Brenna's face. Her eyes were shut and she was so still he started to worry about her. He squeezed her hand, trying to get a response without startling her.

She squeezed back.

He closed his own eyes and tried to relax.

It was a long time before he felt the smooth road become rough. They were jostled around, and Brenna woke, panic in her eyes. Collin smiled and pressed her hand again. "It's okay. Keep still. We're almost there," he whispered.

They were at the outskirts. He let go of Brenna's hand and turned on his back. He felt around on the opposite side for his sword and felt the smooth leather of his sheath at last.

"Scrap delivery," he heard Jacque say.

Someone replied, but Collin didn't understand him.

"I can bring it around. I don't mind."

There was an argument about this and the cart started moving again.

"Be still another moment," Collin whispered close to Brenna's ear.

The back of the cart was being lifted. Collin's hand closed on the hilt of his sword.

"You've parked it in the wrong stall," he heard an unfamiliar voice shout. "Don't fuss. We've got it handled. Help me lift the lining and we'll heave it in. Oy! Something's moving down 'ere! Hit it with a shovel. There's a mouse or somethin'!"

Ayla screamed and pulled herself up as the shovel would have landed directly on her leg.

Collin grabbed his sword and pulled the canvas away from them in one movement. They were face to face with two dumbfounded farmhands. The closest to him was about his height and had the softer features of a Lashaian. The other was taller and obviously a Lightling.

"Don't move and don't scream," Collin warned, lifting his sword level with the closest one's neck.

The other man turned to jump out of the cart, but Jacque blocked him. "You, don't move either, except do drop that shovel." Jacque had his own sword pointed at the man's abdomen. The shovel landed with a soft thud in the refuse.

"Are you alright, girls?" Collin asked without looking at Brenna and Ayla.

"Yes, sir," they both squeaked.

"We're going," Collin said to the two men. "Both of you get out of the cart and stand against that wall. Keep your hands where I can see them."

The men lifted their hands in the air and jumped off the edge of the cart. "What's goin' on?" one asked.

"I told you not to speak. Do it again and you'll lose something that won't grow back," Collin growled. "Jacque, tie them up and gag them." Collin kept his sword close to the farmhands, but they didn't put up a fight as Jacque found a rope in the barn and used it to truss them up.

"Alright, it's okay," Collin sheathed his sword and put his belt back on. He went to the cart where the two girls were staring wide-eyed at the two boys. "Jump down. We have to go."

He held out a hand and Brenna grasped it so she could jump. Ayla followed. "Sir, will they be alright?" asked Ayla.

"I'm more concerned that you won't be. Come on." Collin grabbed a satchel Sacha had packed full of food for the two girls and they ran from the barn. "Those woods are our goal, alright? We have to get to those trees before someone spots us. Duck behind anything you can. Don't stop running."

Collin was beginning to doubt the plans they'd made in the middle of the night. Jacque caught up to them as someone from the farm yelled out.

"Hurry," Jacque shouted and grabbed Brenna's hand to keep her going. Months of training, hiking and mountain climbing had the boys in the shape they needed to be in to make the sprint, but the girls were gasping and bent double before they reached the tree line.

"It's alright. Carry them. We have to get out of here!" Collin said, scooping Ayla up under her knees and holding her tight against his chest. Jacque had to bend over to help Brenna wrap her arms around his neck. He carried her as if she weighed nothing.

Collin was finally getting winded when they reached the trees. He let Ayla back on the ground and Jacque put Brenna beside her. "Hide," he whispered, completely out of breath.

Collin and the girls ducked behind a stand of trees and Jacque crouched low in the brush, watching the farm.

"They've found the farm hands already. They know something's wrong. It looks like they're getting a search party ready."

"Do we stand and fight, or do we hide?" Collin asked.

"First hide, then, if we have to, the other. Come on."

They went deeper and deeper into the trees until the noises behind them all but faded. Collin wasn't scared of it coming to a fight, but he'd rather not kill anyone.

They slowed their pace to let the girls have a rest and Ayla came up to walk beside him.

"They told me you were brave, sir. They said you would help us if you could. I had no idea... I didn't believe a stranger would care that much." Her voice broke and tears poured from her giant brown eyes.

Collin's chest twinged as he remembered Laurelle's tears from the night before. This was why she left him, because he pulled mad stunts like this. "Who told you that?"

"Sacha and Marcole, sir. They've been very kind."

Collin nodded and smiled at her, feeling ripped up inside. "They're good men. I hope I can live up to my reputation and get you to safety."

NINE
THE INN

They walked for a long while without stopping or checking to see if they were being followed. When they took a minute to catch their breath, Collin pulled the satchel off his shoulder.

"There's a change of clothes in here, in case they try to describe us by what we were wearing." He explained. He handed the girls the two dresses he'd got from Laurelle the night before. "These shoes are really good too. They'll keep your feet from getting blistered."

The girls took the clothes and stroked the fabric. Ayla felt inside the shoes. "Where did you get these, sir? We've never had anything so fine."

"From a friend. Someone who hopes you get to safety."

He could feel Jacque's eyes on him and knew his friend had guessed exactly who the clothes came from. "I brought us some stuff too," he muttered without looking up at Jacque. "We should change."

The girls ducked behind a thick stand of trees and the boys took off their things and replaced them. Collin was relieved to shed the clothes smelling of old vegetables and rotten fruit.

"Oy, that feels better," he said, smelling the familiar scent of his trunk.

"What do we do with this stuff?"

"We'll stuff it in my bag for now. Hopefully we can find somewhere along the way to dump it. If someone catches us and tries to find out about the girls, I don't want them to find we're carrying their old clothes."

"We're dressed," Ayla said. She stepped out from behind the tree. Collin felt the need to swallow repeatedly, thinking it would ease the hard lump forming in his throat at the sight of the two girls in Laurelle's clothes.

"Perfect. You look very nice. Use these scarves to hide your hair."

They wrapped the scarves around their shiny black hair and Collin helped them tuck it out of sight.

"Beautiful. You could be anyone now," Jacque commented.

Brenna looked nervous to be dressed as a free Lightling girl and the dress was several inches too long. "We will get into such trouble," she finally burst out. "What are we thinking, Ayla? They'll beat us, or maybe even kill us for this." Her face screwed up, she threw her hands over it and wept into them.

The boys stood frozen at this unexpected outburst, but Ayla wrapped an arm around her shoulder and whispered softly to her in their native tongue.

"I'm so sorry, girls, but we really have to get moving. Is she alright?" he asked Ayla.

"She'll be fine. She's scared this won't work."

"I don't blame her in the least, but it definitely won't work if we don't move. We have to get you somewhere it's common to see Riverfolk walking around free."

"Where does such a place exist, sir?" Ayla asked. Brenna put her hands down and listened.

"There's a place we went to beyond the walls of Halanah. It's a bit of a long walk, but you could get there by nightfall if you get through the wall." Jacque described the village of the River-folk the companions had stayed in when they left for Lashai. Both girls looked stunned to hear such a place existed.

~

COLLIN TALKED AS THEY WENT, unsure if they understood everything he was saying.

"If you think you're being followed, walk in the brook. The water will hide your footprints and mask your scent from dogs—if they use them."

"Find cover before night and don't light a fire right before the sun goes down. They'll see the smoke above the trees," Jacque added.

"Don't light fires at all if you can help it," said Collin.

"I've packed rations for a three-day journey. That's one extra day's worth, but save it anyway, for emergencies," Jacque said.

The girls nodded to them now and then. Collin noticed Ayla seemed to be comprehending more than Brenna. At odd times during the day, tears streamed down Brenna's cheeks, which she wiped away and kept going. Ayla, on the other hand, kept her features set, determined, it seemed, to get herself and Brenna to their uncle's house in safety.

"We're coming to the road," Jacque said when the trees started thinning. "Don't forget to stay hidden, okay?"

There was a bridge ahead where the boys planned to take the road back to Halanah.

Collin knelt and pulled a dagger from his boot. He pressed it into Ayla's hand. "Keep this hidden. If you can't reach the throat, jam it in right here." He patted her on the lower back where her kidneys were. "If you can't get it in there, aim right below the belt. That'll cripple any man trying to hurt you."

Ayla nodded, the same determined look in her eyes. "Thank you, sir. Tell…tell Sacha thank you. I hope he's alright."

"He's much more alright than you two at the moment. I'll tell him what you said, though. Keep each other safe." Collin smiled and patted her cheek. She stood on tiptoe and kissed him.

"Goodbye, Collin of the Borderlands. Thank you, Jacque," she said. Then she took Brenna's hand and led her off under the bridge.

~

THE BOYS TOOK the road in silence for a long time, each absorbed in their own thoughts. Finally, Collin felt Jacque's elbow on his shoulder. "Alright, Armrest?"

"Fine. I'm hoping the girls get out safe."

"They'll be okay, surely. It helps that they look like two women traveling now, instead of ragged, pathetic runaways. You got the clothes from Elle?"

"Yes. I went there late last night after we made our plans. Appearances are everything here, and nobody is better at keeping up appearances than Elle." His voice sounded bitter, but he hadn't meant it to.

"Easy on her, Collin. She's a sweet girl."

"I know. She's perfect. I'm...I should stop talking about her. I'm tired and need some sleep."

"You're in luck then. There's a town not far from here where we can get a meal and a room. I think it's probably best to lie low for a few days."

"We'll miss our classes though. Won't that look suspicious?"

Jacque roared with laughter. "You do realize some kids who come to the Elythium never show up to any lectures in the first place? Your weird dedication to perfect attendance honestly looks more suspicious than you missing a class here and there. When we go back, we'll say we spent our days off having a bit too much fun with the locals. We'll tell them Elle broke your heart and you needed some extra companionship to recover."

Collin didn't like the sound of that. He was relieved to see houses appearing with greater frequency. "Look, the town. Perfect way to change the subject."

They walked a few minutes more before they came to the center of town. There were several shops and stands selling clothes and food, and all sorts of things. There weren't nearly as many shops as in Halanah, but Collin still enjoyed seeing the things people spent their money on.

"Candied almonds," Jacque exclaimed. "Do you want some?"

"No, I want hot food if we can find it."

"One parcel then," Jacque said to the vendor. The man wrapped Jacque's treat in a square of newsprint and handed it to him. Jacque munched as they walked to the place he knew. "Carriage House Inn, there it is."

The inn was built between two other tall buildings. Collin thought that, in the Borderlands, the height would have indicated at least four stories, but here, where everyone was so tall, things were built much higher to accommodate them.

They went through the wooden door and immediately went to a counter. Collin stood on tiptoe, feeling like a small child out with his father. He hated it.

"May I help you, gentlemen?" The man who stood to address them even towered over Jacque.

"We'd like a meal and a place to get some rest," Jacque answered. As he spoke, he reached into his pocket and pulled out a coin bag.

"I'll check on a room for you, sirs. Please make yourselves comfortable in the dining room."

Collin breathed a little easier once they were seated and had ordered a plate of eggs and ham. The cavernous dining room was built entirely of stone and a dark wood that he didn't recognize. The walls were decorated with the antlers and horns of various beasts and, here and there, the stuffed head of a moose or elk. These trophies made Collin's stomach squirm. Why anyone would cut the head off a beast and mount it on the wall was beyond his comprehension.

The lady who waited on their table had ringlets piled on top of her head and her dress was draped so low Collin blushed when she stood near him. Jacque reciprocated her flirtatious banter while Collin drank his tea in much too large gulps.

"Food," Jacque announced, waving a hand in front of Collin's sagging eyes.

"Right. Food. Smells really good." Collin dug into his pile of eggs and took bites of the warm roll. He felt even sleepier once their plates were cleaned.

"My friend is about to fall over in his seat. Will you ask when our room will be available?" Jacque asked their waitress.

"Of course, sir. I saw Milly head upstairs to fix you up, so I'm sure it'll be ready soon." She flounced away, throwing Jacque a smile over her shoulder as she disappeared through the doorway.

Collin raised his eyebrows at Jacque, but his friend's face went serious almost immediately. "I think I know a way to check if the girls got back safe."

"How?" Collin asked.

"Sophie. She has a creekstone, and you have a creekstone. We can ask her to go to the Riverfolk and check in on them."

Collin chewed his lip while he thought about this. "We don't know where she is, though. She said she was heading into Fondair after the mountains. She never said where she'd be."

Jacque shrugged. "People like Sophie always need something to do or they get weird. We'll give her something to occupy her."

Collin nodded. "We can at least ask her. How can that hurt?" He started to reach into his satchel, but Jacque put a hand on his to stop him.

"In our room maybe."

Collin glanced in the direction of Jacque's gaze. A table full of men with worn and dirty clothes sat a few tables from them. Collin didn't think they looked suspicious but figured there was no problem with being extra cautious.

As soon as they were taken to their room, he collapsed onto one of the long narrow beds and pulled his satchel to his side. He felt the smooth, flat stone at the bottom and whispered *souvegelle*. His stone vibrated slightly and he spoke to it. "Can you check something for me?"

He held the stone against his chest, waiting for Sohie's reply. When it vibrated again he looked down and saw the red letters "sure." He smiled.

"Riverfolk, ask about Brenna and Ayla." He waited until she said she would and then closed his eyes and let sleep take him.

NIGHT HAD FALLEN when Collin woke. Jacque was folded up at the side of his bed, holding his hand again.

Collin slipped his hand away and Jacque jumped up like he was being attacked. "It's okay. I'm awake."

"Good lord, my neck," Jacque groaned. "I wish there was another way to get you to stop screaming."

"Sorry."

"Why? Are you intentionally having nightmares?"

Collin shivered. The dreams that had haunted him since his imprisonment at the hands of the Fontre weren't becoming less frequent as Elian had hoped. "No," he muttered.

"Are you cold?" Jacque pulled the blanket off his own bed and threw it over Collin's shoulders.

"Not cold exactly…I don't know."

Jacque nodded and sat at the end of his bed. "Hungry?

You've been out for hours. I saved you some bread and cheese from my supper."

Collin's stomach roared at the mere mention of food. "Wow. Didn't know I was hungry until you said something."

Jacque brought him a tray filled with two different kinds of bread and four cheeses. "Your creekstone vibrated a while back. Sophie's heading to the river."

"Thank the Weaver. Hopefully the girls will be there safe and sound when she arrives. This is delicious."

Something crashed downstairs so hard it shook their room. "What the devil?" Jacque yelped and ran to the window. "You want to come see this."

Collin stuffed another piece of bread in his mouth and rushed to the window. Several horses and carriages stood in the street while men poured into the Carriage House Inn. Collin looked at Jacque's horrorstruck face.

"For us?" he asked.

"I don't know. We should get out of here one way or the other." Jacque darted to his bag and shoved in the few things they'd taken out since they arrived. He tossed Collin his creek-stone from the bedside table.

"Is there a way out the back?" Collin asked as he wrapped up the bread and cheese and stuffed them into his satchel.

"I don't know, but we'll find out."

The boys pulled on their belts and swords last. Collin was still buckling his when Jacque shut their door behind them and turned the key in the lock. "If they are looking for us, at least that'll slow them down a bit."

"Stop this now, my guests are not to be disturbed!"

They heard the innkeeper's voice coming up the stairs on the opposite side.

"We were told they stopped in this town. One's a Lightling and the other's a Borderling. You ain't seen nobody like that?"

Collin recognized the voice of one of the farmhands they'd

tied up that morning. "This way," Jacque whispered, pulling Collin to the other end of the hall. They found an unlocked door there and pushed it open.

The room had no occupants, so the boys hid behind the door and waited.

"Most of these rooms are unoccupied. It's been very slow here since the summer holidays."

They could hear the innkeeper still protesting.

Collin spotted a window across the room, rushed to it and, looking down, saw a considerable drop to the ground.

"There's no one in this alleyway, but it's a long drop. We should have taken a room on the first floor," he muttered.

"We can make that easy. Look, there's stones sticking out here and there where we can climb down. I'll go first." Jacque swung his leg over the ledge and found his first foothold.

"Be careful," Collin whispered. Jacque grinned and dropped his other leg.

Collin could hear the men in the hall getting closer. He didn't want to hurry Jacque in case he lost focus, but he was starting to panic when Jacque's feet touched the ground. He backed away from the building and grinned up at Collin.

Collin swung his own leg out the window, straddled it for a moment, then tried to reach the first stone Jacque had used.

"I have a better idea," Jacque called up. Collin blinked and landed next to Jacque on the ground.

"What the...?"

"The rings. Remember? We can take each other wherever we go."

Collin grinned. "Brilliant. Let's get out of here."

TEN

THE BORDERLING AND THE BYRD

Jacque and Collin rushed through the town, avoiding contact with anyone. When they came to the edge, Collin was on the verge of suggesting they sneak into the woods and avoid the road and Jacque cried out in joy.

"What?" Collin asked.

Jacque pointed to a little house surrounded by carts, wagons and carriages. A stable was situated nearby.

"It's a transit station. We don't have to walk back to the Elythium."

"Jacque, anyone who sees us and drives us all the way back to the Elythium will give us up if they're questioned."

Jacque looked totally deflated. "I suppose that's true."

"But, what if we catch a ride to the next town? There's nothing suspicious about that," said Collin, trying to cheer his friend up.

"They're looking for both of us, right? What if one of us waits here and the other gets a ride? Then we can twist our rings and bring the other to us."

Collin grinned. "Even better."

"I'll go. I don't really stand out here as much as you do.

Without you, I'm any old Lightling looking for a ride. Find a place to hide."

～

THEY WORKED their rings the entire day. Even by himself, Jacque decided to take it town by town, pull Collin to him with a twist of his ring, and then head to the next transit station.

They arrived in Halanah that evening, stopping to get food at a cart on the edge of town. They waited until night fell and then sneaked to Sacha's room to see what the cook's reaction had been to the girls' disappearance.

They walked around the outside of the little house to Sacha's window. Collin peered in and saw his friend was lying on his back, staring up at the ceiling. He tapped and Sacha jumped to his feet. He didn't pull his sword, but he was instantly on full alert. His glance shot to the door, but Collin tapped again and he pivoted to the window.

"Get in here," he whispered as he opened it.

Both boys climbed through and got their first good look at Sacha. His face was darker on the left side and his left eye was swollen.

Jacque's forehead wrinkled. "I see the cook didn't take the news well. Are you okay otherwise?"

Sacha nodded. "It's fine. He didn't believe my story, obviously, but he couldn't prove I was lying either. Did...?" He looked around and dropped his voice to a low whisper. "Did they get away?"

"We think so," Collin whispered back. "We took them through the woods to the bridge over the road to Mahni. We left them there well-disguised. I hope they're okay."

Sacha breathed a sigh of relief. "Wasn't for nothing then, hopefully."

Collin noticed he walked with a slight limp when he moved back to his bed.

"Hey, what did he do to you? It's not only your face bashed up is it?"

Sacha shrugged. "Nothing much. He thought he could beat the story out of me. He's obviously not used to dealing with Fontre boys."

Jacque stopped him with a hand on his arm and lifted Sacha's tunic so they could see his back. Collin let out a low growl. Sacha's back was crisscrossed with welts from something long and thin beating him.

"Good lord, Sacha. Why didn't you fight him off?"

Sacha jerked away from Jacque and straightened his clothes. "It's nothing. The longer he messed about with me, the longer the girls had to get away before he sent out people to search. My back will heal. They suspect something's wrong in your not coming to your lectures today, though. They sent someone to your room. You shouldn't go to class tomorrow."

"Surely, if he shows up tomorrow it's fine. They'll think it would take more than a day to get someone to safety, right?" Jacque said. "Seems it would be worse if he didn't show at all."

Sacha shrugged again.

Collin felt his creekstone vibrate in his pocket. He pulled it out and his heart sank as he read Sophie's reply. "No one knows Ayla or Brenna. Different names?"

"Hey, Sacha, do you know if Ayla or Brenna ever went by different names? I know they sometimes change them when they're taken."

"Try Yasheshwi, one said their mother's name was Yasheshwi."

Collin said the name into the stone and pocketed it again.

"You need rest. We should let you be."

COLLIN WENT to breakfast the next day trying to act as if nothing had happened. He only had one lecture that day but was stopped on his way there by a man he knew was part of the school's security team.

"You're a Borderling, are you not?"

"Yes, sir," Collin said innocently.

"You weren't at your lectures yesterday and we couldn't find you in your room. Would you mind coming with me and answering some questions?"

Collin feigned surprise. "Are students required to attend lectures or face questioning by security?"

The man glared. "Two girls went missing yesterday and we're looking for them. They worked in the kitchens."

"You should be questioning the cook then, shouldn't you?"

"He doesn't know where they are. He questioned one of his staff and the boy hadn't seen them. You're friends with the Fontre boy, Sacha."

"Yes, I know Sacha quite well."

"Then you may know something about the girls he worked with?"

"No, I didn't know them. I spent the day at the home of Laurelle and Marcole. Laurelle and I were..." Collin let his voice crack for emphasis, "...together until recently. I thought I could convince her to see me again. Sorry I wasn't at my lectures." Collin pulled his satchel up over his shoulder and walked away.

THE PROFESSOR in the class was a tall, willowy Lightling woman with black hair that reached almost to her toes. In sharp contrast to the browns and whites of everyone's everyday clothing, her dresses draped in red and pink patterns that swirled through the fabric around golden flowers.

"Good morning, children," she said, smiling as they all shuffled in.

Collin wondered if the two men sitting toward the back, well over thirty, had a problem with being called children. "You may call me Andorra. There's no need to add the formality of Omilitus in our group."

Collin glanced around to see if anyone else thought this strange. No one reacted, so he pulled out his pencils and prepared to take notes.

"Long ago, before any of you were born, there was a man by the name of Onitis..." Andorra's voice was soothing and the story so compelling it held Collin's interest. He strained to hear every word and jerked out of what felt like a stupor when two men stomped in and cut her off.

"We need one of the students in this lecture hall."

"Gentlemen? What is the meaning of this?" Andorra fumed, but the men, both Lightlings – but no one Collin recognized from campus – ignored her as they scanned the sea of students. "You have no right to barge into the middle of my class. Who's responsible for this intrusion?"

"There. He's there."

Collin held his breath. They pointed to him. "I beg your forgiveness, Omilitus Andorra. Senator Byrd requires an audience with that boy at once." The man waved a hand at Collin. "Please come with us, sir."

Collin looked around the room. "Who is Senator Byrd?" he asked instead of rising.

"He's a man of great importance in Halanah, and he wishes to speak with you." Forceful as the man's tone was, Collin could tell his resistance had thrown him off balance.

"Is he connected to the Elythium somehow? Does he have a right to interrupt a teacher during a lecture? Am I under arrest?"

The two men looked at each other. "I...no. I mean, he has a right to do whatever he wants, but you're not under arrest. I need you to comply. We have a schedule to keep like everybody else." Collin suppressed the smile that kept trying to creep to the corners of his mouth. The politeness of Lightlings was amusing at times.

"Your schedule can wait a few minutes, surely. I would like to hear the rest of Omilitus Andorra's lecture."

"Fine. We'll wait until she's finished."

Collin nodded and smiled at Andorra. "Please continue. This is fascinating."

Andorra looked stunned. "Of course. And thank you, my child. What is your name?"

"Collin. I'm sorry to be the cause of a disturbance."

"Not at all, my boy. You gentlemen, take a seat please. I don't enjoy people standing behind me like a couple of specters while I speak."

The men, abashed, slunk onto the nearest unoccupied cushion to wait out the lecture.

COLLIN ROSE when Andorra finished and gathered his things as slowly as he dared. He was pushing his luck with these two... whatever they were.

"The talk is over. You've kept the Senator waiting."

"I didn't catch your names," Collin said.

"I'm Theron, he's Proteus. Come on."

"Why does Senator Byrd wish to see me?" Collin could no longer pretend to be packing up. He slung his satchel over his shoulder as he asked and started off without his escorts.

"He has business to discuss with you."

"Business? Interesting." Collin's tone mocked the men, but he burned with curiosity.

"He's sent a carriage for you." Proteus jabbed his finger toward an imposing black carriage in the courtyard. "You'll be quite comfortable."

~

THE CARRIAGE RIDE through town would have been fun had Collin not been weighed down with a feeling of impending doom. Proteus and Theron rode outside, so Collin had the carriage, with its cushioned, velvety seats and heavy scarlet curtains, all to himself. They whisked past the market square Laurelle and Jacque had taken him to, it seemed like years ago.

They rode through the park where they'd all watched fireworks and then through a part of town Collin had never seen.

Collin thought the senator's house was gaudy. It took them a full five minutes ride from the time they entered the grand gates to them pulling up the horses in front of the house. The grounds were decorated with topiaries cut into birds and beasts of every variety. Scattered throughout were statues of men and women in various compromising positions that made Collin's stomach twist into more knots than he already had.

The house itself was as grand as the Hall of Hospitality he and Julius had stayed in, only built with polished black marble stairs and pillars.

There was a wooden door several feet higher than even the tallest of the Lightlings. Approaching it made Collin feel smaller and smaller until he felt he should crouch a little and crawl under it instead of walking inside like a man.

The door swung in without creaking. The entryway was bigger than the largest meetinghouse in Plahn and opened to two staircases, both of which twisted toward the upper floor.

The carpet yielded beneath his sandals, and he looked down at the grandest rug he'd ever seen. The pile was at least two inches thick, woven with black ravens surrounded by red and purple flowers.

"Fine afternoon, gentlemen. May I take your coats?" A Lightling dressed in a black tunic and starched white pants greeted them. He smiled and Collin felt a little lighter.

"Thank you. I'll keep mine, thanks." Collin clutched his fleece-lined jacket as the two men escorting him handed the man their overcoats.

"We're escorting this boy to an appointment with the senator."

"Senator Byrd is in his study. I'll gladly show him in." The jackets were hung with care. "Please make yourselves comfortable in the lounge." As they walked, the man gave Collin a friendly smile. "I'm Martin, the senator's head butler."

"Nice to meet you," Collin said.

Their footsteps echoed down hallways covered in paintings filled with unclothed people. It made Collin blush to look at them.

"Here is the senator's study, young master. Please wait a moment." Martin disappeared through the door and Collin rocked back and forth in the hall. He heard raised voices through the door. Two men were having a loud argument. He tiptoed to the door and stopped it from closing.

"Our forces are not equal to them, Kriel. An invasion won't work against their defenses."

"The wall is broken. Ruined by their own hand," said the other man.

"I have the Borderling you sent for, my lord," Martin cut in.

Collin stepped away from the door so they wouldn't know he'd heard them.

"Fine. Bring him."

Martin smiled pleasantly at Collin who managed to look innocent. "Senator Byrd will see you now."

"Thank you, Martin." Collin walked into a room almost as impressive as the entrance. The carpet his dirty boots were crushing looked like the blue velvet gown Laurelle had worn to Cassai's coronation. Collin's chest tightened at the memory.

Senator Byrd stood in front of a tall bookshelf, rubbing his long hands together in agitation. Next to him, a bald man with stubble on his chin, glared at Collin. "Good morning, Collin of the Borderlands." The senator's voice grated Collin's nerves. He spoke softly and held his s's too long, so it sounded like he was hissing. "I've been most anxious to meet you. This is Kriel. He's of no consequence to you, of course."

"We'll discuss this later," mumbled the man who looked short as he huffed away from the senator, but dwarfed Collin by half a foot. He slammed the door on his way out.

Everything about the senator, from his overly white teeth to his bright green tunic, was repellent. He looked even less pleasant when he gave Collin a simpering smile and pointed to the chair across from his giant desk.

Collin shoved his hands in the pockets of his brown pants and didn't move an inch toward the offered chair. "What walls were you talking about? Who are you planning to invade?"

"Please have a seat."

"I'd rather stand."

"You're a wonder around here, you know. So brash, so…brave."

The senator started around his desk toward Collin. His hips swayed and he tossed his hands about when he talked. It took every bit of Collin's nerve not to bolt for the door.

Instead, he crossed his arms over his chest. "Your men interrupted a very interesting lecture. I assume there was a good reason."

Another smile. "I would like to recruit your help with a campaign I'm launching. You would be handsomely paid, of course. That cramped little dorm room would be a thing of the past. You'd have a carriage paid for out of the coffers of the Lightling Senate."

"Okay," Collin said again. He felt no need to be overly cooperative.

"You're friends with the new king and queen of Lashai, are you not?"

"I am."

"We're having a spot of trouble with shipments. I wondered if you might speak to them about it."

"Shipments?"

"This and that, nothing to get worked up about." Byrd's unctuous laugh made Collin wish he could punch him in the throat.

"I'm not worked up. I'm curious what sort of shipments you're missing out on."

"Nothing serious. You'd be in the trade relations side of this business. An ambassador of sorts. We had a healthy relationship with the Fontre and we're trying to establish communication with the new monarchy. They've been a bit hard to get in touch with. We'd send you there, of course. All expenses on us."

"What would you want me to say?"

"I would give you letters and so forth. Very confidential, of course."

"What does Lady Ella think of the trade relations? She seemed a diplomatic sort. Why not ask her?"

"We would so much rather use someone with an established connection, you know. Your connections are worth quite a lot, if you know what I mean?"

"I don't. But if you mean the black-market organ trades and the shipments of pink granite mined on the backs of starving, unwilling workers, the answer is no."

The senator's already sallow skin blanched. "Why would you suggest such a thing? We would never engage in anything illegal."

"Interesting what people will make legal."

"Well, leaving all that aside, I've another thing to show you. Feast your eyes on this, won't you? Tell me what you think."

He handed Collin a brightly colored piece of paper. Splashed across the top in bright red were the words: "Malderi" and underneath in smaller letters: "The next generation of household help."

Below the caption three beautiful people smiled brilliantly. They were lighter skinned than any Riverfolk Collin had encountered, but darker than the usual Lightlings. Collin looked at his own skin in comparison and felt a little lump form in his throat. They were precisely his shade of skin. The caption beneath their shining smiles read: "Stronger, smarter, more sustainable servantry."

"I don't understand."

"The slave trade. You despise it so." The man spat out the word 'despise', and Collin took a step away from him. "But this is new and better. More compassionate. It's an infinitely fairer system than the archaic *malderone* traffic of the past. With your help, we'll move people away from slave labor and toward a brighter future for all."

"So, they'll be paid, then? You're hiring workers?"

"Of course, of course, my dear boy. This is much more socially acceptable."

"Where do the *malderi* come from? They look a little different than the Riverfolk."

When he said Riverfolk, Senator Byrd's smile turned sour. Then he hitched it up again. "They're a new breed of worker – stronger, smarter, more driven, and with the longest life-span of any *malderone* ever."

"Breed? So...you're breeding them?"

Byrd realized he had made an error. "Not breeding like animals," he simpered. "It's all very much more...I can't think of the word. It's not economical it's..."

"Ethical?" Collin supplied.

"Ethical," the senator oozed the word from between his teeth. Collin shuddered. "Of course, that's the word, my dear boy. Of course. What a brilliant lad you are." The senator's long clammy fingers dropped onto Collin's shoulder. He could feel their coldness through his tunic. It felt like a dead thing coming to rest on him.

He shrugged the hand away. "For being a brilliant lad, I still don't understand why I'm here."

"You're here to help me sell it, my boy. Show my constituents that this is a better way to live. Better for everyone."

"You're breeding these humans from Riverfolk and, I assume, Kiatri. You're selling them and rebranding them as *malderi*, but this is better and more ethical? Maybe it's my humble beginnings as a normal human being, but I don't understand how I'm supposed to sell that."

"Breeding is not the word, and neither is selling." Some of the ooziness had vanished from Byrd's voice. It was sharpening as he spoke. "As these people have...fallen for one another... they've procreated and birthed an entirely new and beautiful brand of mortal. The *Malderi* are superior in every way, as is our treatment of them. This is a better life, and one well worth convincing people it is right."

"Where's Miriam?" Collin asked.

"Miriam?"

"You probably don't learn names. She's one of the Kiatri you kidnapped in the mountains."

"I'll make inquiries. Of course, you would want a girl of your own. She's not *malderi*, but the next best thing. Kiatri are quite a commodity these days."

Collin's face burned. "I don't want her for my own. Her sister is a friend of mine. I promised to find her."

Byrd looked confused, but tried to quickly recover ground. "I'll find out for you then, shall I?"

"Yes. Let me know when you've found her. You can take this. I won't be needing it." Collin thrust the flyer back into the senator's clammy hand.

"Think hard, my boy. It's a good deal I'm offering you."

Collin laughed. He couldn't hold it in. This man was so ridiculous, yet so despicable and probably dangerous, he could do nothing but laugh. "A good deal? Nice one. Okay, I'm leaving now. Thank you for your disgusting offer."

The senator's hand was back on his shoulder, but this time it was not light. His fingers were strong and they held Collin in place. "The alternative is not as pleasant, I'm afraid."

"How is that possible?" Collin tried to pull away, but the fingers tightened, digging into Collin's muscles.

"I've made alternative arrangements for you." How he still managed to simper, yet look terrifying was a mystery to Collin.

"Let me go."

"I can't. You see, the Light Ones are a people who like things simple. They don't want complicated morals and reasoning getting in the way of their leisure, or entertainment. You're creating a problem here and you must be dealt with one way or the other. You are either part of the solution, or you're a complication no one wants to deal with. Martin," he called out.

The man appeared at the door. "Yes, my lord?"

"Take this young man to the basement and lock him in."

"I want to speak to Lady Ella," Collin said as Martin approached.

"Lady Ella is in disgrace. She too has caused trouble."

"Trouble? Like freeing the slaves? Thinking unwilling organ donations should end?"

"Your life in Halanah is finished, boy. Take him now. Make sure he's secure."

Collin pulled away from Martin, but he felt light headed. Martin turned into two Martins. Then three. Senator Byrd swam before him. "Fight!" his brain screamed. "You have to fight them off."

"I don't understa-" he mumbled aloud as he tripped and fell. He was falling down, down, down. Everything turned to rainbows and then blackness.

ELEVEN
THE MALDERI

Collin lifted his head. His arms were forced above him, manacled to chains in the ceiling. He could barely touch the floor. He screamed and pulled against the chains, but they didn't budge. He felt the skin on his wrists rip. Then his wrist bones broke. No. What was going on? He wasn't pulling that hard. He screamed again.

"Hello, Collin. Did you miss me?" A dark chiseled face. A giant man with black hair and black eyes smiled down at him. An evil, horrible smile. How had Devilan gotten here so fast? He wasn't there a moment ago.

"Cut him open. We need his heart and his liver for a man in Halanah."

The voice of another man made him shiver. Ffastian was there too.

"You loved Josie too, didn't you? You took her away from me." Devilan's eyes seemed to light up.

"No, I didn't. I loved Laurelle."

"Laurelle? The Lightling girl?" Devilan snapped his fingers and twenty Fontre soldiers appeared. "Bring me the Lightling girl called Laurelle."

"No!" Collin screamed. "Let me go! Leave her alone!" He pulled on his chains again. Devilan circled him. There was a whip in his hands. Collin didn't remember him having a whip.

"Let's talk about Laurelle, Collin. Let's see if you remember what I taught you." The whip cracked against his skin. He screamed again.

COLLIN WOKE SCREAMING. He lay on a straw-stuffed mattress. When he tried to roll over, he realized his hands and feet were tied and secured to the creaking iron bedframe. He pulled against the ropes, but there was no give.

His back and throat ached.

A clinking sound came from somewhere. Collin tried to look around and get his bearings, but moving his head was a mistake. He felt like he was spiraling into a black hole. His tongue felt dry as parchment.

He'd been with the senator. He started to remember some of the moments before he'd blacked out. The senator touched him, touched his skin with something and it scratched him. He'd figured out a way to make him lose consciousness.

Basement. The dreadful man had him taken to the basement. Collin's heart rate slowed a little. He wasn't in a dungeon. Devilan and Ffastian weren't coming to hurt him. His wrists were still intact. He was in Halanah. Surely there were laws here against torturing people even if they disagreed with slavery.

Keys jingled. Collin craned his neck to see where the door was. He regretted that when the room started spinning again. He hoped whoever it was had water.

A tall, willowy form slunk into the rectangle of light left by the door, and cast an impossibly long shadow into the room. Collin cringed.

"Good evening, my boy," said Byrd. From the oily tone of voice, Collin assumed he was smiling.

"Let me go," Collin rasped. His mouth was too dry to do anything louder, but he wanted to scream.

"Ah, you see, I cannot do that. You proved uncooperative and that hurts me deeply." Byrd stood next to the bed and Collin thrashed against his bonds, trying to get at him. "Please don't struggle, son. It really is useless. Martin used to run the slave raids to the River for me. If there's one thing he knows very well, it's how to bind someone fast."

"Wow, I guess some people aren't at all what they seem." Collin paused to cough. "Martin seemed a pretty decent sort."

"You sound awful. Here, I've brought you water. I know how the *blight* can dry your throat and mouth."

A cup was held to Collin's lips. He lay at such an odd angle it was difficult to get more than a couple of swallows when it was tipped up. It still filled his mouth with relief. "*Blight?*"

"The chemical agent I used to make you more cooperative. I should have regulated the dose for your size."

"What do you want?"

Instead of answering, Byrd got up and clattered around with something. Collin couldn't see what he was doing until a warm glow filled the room. Byrd came back to sit beside him, setting down a lantern at his feet. "That's better isn't it? I hate squinting at people in the dark."

Collin glared. "Tell me what you want with me."

Byrd smiled and his teeth gleamed in the light of the lantern. "Punishment. I do not appreciate your attitude toward those who've been so generous to you."

Collin rolled his eyes. "Okay."

"There it is again. You're reckless with your false bravado, although it's the sort of thing I need for what I have planned."

Collin didn't deign to reply, which seemed to further annoy the senator. He stared at Collin for a long while, clasping and unclasping his hands, impatient for the boy to react. Collin closed his eyes instead and pretended to fall back to sleep.

"Your other assets, of course, are your experience in combat. Hand to hand combat is an important skill in the arena."

"The arena?" Collin couldn't help but say.

"Indeed. I have you scheduled to train as a gladiator. We do that sometimes with those who are unwilling to assimilate to life as a *malderone*." Byrd made no effort to hide his glee at Collin's reaction.

"I will not be your *malderone*, and I certainly won't be a gladiator."

The man had opened his mouth to respond when Collin felt the familiar sensation of vanishing from his presence.

HE REAPPEARED AGAIN, only feeling disoriented for a moment. He was in his own bed The ropes around his hands were gone, but his feet were still bound.

Jacque sat opposite and grinned. "I've been looking for you for hours. Which library were you in? I looked in two and gave up." The smile died when he looked down and saw Collin's legs wrapped in ropes. "What the devil?"

Collin sat up. All his muscles were tight from being bound. He rubbed his wrists. "Yes, get them off me. I have a lot to tell you." Jacque worked on the ropes, Collin rubbed his pounding temples. "Do you happen to have any water available?"

"I refilled the jug." His friend dropped the ropes on the floor and went to a table that carried a water jug, washbowl and two glasses they'd taken from the dining hall and forgotten to return. The sound of Jacque pouring water made Collin lick his cracked lips. "Here you are. Okay, so out with the story. Why are your wrists chaffed?"

Collin took the glass in shaking hands and drained it before he answered. "Senator Byrd had me taken from one of my lectures." Collin felt like a lightning bolt had shot him through. "We have to get out of here."

"Senator Byrd? Are you putting me on?"

Collin stood up and stumbled around the room, stuffing clothes into his satchel, grabbing Jacque's things and chucking them at him. "Pack. I'm serious. We have to leave. Only take what you need, okay? Like, one pair of shoes. Seriously."

"Now you're being rude." But Jacque went to his trunk and loaded his carefully folded wardrobe into his knapsack. "What did Senator Byrd want? Why would he take you? Did he..." Jacque dropped his voice to a whisper, "...did he find out about the girls?"

"He didn't even ask me about them. He's heard I've made a ruckus in classes about slavery and the *malderones*. He wanted me to champion their new *malderi* campaign, though I'm sure he knew I wouldn't do it. He was getting me out of the way." Collin reached under his mattress, pulled out his sword and laced his sheath onto his belt.

Jacque started to laugh as he finished the last of his packing. "Imagine his face now. Sitting there threatening you and then you up and vanish."

"Yeah, I'm imagining it, alright. Hurry up."

The boys rushed from the room, bags slung on their backs, swords hitting their legs as they ran.

They exited their living quarters and had rounded the corner into the courtyard when Collin smacked into what he thought was a brick wall, but which turned out to be Sacha.

"What on earth?" Sacha said, grabbing Collin before he fell backward onto the paving stones.

"Ow!" Collin caught his feet under him. When he saw it was Sacha, he hooked his arm and pulled him along with them. "C'mon, you're probably in this too."

"What's going on?" Sacha asked, not resisting Collin's lead.

"Bad people are after us," Jacque said in a mock serious tone.

"Bad people?" Sacha asked.

"He says it like it's a joke, but Senator Byrd is behind something really sinister, and they want me, and most likely both of you, out of the way," Collin explained.

"Did they catch on about the girls," Sacha asked in a breathless whisper.

"I've no idea, but they've caught on about who doesn't agree with the *malderone* system."

"Where are we going exactly?" Jacque asked as they cleared the courtyard. Collin increased their pace as they made their way to the gates of the campus.

"Into hiding somewhere. Where can we hide?" Collin asked.

"Outside town is easier. Not as many peace officers," Jacque said.

"Peace officers?" Collin asked.

"Keepers of the peace. You know, the blokes who chuck you into the stocks for misbehaving."

"Right, we definitely don't want to run into them," Collin agreed. "How do we get outside town?"

They had almost made the gate. "I'll go through town and then bring you along with the ring like we did yesterday," said Jacque.

"What about Sacha?"

"He can come with me."

"It's not like he doesn't stand out," Collin argued.

"It's not like I'm not right here and can't speak for myself either," Sacha growled.

"Sorry. What do you want to do?" Collin asked.

"I don't think that'll matter much," Sacha said. "Unless you're wanting to cut some throats for this plan." Sacha had stopped walking and both Collin and Jacque followed his gaze to the gates, which were surrounded both by peace officers and, dead in the center, Senator Byrd himself. Martin stood behind him.

"Good evening, boys."

Collin started to draw his sword, but Jacque put a hand up to stop him. "Don't. If you kill them, our lives are over."

Senator Byrd's words to him in the basement ran through Collin's head. "They're selling us into slavery. Our lives are over anyway."

Jacque turned his back on the men and put his hand firmly on Collin's sword. "Live to fight another day, mate. We can get out of this, but not like that."

Collin looked at his friend's intense eyes and realized he meant it. There was another way out. He sheathed his sword. "Alright then, you've got your man. Leave them out of it. Let them go."

"You involved them. They were aiding and abetting a dangerous criminal," Senator Byrd said.

"Dangerous criminal?" Collin sneered. "What have I done that could in any way be construed as dangerous or criminal besides disagree with you?"

"You are hostile toward the laws of Halanah. You are an unnecessary disturbance to the peace."

"That's actually one of my goals in life, to be an unnecessary disturbance for disgusting old men like you who think people can be bought and sold as property."

The senator's normally sallow face flushed pale orange. "Arrest them," he growled.

Jacque crossed his arms. "I'm a member of the Halanic Race: a natural born citizen of the Light Lands. You can't take us without reason or trial."

The senator seemed to contemplate this. He looked from Collin to Sacha and back to Jacque. "Very well. You're under arrest for aiding this deranged criminal."

Jacque shrugged and grinned at Collin over his shoulder. "Well, that didn't work."

The peace officers advanced and it took all of Collin's determination not to fight them. Sacha seemed to be having similar trouble. A muscle twitched in his jaw and his hand hovered over his sword hilt up to the moment they grabbed them, disarmed them and put them under arrest.

TWELVE
THE ARENA

The boys were forced into a carriage with only one door in the back and a wooden bench on each side.

Through the small, barred window the boys watched the road. They were taken through the streets, past the bathhouse and past the Hall of Hospitality, where Julius had stayed only a few days ago. Collin thought, with an increasingly sinking feeling in his stomach, how different this trip was.

"So we're clear, you can think whatever you want in Halanah, as long as you stick to the general narrative. Right?" Collin muttered.

"Right. Using circular logic is their favorite pastime," Jacque answered.

Sacha glared out the window, drumming his fingers nervously on the sill. "They're taking us as slaves then? We're *malderones* now?"

Jacque chuckled. "I'm sure we'll be labeled as *malderi*. We're the new, improved versions."

"I don't think they'll even consider us as updated versions. I think we're being sold into the arenas."

Jacque blanched. "They're making us gladiators?"

Collin nodded.

"I've heard the food there is awful," Sacha said with obvious contempt, as if this was the most heinous grievance of being sent to the arena.

"Combat experience was a high selling point, apparently. I'm so sorry. This is my fault. I can never keep my stupid mouth shut."

The carriage clattered over a cobblestoned street and Jacque jumped up and looked out the window. "We're heading into the Old Town district."

"What's that?" Collin asked, looking between the bars at the window. The buildings were of different architecture here. Rather than pillars and pink granite, these buildings were made of giant stones mortared together. The rooftops were all red clay tiles, which Collin thought were pretty compared with the black roofs of the newer part of Halanah.

They passed a bath house made of the same stone structures. Up the walls flourished dark green vines, with orange trumpet-shaped blossoms bursting out from everywhere.

"Wow," Collin said, "that's beautiful."

Jacque's fists were clenched on his knees. "Right. Beautiful."

At that exact moment, a group of four men walked past them on the sidewalk carrying something between them. It took Collin a moment to realize it was a man. He was bleeding profusely from one side of his face, which had been slashed from his eyebrow to his neck. Collin nearly threw up when he realized the man was also missing an arm. "Ugh, don't look out that way."

Jacque looked. "Zeno, get me out of here."

Collin felt something vibrate in his pocket. His spirits soared. "Hey, Sophie!" He grabbed the creekstone. His face fell. "The Riverfolk village nearest the wall has been ransacked."

"No," breathed Jacque.

Sacha dropped his head into his hands.

"Wait, it's wiped clear. She's sending something else." The stone vibrated again. "No one's there. She says there's no one." Collin swallowed an enormous lump in his throat. "I guess it didn't work."

Jacque shook his head and said nothing. Sacha let out a stream of swearwords under his breath that Collin was surprised the boy even knew.

"Ellesair," he whispered into his creekstone. "We're taken. Arenas, Old Town." He sucked in a breath and looked up at his friends who were both looking at him. "I don't know what she can do, but if she can do anything, it's worth a try."

The carriage stuttered to a stop and Collin pitched sideways into Sacha, who caught him without comment.

The doors in the back opened.

"Get out." The peace officer glared at them as they climbed out. "Don't even think of trying to make a break for it," he said.

Collin saw Senator Byrd speaking with one of the biggest Lightlings he'd ever seen. Tall, like the usual Lightling, this man looked as though his bulk would have taken up most of the carriage they'd vacated. He chewed on the stub of a cigar as big around as a sausage. His face was scarred from his hairline down to his left ear, which had been mangled beyond recognition. He wore brown clothes covered in dust and something darker —Collin suspected it was blood. A belt rested beneath an overhanging belly and attached to it was a coiled black whip and a sword wide as a normal man's hand and long as Collin was tall.

Byrd's every serpentine gesture made Collin's insides burn hotter and hotter. When the willowy man flopped his long hand toward Collin and said something that made the giant man laugh a deep, raucous laugh, Collin's hand went to where his sword usually was.

The giant man stomped toward them. "Borderling, eh? We've never had a Borderling in the arena before." The man bent down to look at Collin's face and Collin leaned away as far as possible. The man's breath smelled like old coffee. He dropped an enormous hand on Collin's head and gripped his hair to pull his chin up. "He's pretty, ain't he? How much for 'im?"

Collin grimaced at the searing pain in his scalp as the man continued to hold his hair and examine him. Senator Byrd's wide smile split across his face. "He's a soldier, Herolle. The sort you like. Twenty thousand."

The man laughed in Collin's face and flecks of spit fell on his cheek. Collin tried to pull away. "Twenty thousand for this parlor boy? You get funnier every time we speak, Senator. I'll take all three for thirty thousand."

The smile faltered on Byrd's face. "I can't let the trio go for less than fifty. They're all trained fighters. The Fontre alone is worth fifty."

"I still can't believe you've caught another Fontre. Bring 'im over. Let's have a look." Herolle finally released Collin's hair, but his head still ached as Sacha was pulled forward. He too was examined, first his face, then his arms and torso. "This kid ain't true Fontre. He's blue-eyed."

"A distinctive feature for which you may charge extra admission," oozed Byrd.

"What're you playin' at, Byrd? And where are the girls you was supposed to be bringin'?"

"We've had some trouble with shipments. My people are on it." The senator didn't take his eyes off Collin as he said this. Collin wanted to spit in his face. So it was he who'd sacked the Riverfolk's village. Collin was as sure of that as he was that the senator was going to come out of this exchange with far less than his asking price.

Sacha struggled when the man lifted his tunic and started prodding his chest and stomach. "Don't touch me, you swine. I'll kill you," he shouted in a very un-Sacha-like manner.

"Looks like he's had a beating recently." Herolle laughed again and slapped Sacha's face. All three boys jumped at the slap.

Collin felt every muscle in his neck and shoulders tense. "Stop it. Let him be."

Herolle was still chuckling when he put his hand under Collin's chin. "This one's got 'wounded in battle' written all over 'im, don't he? Leastwise he's got some fight in 'im. I like that."

"Yes, he's shown great spirit. Of course, with his ancestry..."

"Right, right, shut up, Byrd. Has anyone ever told you your manners are irksome?" Herolle waved away the senator, whose eyes had turned to slits like an actual snake, but the man bowed his head, clasped his hands in deference and took several steps back. Collin felt a chill at the look on his face. He thought perhaps Herolle shouldn't turn his back on such a man.

"The Lightling of course, the largest of the three."

"O' course he's the largest of the three, you great nutter. He's Halanic. I like all of 'em. I'll give you thirty-five thousand. Final offer."

"That'll barely pay for..."

"For what, exactly?" Herolle turned his considerable girth toward Byrd. "Pay for you to arrest 'em on some trumped-up charge and bring 'em out here? You ain't paid for these boys and you didn't bring no girls as I requested specifically. Take the thirty-five, or take this lot back to their mums. All the same to me, Byrd."

Herolle appeared to take the senator's sickly glower for an affirmative. He nodded to a group of heavily armored men behind the boys. The men marched toward them, slightly out of sync, which annoyed Collin. Hollis would never have put up with such sloppy rhythm.

"Go along quiet boys, and I'll keep the men off you tonight, see? Don't go quietly, and I bought them three new chew toys.

Is there an understanding between us?" This was aimed directly at Collin, who looked at the ground. He didn't struggle when the men pulled him away from his friends and into the imposing round building shaped almost exactly like the arena itself.

As he was hustled down a narrow, windowed corridor, he saw there were tiny cells on one side and a massive round field on the other. The field was filled with men sparring with swords, spears and maces. Along the walls of the training ground hung shields and weapons of every sort imaginable.

A man unlocked the door and shoved Collin inside without a word. The door slammed. Out of the tiny window of his cell, he saw Jacque being rushed past his room. He strained to catch a glimpse of where his friend was taken. He heard voices in the distance, a creaking cell door open and slam, but he couldn't see where they'd stopped. He kept watching, but never caught a glimpse of Sacha's fate.

Collin turned away from watching at the window and looked around the enclosure. The cell looked to be carved out of solid stone. There was no window facing the other direction. On the opposite wall a slab of wood had been installed, which Collin assumed was as close to a bed as he'd get. He could cross the entire space in three steps. The only other things in the room were a wooden bucket filled with water and a dipper, and another bucket, which was empty.

Keys jingled outside the door, the lock turned and two Lightlings marched in, taking up most of the remaining space in the room. Collin tried to back away from them and the backs of his legs hit the bed.

"Wait, are we all rooming together? I was thinking this room was barely big enough for me," Collin said.

"Great, we've got a funny one."

The other Lightling rolled his eyes. He looked exhausted. "I hate the funny ones. Pleased to make your acquaintance, jester-boy. I'm Christopher and this is Mat." He gripped Collin's arm. "Don't put up a fuss, alright?"

Collin realized one carried a stack of clothes. He pulled away and backed into the wall. "What is this? What do you want from me?"

"This doesn't need to be a big thing. It can be very simple. We take those clothes, you put on these clothes and it's done. Or...we can tell Herolle you won't cooperate. He comes in with his enormous fists and doubles you over or knocks you unconscious. Whatever, he switches methods back and forth, but either way, you comply. Do this the easy way, okay?"

Collin considered the two men for a moment. "Is this the arena uniform or something?"

"Yes."

"I'll take my stuff off and leave it for you. Put the clothes on the bed."

Mat shook his head, "We have to search you for hidden weapons."

"Where would I hide a weapon?" Collin demanded.

Both Lightlings had clearly had enough. "Strip, or we'll strip you. That's the drill."

"Get away from me. I'll break your arm if you touch me."

"Right, okay," Mat closed the short distance between them and reached out a hand. Collin grabbed the Lightling's wrist and twisted hard, bringing his knee into Mat's arm. Collin felt the bone give, heard a crack. Mat screamed and sank to his knees.

"You slimy little pond scum," growled Christopher pulling Mat up.

"Wait!" They froze. It was Jacque's voice traveling from down the hall. "Let me talk to him. I can persuade him."

Collin's heart beat wildly. He wondered how much trouble Jacque was about to be in for trying to help him. "Stay out of it, Jacque."

Christopher glared at Collin and left the room. Collin heard the clatter of a lock, a door opening. Jacque was being dragged toward Collin's cell.

Jacque was thrust into the room a moment later.

"Hey, Armrest," Jacque said, out of breath. He glanced at Mat, who held his broken wrist tight against his chest. "Nice one. Listen, okay? Let's think this thing through."

"They said I had to strip while they watch."

"Right, I know they did," Jacque's face was intense. The look in his eyes was scared and calculating at the same time. "Let's do this one thing, Collin. Okay? They have a system. It doesn't hurt. See?" Jacque lifted his own tunic over his head.

Jacque undressing combined with calling him Collin instead of Armrest made tears burn Collin's eyes. "Don't, Jacque."

Jacque put a hand on his shoulder. "They'll kill you, Collin. They'll slit your throat – or worse. I can't face them killing you for something so stupid. Please?"

Collin looked away from his friend's face. He glared out the tiny window bored into the dirty wall of his cell. He nodded. "Alright, Jacque."

"Alright. You'll be okay." Tears spilled from Jacque's eyes. He nodded to Mat and Christopher.

"Wait in the hall," Christopher said.

Jacque was already at the door, wiping his eyes as he went.

"You have less than five seconds," Mat growled at Collin.

Collin frowned and peeled off his clothes. His face burned and he said nothing until he'd removed everything and dropped it on the bed. The creekstone fell out of his pocket. Christopher picked up Collin's last connection to the outside world.

"What's this?"

"A rock," Collin answered quietly.

"Fine." Christopher dropped the stone into his own pocket, then handed Collin the stack of arena clothing, which consisted of a brown tunic that scratched Collin's skin, plain white shorts and black pants.

"He looks like that little street rat what died in the first round last week, don't he?" Mat sneered.

Christopher didn't crack a smile at this. "Your friend is right," he said to Collin, "you need to watch yourself. Herolle don't play around with rebellion." The genuine concern in the Lightling's eyes thawed Collin slightly. He nodded his understanding at Christopher.

Mat's face was drawn with pain, but his mouth drew up in a hate-full grimace as he laid a hand on Collin's cheek. "Here's hoping you die first, street rat." Mat slapped his cheek as they turned to leave.

Collin glared at both as they exited and rubbed his cheek. He hugged his arms across his body, trying to dispel the horrible, awareness of no longer being free.

That was the point of the whole business, he said to himself. They're letting me know they control me now, right down to what I wear and when I wear it.

He collapsed across the hard bed when a wooden flap opened at the bottom of the door. He hadn't noticed it before. A shallow metal plate was shoved into the flap. Collin grabbed it. His stomach grumbled, but not from the proffered fare. The plate held a hard, round roll and a scoop of watery gruel.

COLLIN WOKE TWICE THAT NIGHT, screaming for Elle. The first time, he turned over and drifted off to sleep again. The second time, he woke to someone banging against the other side of the stone wall, shouting for him to shut up.

When they stopped, he heard one faint but welcome voice call out, "It's alright, Armrest. We're alright."

Collin stopped shaking at the sound of Jacque's voice. But every time he shut his eyes the images the dream conjured came crashing over him: The senator, twisting and writhing into the form of Ffastian. Then Ffastian's arms reaching for him and turning into uncoiled black whips as they drew closer.

"Don't," Collin yelled, cringing away from the whips. "Please stop." He looked down at his chest. It was covered in blood.

"Wake up!" Ffastian hissed.

"I can't," Collin cried.

"Wake up, boy! It's time to train!" Ffastian yelled, but the voice wasn't Ffastian's.

A giant fist pounded against his door.

"Get up, boy! Time to test the cut of ya'." Herolle's gruff voice roared on the other side. Collin sat up, his scratchy new tunic soaked in cold sweat. He'd barely remembered where he was when the door opened and Herolle stood in the hall, filling up the entire doorframe. Collin couldn't even see his head and shoulders.

He rolled out of bed and tried to rub the pain caused by the night of sleeplessness out of his shoulders and neck. Herolle bent to meet Collin's eyeline. "Slept well, did ya?" he asked, grinning.

Collin didn't answer. Herolle stepped away from the door and stood to one side. This gesture was unmistakably an order to join the man in the hall. Collin forced his legs to carry him to whatever Herolle had in store for him.

"Heard about your antics last night. Hurt one of my boys again and I'll make sure you don't die quickly." The cheerful tone in his voice made Collin look up. Herolle's scruffy red beard twitched a little and Collin couldn't make out if he was going to smile or growl.

Herolle led him out of the corridor, across a field full of men who were stretching and slicing the air with every variety of sword Collin could imagine. A memory of Devilan's bedroom wall flashed into his mind. Devilan collected weapons. This place would have been Havilah to him.

"The gladiators warming up for the morning rounds,"

Herolle said. "You're not starting with them, though. We'll beef you up a bit before you face the real men."

Collin ignored him. He'd fought plenty of real men, but it was fine with him if Herolle underestimated his abilities for a while.

Herolle took Collin to a door that led to another training area, smaller and square.

"Grab whatever you want from the walls." Herolle waved at the stone walls upon which hung swords and other weapons Collin couldn't name.

Collin nodded and crossed to the wall and began to study the variety of rods, shields, swords, and metal balls studded with spikes dangling from chains which were fixed to wooden handles.

Another man, holding a sword and shield, was there already. He balked when he saw Collin. "I'm training children now?" he asked Herolle in a soft voice.

Herolle chuckled, but not unkindly. "According to the man I bought him off, he's a trained soldier. He's a Borderling though, so – short. Sayin' he's a kid may look good on the posters, though. He broke one of my boys' arms last night. Give him a good run and I won't be mad if you hurt him a little."

Collin's insides churned. He grabbed a sword, a cuff and a shield. He leaned the shield and sword against the wall to strap on the gauntlet, then picked them both up and weighed them in his hands. The sword was too heavy, so he put it back and reached for another.

"Look at him go," said the trainer as though Collin was a particularly interesting dog. Collin ignored him, picked another sword and balanced it in his hand, letting it swish through the air once or twice. "I like his eye. That's a good sword. Dukaian."

Collin turned and faced him, his shield up, the sword ready.

"What's your name, boy?"

"Collin."

"Ugh, Collin's no good for the arena. Let's call 'im Brenna."

The trainer rolled his eyes. "Collin, I'm Starklee. You're off to a fine start. Let's see what you can do with that sword, shall we?"

Collin liked Starklee. His voice was mild and his manner calm. Collin raised his blade and started on offense. It surprised him that after a year of no swordplay, he felt so at ease with the blade.

"Good," said Starklee. "You're putting too much strength behind your blows, Collin. I'm not an opponent right now. Save your strength."

"Harder, Stark. He needs to feel it." Herolle had settled himself on a wooden bench against the wall.

Starklee's next blow was hard enough to jolt Collin's sword arm all the way to his shoulder. Collin gritted his teeth and returned the blow in kind. "I told you to save your strength," Starklee admonished, hitting him again with the same force.

Collin backed up, trying to catch his breath.

"Do you need a break?" Herolle's voice vibrated in Collin's ears.

"No," Collin muttered, raising his aching arm again and facing his captor.

Herolle's beard twitched, this time his smile was unmistakable. "Good. Keep at him, Stark. This kid's got spirit."

They worked for almost an hour before Starklee backed Collin against the wall of weapons. "Yield," he said through his teeth.

Collin could see the exhaustion in the taller man's eyes. He shoved Starklee back and raised his sword. "I won't," he shouted. Every muscle in his body burned, but he stood straight, glaring at the two men.

Herolle laughed, clapped and stood to approach Collin. "Don't," Collin warned, pointing his sword at Herolle's chest.

"Ho ho! This boy may actually make me some money, eh?"

Starklee smiled and rubbed his own sore shoulders. "He might. He has all the right elements."

"What say you to some breakfast, eh lad?" Herolle boomed.

Collin looked at them and took a deep breath. He dropped the sword and slumped against the wall. His arms hung at his sides like limp rags, unused to the workout. Though he hadn't thought of food while they fought, as soon as it was mentioned, food was all he could think of.

Herolle picked up the sword and hung it back in its place. "Attaboy. Let's get you some food."

During the day, a meal was spread out on a table with people serving from the opposite side. Several *malderone* girls were lined up, with ladles filling plates as the men went through.

Collin was given a dented tin plate with an identical meal to the evening before.

"Give the boy an upgrade," said Starklee in his soothing voice. "He's level three."

The girl smiled and reached for the plate. Collin smiled back and handed it to her. She filled a bowl with vegetable soup, added another roll and put a sausage on his plate.

A man behind him, who looked like he was from Lashai from his skin tone and stature, gave him a malicious glare. "Oy. Why does the new kid get so much food?" he demanded.

Collin turned and saw the protestor was at least three times his size. Starklee had moved between the two. "He's level three, Manny," he said in his usual calm tone.

The man swore and took his gruel without another word.

Collin scanned the crowded field for Jacque and finally spotted him sitting alone against the wall opposite.

"Hey, Armrest." Deep purple circles under his eyes told Collin all he needed to know about how Jacque had slept.

"Sorry for yelling last night. Did you sleep at all?"

"No need for apologies. Are you going to sit?"

Collin saw that Jacque had a sausage on his plate, but no extra roll or soup. "How did your morning go?"

"I guess I'm level two now. They said I have potential as an opening act. You?"

"Level three. They're thinking of renaming me or something stupid."

Jacque's eyebrows raised. "Nice. Is your trainer easy on your group? Mine is brutal."

Collin rolled his eyes. "Everything hurts." He shrugged and handed Jacque his bowl of soup. "Here, try this. It's pretty good, though I'm sure Sacha hates it."

Jacque sipped three spoons full before he handed it back. "That tastes like heaven after this gruel."

"I don't mind the gruel."

"How is that possible?" Jacque asked with his mouth full.

Collin grinned. "I grew up with most food being confiscated by the Southern Guard. We ate a lot of gruel. Tastes like home."

Jacque looked pained at this confession and wrapped an arm around Collin's aching shoulders. "That's worse than almost anything you've ever told me about your childhood."

Collin laughed. "Worse than Cobbs beating the stuffing out of me for walking down the street?"

Jacque shook his head. "It's over the top. If you have to get chased and beaten and generally tortured by ugly mugs like Cobbs, at least you should be well fed."

"Where do you think Sacha is?"

Jacque looked around the field full of men. "I don't know. Maybe he's in a different area."

Collin ate a spoon of gruel. "I don't like that."

"I don't like it either."

"I'll ask Starklee after we finish eating. Maybe he's heard something."

"Who's that?"

"My trainer."

"You know your trainer's name? Wow. They didn't tell us. They put us all together and worked us like dogs."

"I'm not in a group," Collin finally admitted, wondering what Jacque would make of this.

"Hmm..." Jacque's eyebrows creased in the middle as they did when he was thinking hard. "I don't like that either."

"Why? What does it mean?"

"Maybe nothing. They tend to baby their elite fighters...the ones they use for serious fights."

Collin sighed. "Fantastic."

"Can I have more soup?"

"Yeah, you can finish it."

Someone hit a large gong at one end of the arena and all the men began to return their dishes to the table, wiping their mouths on their tunics as they went. The boys finally spotted Sacha and jogged over to him before he could disappear again.

"Hey, Sacha," Collin yelled so his friend would turn around. Sacha turned and grinned when he saw who it was.

"Hey, where've you guys been?"

"Here. Where've you been?" Jacque asked.

A shadow passed over Sacha's usually cheerful face. "I'm sectioned off for some reason. They have another Fontre here too and don't want us getting hurt. I think we're a main attraction of some kind. They keep talking about Carnivalle when they think we aren't listening."

Collin chaffed at this. "We have to get out of here."

"Lower your voice, idiot," Sacha snapped. "Do you want to get us killed?"

"Aren't we here to get killed?" Collin whispered back.

"Hey, don't talk like that. We'll figure something out. Keep in mind that we're all fodder and extremely replaceable. Tread carefully," Sacha said.

The boys arrived at the table stacked with dirty dishes, and returned their plates and bowls. "I have to go that way," Sacha waved at a door farther along the wall. He patted their shoulders. "Stay safe."

"You too," Collin said.

"I don't know where I'm supposed to go, but that's the group I've been in," Jacque pointed toward a knot of men filing out of the field.

"You'd better go. Hopefully, I'll see you tonight."

Jacque nodded. The crease still hadn't smoothed out between his eyebrows. "Good luck, Collin."

THIRTEEN
THE PREPARATION

Collin continued training with Starklee until the sun set and Herolle came to get him. Collin noticed most of the men returned to their cells each night and shut their own doors with no protest. He suspected he was being escorted for a good reason.

He noticed a pillow and blanket on the plank of wood and smiled.

Only a few minutes passed before his dinner was delivered through the wooden flap. Most of it was identical to the afternoon fare. Collin's mouth watered at the half chicken included in his meal that night. He devoured every bite and fell onto his new pillow and slept deeply all night. He didn't remember if he dreamed.

The next three days were identical. He got up, trained with Starklee, was escorted through the line for the afternoon meal, then escorted back to his cell to eat and sleep.

The only time he saw Sacha and Jacque was at the afternoon meal.

On the fourth day of their captivity, Starklee interrupted

their few minutes of eating with a look of extreme discomfort on his face. "I need to speak with you, Collin."

Starklee so rarely showed emotion, Collin was alarmed to see it now. "Yes, sir," he stood and followed his trainer away from his friends.

"You're scheduled to fight tomorrow. Not a serious duel, a *tinenarxi*."

"Okay. What's a – what did you say?"

"*Tinenarxi*. An initiation fight for both gladiators. If you win, they'll move you up a level."

Collin nodded.

"All you have to do is draw a surrender. You needn't draw blood if you don't wish to, though most do."

"Who am I fighting?"

"Another new recruit. Don't worry. We'll have you well fixed up for him. He's good, but so are you."

Starklee worked Collin harder than usual that afternoon and he didn't see Jacque or Sacha to tell them about the fight.

He found sleeping difficult. When he finally drifted off, he was haunted by images of Ffastian and Devilan, taking turns torturing him. He woke in the dead of night, drenched in sweat, his throat sore from screaming. Someone was banging on his wall and shouting again.

"Sorry," he called through the wall. He'd barely lain back down when he had the feeling of a black cloth pressed against his face and, when everything became clear again, he saw Jacque sitting on the floor of his cell, and Collin lying in Jacque's bed.

"Evening," Jacque said cheerfully as if Collin appearing in his cell was a normal course of events.

"What the …? Jacque, they'll kill us for this."

Jacque shrugged and scooted closer to the bed. "They're going to kill us anyway. May as well get a good nights' sleep first."

"I'm supposed to fight tomorrow," Collin confessed, sounding much more nervous than he intended.

"Yeah, I heard. Even better reason to get some sleep."

"But you should take the bed. You'll never sleep in that cramped spot of floor. I'm shorter, so I fit better.

"Nah, I'm not planning to sleep anyway. Lie down. I'll keep the monsters off you for a little while."

Collin bit his lip. "Thanks, Jacque." Collin lay back and felt more comfortable than before even though Jacque had no pillow. He did have a blanket, which he covered Collin with, then sat on the floor again, tall enough to rest his arms on the bed and lay his red head on them. "G'night Jacque," Collin said, wondering why he wasn't more nervous about the consequences of this reckless act of kindness.

"Goodnight, Collin."

THE BOYS WERE AWAKENED the next morning to the voice of Herolle booming through the corridor. "You find 'im!" Collin's heart rate kept pace with the boots marching off in every direction. "I wanna' know who helped him escape and when I find them, they're deader than dead."

"Here! Herolle! I'm in here with Jacque," Collin yelled out. Jacque had scrambled off the floor and sat next to Collin now, pressed as hard as possible against the back wall. "It's okay," Collin tried to assure him.

Herolle swore as he stomped up the corridor. "Get this door open!" Keys clattered in the lock. He stormed into the room, taking up all the remaining empty space. "What the devil is this?" he demanded, jerking Jacque up by the arm. Collin couldn't believe anyone could make Jacque look small, but against Herolle, right at this moment, he looked like a scolded schoolboy.

"It's nothing. I couldn't sleep." Collin rushed to explain.

"How'd you get out of your room?" Herolle roared still, his voice bouncing off the stone walls so loudly it made Collin's ears hurt.

"I…picked the lock," Collin mumbled.

"Picked the bloody lock? What is wrong with you, boy? Trying to get yourself killed before your fight today?"

"N…no sir. I couldn't sleep. I'm sorry. It's not Jacque's fault." He hoped he sounded submissive. He could tell that, at least in this moment, Herolle was mostly bluster. Herolle wanted the match to continue this afternoon as much as Collin wished he could actually pick locks.

Herolle set Jacque back on the floor with a growl. "You better win today, boy. I swear…" But he didn't finish. He grumbled incoherently as he grabbed Collin and pulled him down the hall.

"We can't find…oh, you found him," the guard stammered.

"Go tell the lads he's here and safe. Though maybe not for long," Herolle said, giving Collin a shake.

"Yessir." The guard went off in the opposite direction.

"What's all the commotion about?" asked Starklee when Herolle thrust Collin into their training room. Starklee didn't bother to look up from the fire he was stoking.

"Picked the bloody lock to his cell last night," roared Herolle. Collin shoved his hands in his pockets and didn't make eye contact with Starklee.

"Did he now? But didn't escape?"

"Nah, didn't even try to, lucky for his skin. Broke into his friend's room and went to sleep, the little idiot."

Starklee finally looked at Collin. He looked sad and Collin wondered who he was fighting today. He must be someone Starklee was worried about.

"Are you staying for this? I may need your help holding him," said the trainer quietly, still turning something in the fire.

"Holding me? What?" Collin took a step back without realizing he'd done it.

"It's no great matter for someone like you, Collin. A bit more pain. Hard to stay still enough not to do excess damage though." Collin realized with a jolt that Starklee wasn't poking the fire with the usual steel rod they used. Instead, the man turned a red-hot brand in the flames.

"No," Collin murmured and backed into Herolle.

"It's alright, boy," said Herolle, sounding uncharacteristically fatherly.

Collin wanted to beg and cry and run, but he knew none of this would make the two men relent, so he pressed his lips together and set his jaw.

"Let's sit him over here on the bench," Starklee's calmness washed over Collin. Herolle led him to the bench and stood behind him.

"Let's off with this shirt, eh?" Herolle said softly. Herolle pushed up Collin's tunic and bunched it at his shoulders.

"Well, that's a regular mess, that is," Herolle said when he saw the scars on Collin's back.

"Yes. His back's out of the question. I think we should brand his breast." Starklee approached and touched the spot. "It'll distinguish him from the others. That's what we want anyway."

The two men discussed Collin's body like he wasn't present. He tried to block them out altogether. Unfortunately, the clinical way they spoke of branding him was so unnerving he couldn't detach from the situation. "Arms up, there's a good lad," Herolle said. Collin felt his arms lift as Herolle tugged his tunic completely off.

"There, I think." Starklee's finger circled the skin on the right side of Collin's chest. It took all Collin's resolve not to jump away. "Are you nervous? You put on such an air of invincibility," said the man in a kind tone.

Collin took a deep breath and let it hiss slowly through his teeth. "I don't...no. It's just...I didn't realize branding was a part of it," he stammered.

Starklee patted his cheek. "It'll be done in a second. You'll be alright. It might be easier to hold him if you lay him back."

Herolle's heavy hands pushed Collin backwards until he was flat against the cold bench. He braced himself as his trainer walked toward him with the iron brand: almost a complete circle with a dapplenut leaf at its center.

It felt like they were scorching a hole straight through him when Starklee touched the red-hot metal against his skin. Through Collin's stiff lips came a guttural moan he couldn't suppress no matter the effort. It hurt worse than almost any pain Collin could recall. Burns didn't hurt the same as whips or even sword wounds.

"That's good. You're doing great, boy. It'll stop burning in a moment," Starklee's soothing voice broke into the haze of blistering pain.

Herolle pressed a cold cloth against the spot. First Collin tried to jerk away. He didn't want to be touched, but then the coolness registered and he tried to relax. "By Zeno, I've seen full grown men who didn't take that so well. He's a brick wall, this one," Herolle exclaimed. "Hold this against it for a while."

"We'll let you be for a moment. Would you like someone to...? Jacque!" Starklee said as though he'd had a revelation. "Do you want Jacque to come sit with you? There's no training this morning. The branding and ceremonial things."

Collin nodded but still didn't dare speak. He knew his eyes were full of tears and if he spoke, they might break free and never stop coming. The two men nodded, giving him a bracing pat on his shoulder as they left the training room. Collin closed his eyes and pressed the cold cloth harder against the wound.

He sat there for only a few minutes before he heard the door open again and Jacque burst in looking ready to enter the arena himself. At the sight of Collin hunched over with a rag pressed to his breast, Jacque let out a stream of curses that, under normal circumstances, would have made Collin grin.

As it was, Collin looked up and his friend went blurry. "They told you?" he murmured.

Jacque's anger vaporized. Collin noticed he held a squat clay pot and a piece of white sheep's fleece. "Bloody *noaminis*."

Collin did grin this time. "I guess I don't need to ask what a *noamini* is."

"I can speak more plainly if you like. This is supposed to help with the burning, but it won't heal you because, apparently, that's not the point."

Jacque knelt in front of him and moved Collin's hand. Collin braced himself. As soon as the cool cloth lifted, the unbearable burning continued. "Jacque," he whimpered.

Jacque put the medicine aside and pulled Collin into his broad shoulder. "It's okay, Armrest. It's going to be okay; I promise. We'll figure some way out of this."

Collin broke and sobbed into his friend's shoulder until he had the hiccups. "Sorry," Collin said between jerky breaths. "I got your shirt all wet."

"And this was my favorite tunic," Jacque feigned indignation. Collin let out a choked laugh. Considering his own disdain of the arena tunics, he couldn't imagine Jacque's reaction to them.

"Arena dirt looks really good on you," he said.

"Doesn't it? I'm not even looking forward to changing day, which I'm told happens only twice a week here. Twice a week to change clothes! You think *you've* got problems," Jacque was making him laugh so much, Collin didn't notice he'd started to rub the medicine on his burn with the soft sheep's wool.

Collin sat still and tried to stop the jerking in his sternum every time he hiccupped. "Ugh, that hurts," he moaned.

"Sorry. They said this would help, but I wouldn't put it past them to give me something nasty instead."

"You know what's odd? They tortured me as much as

Devilan or Ffastian, but they were so nice about it. This place is weird. They were all, 'It'll be okay. You're doing so great,' as I was ready to scream my stupid head off."

Jacque shook his head. "What was I thinking letting you come to the Northlands? I knew the sort of nutters they are. We should have run as fast and as far from this place as we could possibly get."

Collin sighed. "It's okay, Jacque. I wanted to come. I thought we could help them do better, you know? I thought they'd let their slaves be regular free humans. What was I thinking? People don't change like that. Now look at us. Slaves ourselves, but better fed. And you with no opportunity to show your fashion sense."

Jacque worked to keep his lips from twitching upward. "The greatest crime of all."

A MALDERONE GIRL brought the boys a meal and they didn't leave the training room until late afternoon.

Starklee returned as the shadows were stretching across the arena. He seemed excited to pit his new prodigy against whoever they had chosen.

"You look much more cheerful," he commented as he entered with a stack of clothes. "Ready to get cleaned and dressed?"

Collin grinned at the look Jacque gave the fresh clothes. "Yes, sir."

"I brought a special pad to keep the armor from pressing too hard against the brand. You won't need it after this time. Brands seal off pretty well. Let's get you to the bathhouse."

"Is …is there something ceremonial about the bath or can I take one alone?"

"There's something ceremonial about everything," Starklee assured him. "Jacque can come if you'd like."

Collin groaned. "Sure. I'd love that," he said sarcastically.

"Hey, no need to be snarky. I was there for your first washing ceremony. How different can it be?"

Very different, Collin discovered as they walked into a large bathhouse, deserted except for four *malderone* girls wrapped in identical white dresses, their brown feet wrapped in golden sandals. Their shining black hair was braided elaborately and woven with gold threads all the way down their backs.

Two girls held large white towels thicker than any fabric Collin had ever seen. One held a basket of soaps that smelled like lavender and something else that made Collin want to throw up. The last held a jar of oil. It was sealed, but Collin was willing to bet it smelled like some sort of flowery nonsense.

"I don't want to do this," Collin said, backing toward the door.

"Nonsense. You can take a branding without a word of complaint, but lose your nerve at a washing ceremony?" Starklee mocked him gently and pushed him into the center of the four girls.

"You're to stand back, sir," one said to Jacque, who bowed his head to her and stood to the side.

"I'm actually…" Collin was cut off when the girl put a gentle hand against his mouth.

"We have a song for you, Collin of the Borderlands." They laid down the towels, soaps and oil.

The girls surrounded him and Collin forgot Starklee and Jacque even existed. One began to sing and the others joined in. Their voices blended in a haunting harmony.

Far across the world you've come,
Powerful and fair.

Never in your dreams did you,
Imagine such a lair.
The dragon's flying toward you now,
Just listen to his cry.
Draw your sword and hold your shield,
Or you will surely die.
Never spare the dragon's life,
Do not hold back a blow.
Spear the dragon's golden heart,
And make your own heart glow.
You will fight to victory,
Powerful and fair.
You will slay the beast of old
And take the dragon's lair.

AS THEY SANG, their hands worked without ceasing. He felt lightheaded with the notes echoing off the water and the cathedral ceilings. They undressed him, but he barely noticed. They led him down several steps into the water and swirled around him, singing and pouring water over him in a ritual almost like a dance.

The girl with the cake of soap worked it into a lather and wiped it over his skin. Collin closed his eyes tight against the pain when her hand brushed lightly over the fresh brand. The soap didn't burn as he'd thought it would. The lavender eased the pain and their voices continued to sing in perfect harmony long after the words were finished.

The spell broke when they pulled him from the water. They wrapped him in one of the snowy white towels and led him to a separate room that glowed with a faint pink light. They stopped singing and one of the girls smiled brightly.

"This is the salt room, sir," she said.

The walls of the room were slabs of pink salt, and the air itself tasted of it. Collin gulped a little when they directed him to lie on his stomach on a padded bench. "Wait, what do you do in here?" he asked.

"We oil your skin and scrape you dry. Then you lie here and breathe the salt into your lungs. It's very healthful. I'll play for you as you wait." She held up a curved wind instrument with a lady carved into the delicate wood.

Collin smiled at her and nodded, still filled with reluctance. He wished Jacque had stayed to lighten the mood as he unwrapped and lay down. "Could I, erm … wear something in here?"

The girls laughed a beautiful twinkling sort of laugh. Collin wondered if they were part fey. "Of course you shouldn't wear anything. The oil is for your skin not your clothes."

Collin grimaced and buried his head in a circular pillow open in the center so he could breathe.

He felt oil trickling down his back and the girls tittering about his scars and the stripes that didn't heal. They discussed something in their own language and the room filled with the scent of flowers.

"Helichrysum oil, rose and lavender," said one of the girls. "They'll help your back to heal."

"Thank you," he muttered into the hole in the pillow.

"You're very welcome, Collin from the Borderlands."

All he did for a long while was lie still and breathe and try not to think what anyone in the Lashain army might think if they saw him at this moment.

FOURTEEN
THE TINENARXI

The girls dressed Collin in a dark red tunic embroidered with gold thread in a pattern of intertwining vines and leaves, which he thought were dapplenut to match his brand.

They met Jacque outside the bathhouse. The Lightling man snickered as he informed Collin that both the brand and the embroidery were cannabis leaves.

"What the devil are cannabis leaves?"

Jacque grinned and very lightly patted the padding covering Collin's brand. "Something that would make you feel a lot better about this."

Collin cringed away from him. "Don't do that. They put something on it to make it stop throbbing."

The girls saw them to the bathhouse's exit. Starklee and Herolle waited, as they always did whenever Collin went anywhere.

"Now they've got you all prettied up, let's get you some armor and weapons. Nothing makes you feel less manly than having girls dribble oil all over you. Am I right?" said Herolle.

"Yes. You couldn't be more right," Collin grumbled.

"I find the washing ceremony rather enjoyable," said Starklee. "It gives me time for contemplation, while I know the job of cleansing my body is being done properly."

"You were a gladiator?" Collin asked, fascinated that such a mild-mannered man had ever fought anyone to the death.

"I was, long ago." Starklee said no more. Collin saw from the look in the older man's eyes that he shouldn't pry.

"Here we are. Weapons and such. We'll get you covered up with armor and hope no spears get you in some place we ain't thought of, eh?" Herolle burst out in a throaty laugh and slapped Collin on the back so hard it nearly knocked him down.

After he was fully dressed in armor, Herolle scanned the wall of weapons. "Which sword do you like, boy? You picked a beauty that first day, but I can't for the life of me remember which it was."

"This one," Collin pointed to his favorite sword. "Can I have a dagger as well?" he asked. He thought of Elian and the dagger he always had in his boot.

Starklee nodded. "It's a bit unconventional, but in a last-ditch effort a dagger can be useful. Here's a pretty thing." Starklee handed him a sparkling white dagger with a scarlet handle.

"Made, they say, by the old wood elves what used to roam these lands," said Herolle.

"There were elves in Lashai? Why did they leave?" Collin asked. He turned the blade over in his hand, then knelt to slip it into his boot.

"Fairies came, and they don't play too well with others. Drove 'em out. Killed a whole slew of 'em in the process too. Nasty business it was. Fey don't exactly fight fair."

"I know," Collin replied, recalling his friends' stories of the battlefield full of dead bodies and fairy blades.

They marched him through a crowded corridor and into the arena.

Instead of grass, this giant, oval field was floored with sand.

"Soaks up blood better, you know? Grass is nice fer training, but ain't nothing better than sand for drinking up blood," Herolle explained as if they were speaking of the price of beans. Collin shuddered.

"You leave him here, boy," Herolle said to Jacque.

"Good luck, Collin. You'll take this guy. He's nothing compared to fighting off the Fontre."

Collin grinned at his friend. Jacque went off to the stands where Collin saw him join Sacha. All the spectators were men they'd been training with that week.

Collin had been thinking only of his own fight, but through the wooden slats of his holding cell he could see they were marching other men into similar holding cells and locking them in until it was their moment to fight.

"Don't focus on the fights leading up to yours, my boy," Starklee said quietly. "When it comes to your own fight, remember cause and effect. What your opponent does must have an equal or greater consequence. If there are consequences for every blow, he will stop delivering them."

Collin began to feel the familiar pre-battle nerves. He toyed with his sword, fiddled with the fringe on his tunic and finally stood and paced the dirt floor of the confinement.

The brand on his chest hurt. "Could I have a drink of water?" he asked Starklee above the roar of the crowd.

His trainer handed him a canteen much like the ones Collin had from the army. He drank until water dripped out the sides of his mouth. Fights were fought. Most ended with very little bloodshed. They grew bloodier as the evening wore on.

"Your battle is next. How do you feel?"

Collin took a deep breath. "Fine."

"No matter what, don't surrender. Cause and effect. Don't forget."

Collin nodded.

"And now," shouted the announcer. "Coming to the arena for the first time in his short life, we bring you a boy of only thirteen."

"I'm seventeen," Collin muttered to Starklee.

His trainer smiled mildly and shook his head. "They always choose an angle for the crowd. Yours must be your extraordinary youth."

"I give you, the child, the soldier, and now...the gladiator! Collin the Bloodletter!"

The crowd roared and stomped their feet as Collin was shoved from his confinement.

"Facing him is someone you'll all come to know and fear." The arena fell silent. "He comes from the farthest regions of the North Country, where he fought massive bears, lions and giants of extraordinary proportions..." Collin wondered, his heart pounding in his chest, how much of that was true. "Gentlemen, I give you, Caine the Savage Slayer!"

Collin's head throbbed from the roar that filled the arena as a Lightling sauntered out of his holding cell. He wasn't broad like Herolle, but taller than Jacque. Animal pelts were layered over his armor. He wore a helmet of hammered copper. Collin thought he should have worn one as well. He made a mental note to remind Starklee next time.

"Good luck, gentlemen. May the gods have mercy on your souls."

Caine strutted to the center of the arena, so Collin walked to the center as well. Collin felt shorter and shorter the closer he came to the Lightling. Caine lifted his sword; Collin lifted his.

"Begin!" shouted the announcer.

Collin ducked and Caine's sword glanced off the side of his

shield. Collin aimed a blow at the man's side, which he blocked. Caine swung, but Collin was too quick.

They sparred for almost no time at all when Collin realized that if Caine landed a blow, he'd sever a limb with little effort. However, Caine's size made him slow and it was easy to anticipate his moves.

Collin waited for Caine's sword to strike his and flicked his blade, twisting the weapon from Caine's hand. As the long, heavy sword hit the sand, Collin somersaulted over the top of it, dropped his shield and gained his feet with a sword in each hand.

The crowd roared their approval.

Caine's mouth gaped. He pulled back. Collin charged him.

The Lightling knocked the blades aside with his shield. The Lightling sword was heavy and Collin wasn't sure how long he could keep holding it aloft, never mind swing it. Caine managed once more to knock both blades to the right, in the moment it took Collin to pull them back to center, Caine punched his left side.

Agony ripped through Collin. He stumbled backwards. The sand squished under his sandals and made it hard to find purchase. He dropped Caine's sword, but the gladiator didn't reach for it.

"Cause and effect," Collin said aloud to distract himself from the pain. Two deep, slow breaths and his head cleared. Good, he thought, because Caine was there again, fist raised, ready to strike.

Collin ducked and felt the air swish past his cheek. He drove his elbow up into Caine's stomach. Caine doubled over, coughing, his face screwed up in pain. Collin took advantage of his opponent's moment of weakness and kicked him hard in the shin. This threw the tall man off balance, enough for Collin to ram his shoulder into him and knock him to the ground.

He fell with a thud and Collin straddled him, his sword tip pressed against Caine's neck.

Caine strained away from the sword and yelled, "I yield."

Collin grinned and sheathed his sword. The crowd of men erupted in applause. Collin felt his stomach clench. He nodded to the crowd and walked back to Starklee, whose smile was so broad Collin could see his broken, yellow teeth.

"Well done, Collin. Really well done, boy."

Collin dipped his head and walked toward the enclosure where he'd started, but Starklee put out an arm to stop him. "Go and take your praise from the crowd and we'll walk out through the main entrance. You're the winner. Look happy."

"This is nonsense," Collin muttered.

"This nonsense is keeping you alive," his trainer said, bending down to speak in his ear. "Play the game, boy."

Collin took one more second, turned back toward the crowd and waved. He couldn't muster a smile, but no one seemed to care. The crowd clapped and roared louder than ever. Flowers rained into the arena and someone started to chant, "Collin! Collin! Collin..." Everyone joined in.

"Good. That's a good show. Nice name that rolls off people's tongues," Starklee whispered. "Now we'll head straight through those big iron gates and you can go to your room. Your friends can come see you if it'll make you feel better."

"Okay," Collin said and the two walked across the blood-stained sand to the grand entryway. The crowd continued cheering until they were out of sight. Then they turned, circled the building, and went back into the main corridor surrounding their grassy training field.

"Why do they cheer? Why take me through the main entrance? The crowd are men who train with us. They know I'm coming right back here."

"Doesn't matter what they know, it matters what they see. They see you leave by the main entrance, and in the deep, strange places of their minds where automatic thought takes over logic, they think: 'If I win, one day I may walk out that door. I may be free.' "

Collin sighed. "Alright. So, Jacque and Sacha can come now?"

"Yes. I'll send them to you."

"Thank you."

"Thank *you*. Every time you win, so do I. You're going to do well here, Collin." Starklee turned to leave and Collin stepped back out of his cell.

"Starklee, is it true?"

The trainer stopped. "Is what true?"

"If I keep winning, is there a day I'll be set free?"

Starklee gave him a sad smile. "Of course."

As he disappeared around the curve of the corridor a realization struck Collin like a fist to the chin; Starklee had once been a gladiator, now he was a trainer. Neither he, nor Collin would ever be set free.

JACQUE AND SACHA appeared at Collin's open cell door as men began to filter into the living quarters. Jacque was annoyed by the noise, so once the three had squeezed into the tiny cell, they shut the door.

"Look at you, taking over the arena," Jacque said, hitting him on the shoulder.

"Please help me out of all this stupid gear," Collin said.

Sacha turned him and started unlacing the pauldrons so he could lift them off his shoulders. "They say a match like that could move you up a couple of levels."

"I don't care about moving up a couple of levels. I want to get out of here." Collin spoke quietly in case the men in cells beside his could hear.

"I've been working on that, but it's a conundrum. I can

figure out how to get one of us out, or maybe even two. But all three of us...I haven't worked out," Sacha said.

Once the armor was removed, Collin sat in a corner of the wooden slab of a bed, and Jacque folded himself onto the patch of floor. Sacha stood, showing no sign of wanting to get comfortable.

"What is your idea for getting one out?" Collin asked.

"There are two weaknesses in the compound, but both are well guarded. There's a back door that no one ever uses except to dump laundry and we could hide someone in the laundry, possibly. But there are guards as the truck leaves, so I don't know if we can pull that off. If we get one of you two out, the other will be as good as free because of your rings."

"The guards search the laundry," Jacque said.

"How do you know? I haven't been able to catch a glance."

Jacque shrugged. "I was on laundry duty two days ago. Also, two of us can't escape by ourselves. If we disappear, they'll kill Sacha outright. That's the way they work here. Someone suffers for everything." The haunted look in Jacque's eyes told Collin all he needed to know about whether Jacque knew what he was talking about.

"Alright. So we don't get out that way. But what else is there? We can't stay here for years fighting for these lunatics."

"Can't we? Do you have some other pressing engagement?" Jacque asked with the hint of a grin.

"The food alone..." Sacha let this sentence hang, but it made Jacque and Collin laugh.

"We knew you'd hate the food," Collin said.

"Everyone hates the food," Sacha countered.

"Collin's okay with it," Jacque said, pushing Collin's leg.

"What?" Sacha asked in a tone of deep betrayal. "How is that possible?"

Collin grinned at his friend. "I grew up with practically no food at all. All food tastes good to me."

Sacha shook his head. "That's a pathetic excuse for having no taste."

The three boys laughed and were still laughing when the door to the cell opened and Herolle poked his head in. "Visit's over, lads. Both of you back to your rooms for dinner. Collin, good show today, boy. Well done."

Collin felt considerably deflated as Jacque and Sacha exited, but he managed a smile. "Thanks."

Herolle came in as they left. He picked up the discarded pile of armor in one clattery sweep. "Ah, your reward is on its way. You'll enjoy it, I think. Goodnight. Have fun." The giant man disappeared. The cell door shut once more.

Collin sat still long enough to feel the aches and pains of the fight. The bandage they'd pressed over his brand felt hot. His wound throbbed beneath it. He only wanted to sleep.

His head had barely touched his pillow when the flap of his door opened, and his dinner was shoved through. He thought he'd ignore it, until the smell of seared beef hit his nose. He sat up and saw a platter of steak, potatoes with butter and a large, soft roll.

He smiled and picked up the food, wishing his friends were still here to share it. The steak was huge. His stomach roared as he tucked in. Maybe winning did have advantages after all.

He'd sopped up the last of the steak juices with his roll when, to his surprise, the cell door opened. A guard stood in the doorway with one of the girls who'd been at the bathhouse that afternoon. She held a basket in front of her. She was trembling.

"What is...?" he began, but the guard shoved the girl through the doorway, shut the door and locked it without another word.

Collin stared at the locked door, his mouth slightly open, the unasked question still at the tip of his tongue.

"Congratulations, sir," the girl said. "I'm Amatha."

Collin finally looked at her. "S...sorry. I'm Collin and I'm a little confused."

The girl looked at the floor, color rushed to her cheeks. "I... I'm your reward, sir. Sorry. You get better girls as you move up."

Realization dawned on him. "No, sorry. I didn't know why you were here. I'm starting to understand."

She smiled. Collin caught his breath. She was beautiful. "I have medicine." She held up the basket.

"Okay. It's fine. Um...I don't know exactly what I'm supposed to..."

The girl nodded her understanding. She put her basket in a corner, then reached behind her back to untie the top of her dress.

"No!" Collin yelped. "Good lord, whatever you do, don't do that. Please." He didn't seem to be able to get air into his lungs. He realized he'd frightened the girl. She backed away from him into the wall, still holding the ties to her top behind her head. "It's okay. You're not doing anything wrong. You said your name was Amatha? That's a pretty name."

The girl's face relaxed. She let go of her top and lowered her arms. "Thank you."

"Okay, let's sit down. Is that alright?"

Her eyes glittered with what Collin feared would turn to tears. "Yes."

"Good. There you go. It's okay. I'm not upset with you or anything. Sorry. I'm tired. It's been a long day."

Her face lit up. "Yes, sir. That's why they sent me. You won the match. I'll relieve your stress and you'll sleep very soundly. I promise. They always sleep soundly."

His stomach churned. "Right, no. I'm sure you're wonderful. Trust me, you are not the problem." He realized his knuckles were white he was clenching his fists so hard. He relaxed his fingers. "I fight against this stuff. I'm their prisoner because I fought it. You ... you should be free to decide who you want to be with and not thrown at some bloke because he won some-thing. I can't...take advantage of you like that."

He wasn't sure how much of this she understood, but the tears had made their appearance and he wished the ground would open and swallow him.

"I'm fine. Please don't worry about me, sir."

"Collin. You can call me Collin instead of sir." Collin put a hand on her slight shoulder. "Sorry I'm flustered. They didn't tell me this was part of it. How long do they leave you in here?"

"Through the night, sir - Collin. If I don't serve you, I'll be whipped. I promise you, I'm very nice."

Collin's felt like the steak he'd eaten might make a reappear-ance. "Right. No, that's fine. Of course, I don't want you whipped. Do they look for...evidence?"

She looked surprised. "I don't know. I've never n...needed anyone to confirm."

"Good. Then you can make yourself comfortable here on the bed. I'll...I guess I'll sleep on the floor. I sometimes scream in my sleep. Sorry if I wake you."

"I don't understand, sir - Collin. You don't want me, but I'm to take your bed?" Her lip trembled and her shoulders started to shake.

Collin wrapped an arm around her and cradled her head on his shoulder. He felt the brand on his breast burn as she pressed her head against him. He ignored the pain. "Please don't cry. You're safe here with me, okay? I promise. Hey, do you like stories? Lie on the bed and close your eyes. I'll tell you a story." Collin's chest tightened a little when he remembered why he'd thought of this. It was Devilan's good side, he reminded himself. It was one of the only good things about him.

Amatha nodded, her face still stamped with fear and confu-sion. She lay back on Collin's pillow and he draped the blanket over her. She gave him one last frightened look before she shut her eyes.

"Years and years ago, there was a young Kiatri named Hollis. Hollis loved learning, and he loved adventures…" Collin kept his voice low and soothing. As he told Amatha of Hollis' adventures with werewolves and fey, he saw her chest rise and fall in a steady rhythm. Her hand, which had been clutching the covers tightly, released them and she fell fast asleep.

FIFTEEN
THE LOTTERY

The next morning Collin woke as soon as weak rays of light streamed through his windows. He crawled into his bed beside Amatha, trying not to wake her. He'd barely settled in when the door opened, and a guard walked in.

"It's morning," the man growled. He pulled Amatha up by her arm and dragged her to her feet. "She do alright for you, boy?"

Collin glared at the man. "She was perfect."

The guard nodded and exited with her. She cast a grateful look over her shoulder as his cell door slammed shut and the lock turned again.

The aches and pains from the fight yesterday made Collin reluctant to get moving. Food was pushed under his door, different from previous mornings. He picked it up. It was soft, buttery rolls in some sort of creamy gravy that even Sacha wouldn't have turned his nose up at.

The guard returned to take Collin to training. He munched his roll as they walked along. He'd never been fed before training. He guessed he really had moved up a level.

Starklee smiled when he entered the ground; the same sad

smile that always made Collin feel he knew something bad was coming.

"Good morning, Collin. Did you enjoy your evening?"

Collin shrugged and nodded.

Starklee's eyes narrowed. Collin shifted uncomfortably under his scrutiny. "You didn't sleep with her, did you?"

"What? How can you know that?"

The older man ruffled Collin's curls. As much as he usually hated this gesture, Starklee's face looked so kind and fatherly Collin didn't duck away. "I've lived a while, boy. I can tell the difference between someone who has and hasn't."

"Please don't get her in trouble. She was willing. It was my fault."

"I have no interest in hurting the girls who work here."

Collin shoved his hands in his pockets and looked away, wanting to change the subject. "Will you train me with some other weapon today?"

"Of course. Choose whatever you like."

Collin went to a wall with every size and weight of ax possible. The large two- headed ax reminded him of AJ. He smiled. "I think I'd like to try the double-sided ax."

"Very well. First time with an ax?"

"No, but pretty much. I wasn't any good with it."

"Axes have a very particular swing for maximum efficiency."

They worked with the ax all morning. Muscles that he hadn't known existed ached in Collin's arms by the time the gong sounded for the midday meal.

Starklee walked with him again. "Your fight moved you up to level five. You go to this table to get your food now." He pointed out a smaller table, with a large slab of meat in the center surrounded by roasted vegetables. A platter of fresh bread graced each end.

"Wow," Collin murmured.

His trainer smiled and picked up a plate. "Your advancement

benefits me as well. I wasn't sure how much longer I could handle gruel."

"You have to eat gruel? Surely you were as advanced as could be?"

"A trainer stays at the level of his trainee. It's our honor at stake as well, you know."

"I don't see how there's any honor at stake at all." Collin spotted Jacque and Sacha. His outlook brightened considerably. "I'll see you in a few minutes," he said to Starklee and jogged across the grass.

"There he is, the conqueror of...what level was that bloke, two?" Jacque said, punching his arm.

"Hey, mock if you want. I got this for lunch today and you've got that." Collin nodded at Jacque's plate.

"Hey, I've got my own bowl of soup today. I'll have you know I've been moved up to level three. I slept with a pillow last night."

Sacha said nothing.

"You're quiet," Collin said as they sat in the soft grass.

"Is that pumpernickel?" Sacha asked.

"I don't know. Do you want it? I'll take your roll." Collin handed over his slice of hot bread, which Sacha took as though greeting a lost love.

"Hey, boy," someone shouted at them. It was Caine and two other burly men Collin knew only as the man's bookends.

Collin nodded to him and took a bite of meat. "Good match yesterday," he muttered.

"Shut up, boy. You made me look a fool."

"You did the majority of that yourself, Caine," Collin couldn't help but snap back.

The man drew closer. Collin and his friends stood: their food forgotten. "I've been pushed back a level because of you. I think maybe I'll take a bit of your lunch, eh?"

Collin glared.

"No fighting here, Caine. Settle this at the next match. Back off," Sacha growled.

"Don't speak to me, Fontre. I won't take lip from the spawn of the Fontre Temples. Who was your mum, again?" Caine spat at Sacha's feet.

Collin had never seen Sacha snap; never even seen him lose his temper. The Fontre boy's dark face turned crimson. He shot toward Caine before either companion could grab him. His fist drove upward into Caine's ample belly and, as the man doubled over in pain, Sacha wrapped around Caine's head and neck and swung onto his back. Caine's face was turning red as Sacha held an iron forearm against his windpipe.

Collin joined in, Jacque on his heels. Collin cocked his fist, ready to sink it into Caine's nose, but Jacque threw out an arm and the fist hit him instead.

"No, Collin. Stop, Sacha. He's not worth it," Jacque screamed. "Get off." Jacque moved behind Sacha and pulled his arms, trying to force a release.

"Let me go, Jacque. I swear by the Weaver I'll…"

"You'll what?" Jacque challenged, out of breath. He'd taken hold of Sacha's midsection and pulled at him uselessly.

In his peripheral vision, Collin saw arena guards moving toward them. He tried to pry Sacha's arms off Caine's neck. The boy's grip was steel. "Don't, Sacha. You can't. The guards are coming."

Caine's face had turned purple. He flapped his arms toward the younger man choking the life out of him.

"Oy! What is going on here?" Guards descended on them from three directions. Two dragged Collin away from Caine.

"I wasn't fighting. I was trying to get him off," he yelled as they pulled him. He watched as one hit Sacha hard in the side. Another brought a long bamboo rod down heavily on Sacha's back. He groaned in pain and finally let go.

"You're done, boy," one of the guards huffed at Collin as they pushed him toward the corridor.

"No, I want to finish training. It's over. I wasn't fighting," Collin protested as they thrust him into his cell and slammed the door.

~

COLLIN PACED his tiny floor for an hour before he heard the lock click. Starklee and Herolle both stood in the corridor. Starklee looked worried and Herolle looked furious.

"What is the meaning of this, boy?" roared the larger man.

"I didn't..."

"Shut your mouth! Get out here."

Collin mutely obeyed. Each man gripped an arm and they marched him down the hall. He wondered what the punishment was for fighting. He trotted to keep up pace as they dragged him back to the training room.

"You was showing real potential! What are you playing at?"

"Caine is a weasel. He was being really cruel to Sacha," Collin explained breathlessly.

"Sacha is a whole 'nother matter," Herolle fumed back. "You realize fighting outside the arena is a serious infraction? Could be punishable by death if you catch me in the right mood."

Collin felt like he'd missed a very large step on a set of stairs. "Death?"

"Of course, death, you idiot. You men are trained gladiators. What do you think happens if we let fights break out whenever and wherever you like?" Herolle's face was less than an inch from Collin's.

"It was my fault. Please don't take it out on Sacha. Caine was angry at me and trying to provoke my friends to get a rise. I promise you, sir. Sacha was there, an easy target."

"Naturally Caine is angry at you, Collin," Starklee's own

voice held an edge that made Collin shake. "You beat him in a very important trial. You advanced and he was denounced. You're half his size and half his age. He's been here a year trying to make a name for himself. Any man would be furious at you."

Collin nodded. "Okay. So...my fault? We all agree on that, right?"

Herolle deflated slightly. "You're too attached to your friends, boy. It makes you a liability."

"Punish me then. I'll take it."

"You'll take it if it's your neck I decide to break, won't you? You'll take that?" Herolle's face was an inch from Collin's.

Collin stepped back. "Whatever you have to do. Please leave Sacha out of it. He's a brilliant fighter. He can make you money."

"*You're* a brilliant fighter," Herolle roared. He backhanded Collin. Bright lights popped before his eyes and his right ear felt like it would burst. "You were going to make me money, you little prat."

"I'll deal with him, Herolle," Collin heard Starklee say through the buzzing in his head.

Herolle shook his head, raised his hand once more. Collin braced himself for another blow, but Herolle stared at him for a long moment, then lowered his hand and stormed from the room.

Collin massaged his ear. "What's going to happen to Sacha?"

Starklee shook his head. "He'll be moved up in the fight rotation at the very least. Probably flogged. He almost killed Caine."

"What about Jacque? He tried to pull Sacha off. He didn't fight," Collin said.

"Your friend Jacque is the only one capable of keeping his cool, apparently."

"Am I going to be flogged?"

Starklee sighed. "Would it do any good? From the state of

your back, that's been tried more than once, and yet, here we are."

Collin stiffened. "What's my punishment then?"

"No food tonight. Water, but no food. Slip up again and I'll slit your throat in front of all the men to set an example. Understood?"

Collin nodded.

"Your real fight is in two days, and we have work to do. Get your ax or your sword or whatever you think will help you fight me off." He still sounded so calm and sad Collin had the distinct impression of being a pig about to find out ham is on the menu.

He grabbed the ax he'd been working with and prepared for a tough afternoon.

COLLIN WASN'T ALLOWED to leave Starklee's side for the next two days. His trainer picked him up in the morning, marched him to training and brought him food in their training room. He didn't bring Collin anything as good as the food in his moment of being at level five, only enough meat and gruel to keep him fueled for training.

Starklee talked constantly of the upcoming match in which Collin would be featured as a rising child star in the arena. Intensity heightened when Collin discovered he would be fighting in a death match.

In addition to the ax, which Collin was comfortable with by the second day, Starklee taught him basic techniques for evading a mace. "You've no experience at all with this weapon. What if your opponent chooses it?"

Collin took the spiked ball attached by a short chain to a club handle. "Well, that's pleasant," he said, dryly.

Starklee chuckled. "It's even less pleasant when it's sticking into your gut, so pay attention."

He spent the next few hours on maces and then escorted Collin back to his cell.

"What happens if neither of us is killed in the match? What if someone surrenders?" Collin asked quietly as they walked.

"If he surrenders to you, kill him. The jugular slice I showed you is the most humane. A stab in the abdomen is effective, but a terrible way to die."

Visions of Devilan lying on a couch with an arrow sticking out of him flashed in Collins mind's eye. He shuddered.

"You do not surrender. You keep fighting no matter what. Even if you're an inch from death, there are healers here who can bring you back. Never give up."

"Who is my opponent?"

Starklee shook his head. "You'll draw a number tomorrow before the event. Whoever draws the same number is your opponent."

"Any other things I should know? There's not...like a ceremonial flagellation I have to attend before the match or anything?"

Starklee laughed. "No. You've been branded and you're ready to fight. You'll get better food tomorrow. You'll get your bath and wait for the match."

"I don't want a girl brought to me after, if I live."

His trainer stopped halfway to unlocking the door of his cell. "Why? It'll be a better girl than last time. Amatha is very inexperienced."

Collin felt his face growing hot with rage. "Amatha is a wonderful girl. I … I don't want one, please. Can I have Jacque or Sacha come visit me instead? I haven't seen them all week."

Starklee gave him a hard look that Collin didn't understand. "We'll see how the match goes and then discuss it."

Collin nodded. "Right."

The cell door unlocked, and he was put inside for the night.

THE DAY of the fight was much less painful than the *Tinarxi*. Collin trained in the morning, but only to hone his technique. Starklee wanted to spare his strength for the evening.

The washing was as haunting and uncomfortable as before, but this time, there were multiple men in the bathhouse with him, including Sacha.

Collin avoided eye-contact as the girls wound around him, washing him, and singing their beautiful song. The girls washing the other men sang too and the harmony gave Collin gooseflesh.

The worst part of the afternoon was being dressed in the armor, which looked more like a costume to Collin.

Strips of leather hung off the pauldrons like a fringe, and much of his torso and legs were left bare. "It's to give people a chance to enjoy your body," explained the girls, who were strapping items on piece by piece.

"Fantastic," Collin muttered. "And give my opponent a clear shot at my stomach?"

The girls giggled. "You should see what women wear when they're made to fight."

"They make women fight?"

"Sometimes. There are no women on the list tonight, though."

One laced something to his breastplate that looked like a metal skirt.

"What is this?" he asked.

"It's a cuirass. It'll protect your...um...areas below the belt."

"So...what about the leather breaches I wore last time?"

"Herolle wants to show off your legs as well. Don't worry sir. Blows to the legs are rarely fatal."

"Unless they get infected," another girl added.

"Good lord," Collin grumbled again as they laced sandals all the way up to his knees. "I look like an idiot."

The girls giggled again.

Amatha blushed. "I think you look beautiful."

THE GLADIATORS for the evening were herded into groups. One group was enormous, and Collin saw Jacque was in it, dressed in a blue and red outfit with puffed sleeves, and red and blue striped pants that ballooned out to his knees and then gathered above his shins.

Collin waved briefly and wanted to jab him about his outfit but, before he had the chance, he was shunted off to his own, much smaller group.

He saw with a sinking heart that Sacha was also in this group. He had a bruised cheek and a scab on his lip that looked like it had split recently. His armor was a strange cut-out version of black leather Fontre fighting gear. His torso was bare, as Collin's was, but, Collin noted, at least he got to wear full leather pants and boots.

"Hey," Collin called to him. He smiled and trotted over.

"Hey, yourself."

"You look great," Collin said.

Sacha rolled his eyes. "I'd hit you for that, but I'd probably get run through on the spot. Besides, I wouldn't talk if I were in *that* getup. Did you hear about this nonsense they're putting us through?" Sacha waved at the hat holding paper slips with the numbers they were to draw.

Collin's smile flattened out. "Be careful, okay? They're certainly not joking about the brutality of this one."

Sacha nodded, but didn't seem able to say anything.

"Gladiators," shouted Herolle as he walked into the middle of the group holding a large reed basket. "I will pull your numbers from this basket. The lottery is random. When I call your name, step to the front. The other fighter with your number is your opponent."

Collin's eyes darted to Sacha. The Fontre boy put an elbow on Collin's shoulder while they waited for their numbers. Collin looked across the group and saw Caine glaring at them. Herolle continued to call out names and numbers.

Please don't let me get the same number as Caine. Please. Please don't let me get him again, Collin prayed silently.

"Collin of the Borderlands," Herolle pulled a number out of his basket. Collin stepped forward and held his breath. "Number 6. Your opponent..." he pulled another number and handed it to Sacha. "Sacha of the Fontre. Good luck. May the best man win."

SIXTEEN
THE ARENA

Sacha held the slip of parchment, frozen as he stared at the number six.

Collin shook his head. "This isn't random. The lottery is rigged."

"Punishment for the other day. I had a feeling that's what they were up to the moment I saw you in this group." Sacha's eyes were black, and his muscles tense.

"But … what are we going to do?"

Sacha grabbed his arm. "I'm meant to die tonight, Collin. They're going to kill me one way or the other."

"No."

"Collin," Sacha pleaded.

"You can't ask me to do that."

"It'll move you up the ranks. Maybe gain their trust. Maybe you can slip away from them and free Josie's little sister after all."

"Sacha… "

"Gladiators, get moving," barked Herolle. "No communication from this moment forward."

Collin looked at his captor, stared hard into his eyes and Herolle stared back. "I told you, friends are a liability."

Hard hands gripped Collin's shoulders, propelling him back to the maze of corridors that made up the inside of the arena. "Move along, boy. Let's get you to your holding cell." Starklee was there. Collin hadn't seen him join the group.

"Herolle is … he says I've got to fight Sacha," Collin said, dazed as he was marched away from his friend. "I can't do that. I won't. They can't make us fight."

"You'll both die if you don't."

"Fine. I'll die then."

"You'll be tortured to death, boy. You cannot make fools of these people. You are not free to do as you like. That's their point. Learn from your mistakes, do as you're told. Remember the jugular is fairly painless."

Collin glared and squared his shoulders with his trainer. "I've been tortured before."

Starklee's eyes filled with sorrow. "I'll be forced to do it. They'll make me torture the life out of you. Do you understand? Your fate and mine…they're linked. There's nothing I can do about it, boy. Nothing."

Collin had never heard his trainer's voice waver even a little. It was shaking now. His hands were shaking too.

"Okay. I'm sorry. I…I figured I'd be fighting someone who'd been here a while. I know they want me dead, but…I didn't know it would be this."

"They don't want you dead. Survive the fight and they'll take good care of you." He opened a heavy metal door. There was a manacle on a chain bolted into the wall. "You stay here until the fight begins. Do you need food or water?"

Collin shook his head. Starklee took Collin's right wrist and locked it in the manacle. Collin felt so ill, even if this was the last time he would ever see food, he couldn't touch a bite.

Starklee patted his shoulder and left. The door shut. The lock turned.

Collin looked around. His holding cell consisted of four walls and a floor, and one small window about ten feet up. Cramped as it was, it was bigger than the room he slept in. He could see the last of the daylight through the window that even a Lightling wouldn't be tall enough to reach. He gave the manacle an experimental tug. It didn't give in the least. He'd learned better than to pull until his wrists were chaffed.

The sigh that escaped him felt like it came all the way from his toes. He paced the dirt floor—as far as his chain would allow—trying to figure out what he should do.

"You can do this, idiot. You can find a way out." He looked at the window again.

After an hour that seemed like ten had passed, he finally landed on a terrible idea, but maybe the only answer in his impossible situation. I'll slit my own throat, he thought. I'll walk into the arena and die as they want, but Sacha won't have to do it.

He trembled thinking about it. He could do it, though. They would probably still punish Starklee but, he hoped, not as harshly. Maybe they would even consider it a victory for Sacha. "Maybe they'll let him live," he mumbled.

"You know what they say about talking to yourself?" Sophie's voice slammed into him like a physical thing. He spun around to see her perched behind him, on the windowsill ten feet above.

"Hey, kid," she said, grinning.

"Sophie, what on earth? How did you get up there?" Collin's spirit's soared.

"You look like an idiot. Who dressed you in that getup?"

Collin glared at her. "That's all you have to say right now? I'm supposed to go and fight Sacha to the death and you're mocking my outfit? Get me out of here."

"Sorry, the outfit's so terribly mockable. Where's Jacque?"

"How the devil should I know? They've got us all split up and they're making me fight Sacha. Did you catch that part?"

"I caught it. They're almost to your name in the lineup. The blokes they've got fighting now are pretty ridiculous. Only one or two are actual fighters."

"Hey! I can get Jacque," Collin said. He grinned at Sophie and twisted the silver ring on his finger.

Jacque lunged into the cell, covered in dirt, his nose bloodied. They'd summoned him mid-swing. Collin jumped out of the way to avoid his enormous fist.

"Oy!" Jacque shouted, figuring out what had happened.

"Woah, Jacque, it's us. Oh no. Did I disappear you from the arena?"

"Hey, Soph," Jacque said, as if he regularly encountered his friends in windows around the compound. "Nah, the arena bit is over. I was fighting. They were taking bets. I was teaching them a lesson."

"Who were you fighting?" Collin asked.

"The other men in my group. You're up next and they were wagering on you or Sacha."

Collin rolled his eyes. "Nice."

"Instead of talking about it, let's get you all out of here, shall we?" Sophie suggested. Collin heard footsteps and jingling keys on the other side of door.

Jacque ducked outside the door, pressed against the wall to take the man by surprise. Collin twisted his wrist around the manacle, which despite his care, had rubbed him raw.

"Aw, look at the boy wonder," jeered the Lightling jailer who sauntered in followed by two other armed guards.

One Collin recognized as a Lashain, no taller than he. The other was a Riverman, powerfully built with a beard and mustache so bushy the only part of his face visible was two beady brown eyes and a long thin, nose.

"Not so tough in chains though, are ye?" jeered the jailer.

Collin scowled. "Not very tough, no. Just tough enough for you to need three guards to fetch me."

"One more word, boy, and I swear by Zeno..." The jailor approached Collin, and wiped his hand down Collin's face.

Jacque waited until all three men had entered before he slammed the door, making them jump and twist around.

"Evening, gentlemen," Jacque said, touching his forehead as though doffing a cap.

"How in the burning pit of Hades did you manage this?" shrieked the jailer. His face had gone pale, as if he suspected the boys were ghosts who could walk through walls.

"Magic," Collin said.

The jailer threw Collin a dirty look and an arrow whizzed from above and shot the jealer through the shoulder blade. He screamed.

"We can fly also," Sophie quipped. She jumped from the sill and landed soft as a cat on the dirt floor.

"What the bloody-?" The Riverman's curse cut off as Jacque grabbed him in a chokehold.

Collin lunged for the Lashain and wrapped the chain from his manacle around the man's neck. "Give me the key, *Nordian*, or I'll snap his neck like the twig it is," Collin growled.

Sophie had knocked the jailor off his feet and pinned him to the wall beneath the window.

"Snap it then," said the jailer in a weak voice, breathless with pain. "If we let you go, we're as good as dead."

"Good to know," Sophie said, pushing the arrow deeper into his shoulder. His scream reverberated off the stone walls of the cell and Collin cringed. Sophie took the opportunity to relieve the man of his bunch of keys. She tossed them at Collin's feet.

Collin pulled the chain tighter around his captive's neck. "Don't," wheezed the Lashain. "Please don't kill me. I've got a family."

"Really? Any sons around seventeen you'd like to see sold into the arena?" Collin asked.

"I'm sorry. I'm doing my job. Please." The man was almost out of air.

Collin shoved him to the ground. The man gasped and massaged his neck but made no move to rise.

"It's a lousy job. Everything is available to you in this city and you choose to enslave your fellowmen and pit them against each other in the arena like animals? Pathetic." Collin picked up the keys and tried four before the manacle fell away.

They heard a roar from the crowd in the distance. Collin wondered if that meant Sacha had been thrust into the arena. "We've got to go," Jacque said.

"Right. What do we do with them?" Collin asked.

"If they're fated to die anyway, maybe we should, you know, help them along..." Sophie gave the arrow a twist, tearing a sound from the jailor that couldn't be human.

"Stop, Soph. Good lord," Collin rubbed his own shoulder in sympathy. "Lock them in and let's go."

Jacque released the man he held with a hard kick to the ribs. "Don't get up," he said. The man groaned.

Sophie ripped her arrow from the jailer. "Good luck with your owners, idiot."

"Stop," the jailer whispered. "Please kill me first. They'll show no mercy."

"C'mon Sophie," Collin insisted.

But Sophie ignored him. She walked to the jailer and pushed her boot into his wounded shoulder. "What makes you think I'd show mercy? These boys you almost killed, they're my friends, and I don't have many friends. You should pray they kill you. If I see you again, I'll introduce you to a technique called 'death by a thousand cuts.' "

Collin shuddered at the look on her face when she turned from her prey and preceded him through the door. "She's secretly hoping we run into more people to kill, isn't she?" he whispered to Jacque.

"Shut up and walk, Collin, or you're next," she said over her shoulder.

"Right. Coming."

Sophie wiped the blood from her arrow on her brown pants and nocked it back into her bow. Collin noticed her gait was exactly the same as her uncle Hollis'. The hallway ended with a corridor that went in both directions.

"Which way is out?" she asked.

Collin tipped his head to the right. "I think it's that way. I don't know. It's a maze in here. What about Sacha?"

"Where did they take him?"

"The opposite direction to me. So, I think that way."

"I think he's already in the arena," Jacque said.

"We can't leave him behind," Collin said. "They'll kill him outright."

"You two have no faith in me at all, do you? I've broken in once. I can come back for him." In the middle of the curving corridor was a heavy wooden gate. Sophie kicked it, sending up a cloud of dust that made Collin cough. "Didn't budge," she huffed.

"I've got this, Soph." Jacque threw his body against the gate. The door rattled and the hinges whined.

"Do that once more and I think we've got it," Sophie said.

Jacque grunted and rubbed his shoulder. "Ugh, alright, stand back." He screwed up his face and rammed the gate again. It fell flat to the ground in a cloud of sand and dust.

Jacque yelled in triumph, and the three charged into the cloud. Heavy footsteps pounded behind them and Collin heard a gruff, "Oy! They've broken the gate!"

Collin and Jacque heaved the gate back up and leaned it against the posts.

"That'll hold them for less than a second," Collin panted.

"Um…boys…" Sophie muttered.

"We're good. If there's not many, we can fight them off," Jacque said.

"I found Sacha," Sophie said.

A crowd behind them exploded into a roar.

"Zeno."

"Crap." Collin had turned from the gate and seen the reason Sophie's face was white. They'd knocked down the gate that led into the arena. Sacha stood at the other end. a dazed look on his face.

"Anyone got a spare weapon I could borrow?" Jacque shouted over the mass of humanity screaming around them.

Collin drew his sword and handed it to his friend. Jacque shook his head. "That's all you've got."

"It's not." He pulled a double-headed ax from a strap on his back.

"Got a dagger in your girdle as well?"

"Nope. The dagger's in my sandal straps. Remind me to kill you for that later."

Jacque grinned and took the sword. "Ready?"

"As I'll ever be," Collin answered.

An announcer stood in the middle of the circle slowly recovering from the shock of their sudden appearance. "We've three challengers it seems," he roared and waited for the crowd's reaction.

No one in the crowd seemed to have realized something had gone amiss. They screamed and clapped and jumped to their feet.

"Savages," Sophie snarled.

Sacha took a few steps toward them, but the announcer threw up a hand so he could work the crowd into a greater frenzy. "They must know the extraordinary strength of their champion would be too great for one soldier," shouted the announcer. The crowd screamed louder.

Collin shook his head. "What are we supposed to do?"

"Grab Sacha and find a way out," Jacque yelled over the racket.

The gate crashed to the ground behind them and half a dozen men, armed and glowering, blocked the way they came in.

The three backed toward the center of the arena. Collin stepped on something and almost fell. When he looked at his feet, he saw someone's severed hand, half buried in the bloodied sand. Bile burned the back of his throat.

The announcer had reached them now. "What the devil is going on here?" He grabbed Collin's arm to drag him away from Jacque and Sophie.

Collin yanked his arm. "Get out of here now, while you still..." His words choked off in horror. A black-feathered arrow was sticking out of the announcer's neck.

The man's eyebrows knitted together, and his mouth froze, opened wide in a horrible silent scream. Collin jumped away from him. When the man fell, Collin saw Sophie aiming another arrow, this time at the guards.

"Let us out, or choose which one of you dies next," she shouted.

The men behind them took a few tentative steps forward and Collin almost laughed at the confusion on their faces. They weren't used to things going wrong. The arena was a fortress, a well-oiled machine.

Collin raised his ax and Jacque winked. "Here comes Sacha."

"Fontre, fight for us and we'll see to it you take the highest honor in the arena," yelped one of the guards.

"Fantastic. I'll kill my friends and pop over to your side. Naturally," Sacha sneered. "Save the one on the right for me, okay? He did this," Sacha said, pointing to his battered face.

The crowd had finally silenced. The death of the announcer was unusual enough to stop them.

Sophie glared at the men and shot an arrow at the one in the middle. It hit his left breast and sunk through the make-believe armor they wore. He swore and fell to his knees in agony.

"Thank you for making simple choices. Which one next?"

The guards scuttled away from the dying man, took one last look at the group of gladiators and bolted back through the broken gate's opening. Sophie laughed and hit one man in the back of his thigh. The man screamed and Collin saw every muscle in his neck stand out.

"What is wrong with you Northlings?" Sophie shouted at the crowd.

She marched to the dead announcer, wrenched her arrow from his neck and left the way they'd entered without another word.

From the opposite end, where Sacha had emerged, the gate opened. Into the gaping hole stepped Senator Byrd, his beaky nose creased in fury. "All of you— halt!" he screeched. "Get them!"

"Let's move, Sophie," Collin yelled as a group of guards surged toward them.

The companions ran for the broken gate. Boots pounded behind them, the crowd urged them forward.

The guards who'd fled the arena were a few yards ahead, and Collin felt like a sheep being herded from one pen to another.

"You!" Sophie shouted at a guard as they ran toward the group. "Lead us out of here. The rest of you get off while you've still got your limbs in working order."

To Collin's amusement, more than half the men ran for it, leaving a few frustrated guards to hold the line. The man she'd singled out grimaced as they bore down on him.

"You think you're tough with that bow and arrow, girlie? Why don't you try taking one of us on without it?"

Sophie laughed as she had in the arena and shot him in the foot. "Do I look like some half-baked man-child in tights with a burning need to prove my mettle? I'm an actual soldier, idiot."

Collin thought the man probably wasn't listening. He'd crumpled to the ground, clutching his foot. Tears streamed down his cheeks.

They'd reached the group. Sophie kicked the man she'd shot. "Pull yourself together. It's only your foot. Since that one can't walk now, you'll show us out."

The guard she pointed to nodded and put his hands in the air. "Please don't shoot me."

"Get us out of here and I might not. No promises."

"Get moving," Sacha shouted at the guard.

Collin couldn't hear footsteps pounding toward them anymore, but for some reason, he didn't feel comforted.

"Collin." A calm, familiar voice made Collin flinch. He turned to see Starklee standing at the other end of the hall. More arena guards stood behind him, swords raised, motionless.

Collin realized Starklee expected him to comply. The certainty in his trainer's eyes made breathing even harder than before. "We're going. We don't have time. I'm so sorry."

"They'll kill me, Collin."

"Come with us then. We're getting out. You could be free."

"You'll never be free. You bear their mark. They'll hunt you to your dying breath. Everywhere you go, they'll be right behind you. You can't live like that forever, my boy."

Collin hesitated. Sophie stood beside him, her arrow now pointed at Starklee. "Someone I can dispatch for you, Collin? Is he the one who chose your outfit? That's certainly a capital offense."

"Don't," Collin laid a hand on her arrow and lowered it. "Don't shoot him. I'm sorry, sir. I wish you would reconsider. We could help you."

Starklee gave him his usual sad smile. "I can't, my boy. I'm sorry too."

Collin nodded and turned to the rest of his group. "Let's go."

SEVENTEEN

THE FUGITIVES

The companions fled through the crowded streets, weaving in and out of the masses without looking back to see how many arena guards followed. People's heads swiveled as Collin passed, taking in his ridiculous clothing, then Sacha's and Jacque's.

"We have to get normal clothes from somewhere," Collin finally said to Sophie, who led the way through the streets as if she'd grown up there.

"Come on, there's a back alley this way." She cut between a bathhouse and a market building and the others followed.

Baskets piled high with laundry in various states of filth filled the alley on each side. The group stayed in the center as much as possible. Sophie slowed down when they reached a mound of dirty clothes taller than Collin.

The companions leaned against the stone wall of the bathhouse, breathing heavily. Except for Sophie, who, to Collin's annoyance, didn't seem winded.

"There's surely something here you can put on until we get someplace less dangerous," she said. She nudged the pile with her boot and both Collin and Sacha began rifling through it.

Sacha found a brown tunic. "This one looks okay. A bit dusty, but it'll be better than this." He waved his hand at his fight costume.

"Get something to cover your black hair. Maybe we can get away without people realizing we're traveling with a Fontre and a Borderling." Jacque pulled things out of the stack as he spoke. "Here, Collin." He handed Collin a blue tunic and a pair of brown linen pants. "These should cover you."

Jacque grabbed clothes for himself and pulled off his costume, which, ridiculous though it was, seemed considerably more substantial than Collin's. Collin helped him undo the strings in the back and the leather straps holding on his colorful breastplate and pauldrons.

"I hate stealing things," Collin muttered. "Sophie, could you...keep your eyes over there for a moment?" Collin felt exposed enough without a girl watching while he tried to dress.

"What? Your body is good enough for those arena girls, but not good enough for me?" Sophie asked.

Collin pressed his lips tight and nodded without comment.

She rolled her eyes. "Fine. I've seen you with fewer clothes than that, though. Remember we were in a war together?"

"Leave him alone, Soph. Come here, Collin." Jacque pulled him around to unlace the fringed pauldrons and untie the leather straps holding up the metal skirt. "This armor is ridiculous. What if he went straight for your gut? Clean shot," Jacque muttered.

"Yeah, the girls said it was so the crowd could enjoy my body. Nice, aren't they?"

"If any true Fontre saw me in this, they'd kill me instantly." Sacha shook his head at the cut-outs in his black patchwork gear.

"Brings out the color of your eyes, though," Collin teased.

Sophie laughed, her gaze still on the end of the alleyway.

"Can you pretty boys hurry up, please? We didn't lose those guards for long."

"So, what was your plan if Sophie didn't save you?" Jacque asked Collin.

Collin shuddered, but he tried to pretend he was merely shrugging. "Didn't have one. I knew Soph would come through."

Sacha snorted at this. "You did not, liar. You were going to lay your sword down and get yourself killed or something else equally stupid."

"Better than your plan. 'Kill me, Collin. Go find Josie's sister.'" Collin meant this as a joke, but his voice choked, and he couldn't hold his grin. Sacha looked at the ground.

Sophie turned around and both boys scrambled to cover themselves with clothes.

"Oy! What the devil, Soph?" Collin croaked.

"Shut up and put those on. We have to go."

A group of arena guards walked past.

Collin jerked the pants up and pulled the tunic over his head.

"Cover your hair," Sophie said, grabbing a cap that Collin regularly saw Lightling little boys playing in.

"That's a child's cap," he protested. Sophie shoved it onto his head.

"What do you think those clothes are? They obviously belong to a Lightling kid," Sacha said, pointing to the brightly embroidered tunic. Collin frowned.

"Go." Sophie pushed Collin so hard he almost fell.

They darted into another street, looking in every direction for their captors.

"They're at the end of that street," Sacha muttered. He pointed through the crowd at a group of arena guards who were much bulkier and well-armed than the group who'd fled from Sophie. Collin's heart sank when he spotted Starklee in the center of the group.

"Don't run," he said suddenly. The group froze, awaiting further instructions. "Blend into the crowd. Walk normally like everyone else."

"Good idea," said Sophie. "But let's walk normally heading in the opposite direction, right?"

"Yes. Definitely, let's go this way."

No one was breathing hard anymore. In fact, Collin wondered if they were holding their breath like he was, waiting to hear the guards scream for the people to stop them.

They had almost reached the next corner when Collin heard — "There! I think I see them," from a few yards away.

He spun and saw Starklee squinting over the heads of shoppers. Collin's heart jumped when his trainer made eye contact with him. "Run!" he screamed.

The companions broke into a run and followed Collin around the corner. He darted into a building full of racks, and shelves of clothes and shoes. Collin ducked behind a shelf of books and peered out to get a view through the window without being seen.

"Is there a back entrance to this place?" Sophie barked at a Lightling woman sitting at a little desk in a corner of the shop. Her eyes widened at being addressed so harshly. She nodded and pointed at a narrow hallway in the back.

"Great."

The boys darted to the back of the store.

"This isn't working. We need a real way out," Collin said as they pressed against the building on another busy street.

"Follow me," Jacque said. He walked calmly into the flow of shoppers and Collin followed, hoping he had a plan. Jacque passed an expensive looking carriage, looked both ways, doubled back and ducked inside it. Collin recognized the carriage as Senator Byrd's luxury ride.

Collin held the door open for the rest of the group. "Get in. Quick."

"Woah, who's driving this monstrosity?" Sacha demanded.

"I'll drive it," Jacque whispered. "The driver is over there grabbing food." Jacque nodded across the street to a stand covered with delicious-smelling kabobs. A man in a squat blue cap chatted with a *malderone* girl behind the counter while she made his dinner.

Sacha rolled his eyes. "I've ridden with you at the reins before. I'm driving." He swung himself onto the driver's perch and clicked his tongue at the horses. They whinnied and tossed their black manes as they cantered down the street.

Collin took a breath as they moved quickly through the crowd. No one dared stop them or even looked twice at the imposing carriage as they picked up speed.

"Hey, genius," Sophie said. "Don't put your face in the window. I don't know who's ride this is, but I guarantee they don't look like you."

"I know whose it is." Collin sat back. "I rode in it a few days ago."

Sophie's right eyebrow raised. "Did you now? Dinner with a queen perhaps?"

"More like drugged tea with Senator Byrd. I don't think Lady Ella is calling the shots anymore. Senator Byrd had big plans for Carnivalle and nothing and no one was going to stand in his way."

The crowd grew thinner as the carriage jostled down street after street and finally bumping onto a gravel road at the outskirts of the city.

Collin unclenched his fists and let himself sit back and relax. "Thanks for the save, Sophie," he said with a grin.

"I run into you in the most interesting places," she replied. She emptied her quiver of arrows and went to work rubbing the gore off the tips with a rag she pulled from her pocket.

Collin looked away. He wasn't sure whether the jostling carriage or the bloody arrows made him queasier. "Speaking of interesting places, I don't suppose you know any more about Brenna and Ayla."

Sophie's face had been screwed up in concentration. Now the lines fell, replaced with sorrow. "All the outlying villages were ransacked.; the river folks gone or taken, and huts burned beyond repair. The farther they were from the Light Lands, the better they fared."

"Ransacked?" Now Collin genuinely felt ill. "Who would ransack the Riverfolk? They fish and make beautiful things." His mind wandered back to the night they'd spent eating and dancing around the bonfire with the Riverfolk on the edge of Fondair. "They don't have enemies."

"Don't they?" said Sophie. "What would you call it if you had to always be on your guard so you didn't get nabbed by another race of people and forced into slavery?"

"Right, good point. But, why burn down their village? Why are they taking so many? I thought taking slaves was a seasonal thing," Collin said.

"It is the season. Carnivalle," Jacque replied. Collin didn't realize Jacque was listening to their conversation. He'd leaned his head on the side of the carriage and closed his eyes. He didn't open them now. "And burning down their homes is a way of assuring they have no home to return to. It's easier to control the disheartened and disenfranchised."

"Where do you think Sacha's going?" Collin asked, eager to change the subject. He looked up at the driver's window.

"As far away as we can get," Sophie said.

They rode until the moon was high over their heads, lighting the road. Sacha halted and poked his head in the door. "We have to stop. The horses are too tired to continue. I'd bet they don't ever have to run like this. There's a farm over there with a barn. We can hide out. I'm going to let the horses take the carriage and go home."

"What if they don't find their way?" Jacque asked.

Sacha gave him a look which Collin recognized as him thinking Jacque was a true imbecile. "They're horses. They know how to get home."

"Okay, sorry I asked."

They filed out of the carriage and Sacha went to the front, caressing the noses of the jet-black mares, speaking softly to them.

"What's he saying?" Sophie said, her disdain for speaking softly to horses clear in her tone.

"Probably thanking them for getting us away safely. Sacha's funny about animals," Collin said.

The horses whickered, nudged at the Fontre boy, then turned and trotted down the road the way they'd come.

THE COMPANIONS SNEAKED through the field toward the barn, Collin praying the entire time they wouldn't wake anyone in the house, but they reached the barn without incident.

Sacha and Jacque pulled the door open. It groaned on unoiled hinges and they all froze. When there were no signs of life from the farmhouse, they walked into the darkness of the barn.

Each side was lined with stalls holding several animals, which none of them could identify in the dim moonlight peeking through the slats in the walls.

"There's a loft," Collin whispered, pointing out a ladder leading to a second story. "Maybe there's some hay we can rest in." He grasped the ladder and struggled up the rungs spaced far apart to accommodate the long legs of the Lightlings.

"Do you want me to give you a boost?" Sophie snickered as she followed him up.

"Shut up." Collin pulled himself through the hole. As he'd

hoped, large stacks of hay were tied and pressed together in bales, waiting to be fed to the farm animals.

"There's a couple bales over here already burst. We can sleep in them."

The others joined him, and they settled into the scattered hay.

Collin was so tired every muscle in his body ached. In the fog before he drifted off to sleep, he wondered what was happening at the arena. What were his captors doing to Starklee? His chest felt tight at the thought, but it eased a little as he remembered seeing his trainer searching for him with a group of deadly guards.

He felt he'd barely slipped into the velvet blackness of deep slumber when he was prodded awake by something sharp.

"Oy, get off," he growled, turning onto his back and grabbing at the thing. He opened his eyes. A wide-eyed *malderone* boy stared back. The boy held a three- tined hay fork.

"Get out of here! I'll call my master," the boy threatened.

The other companions woke at the sound of his voice.

"Hey, it's okay. We're not trying to hurt anyone. We were traveling along the road when…our horses got too tired to carry on. We only needed a place to sleep. We haven't stolen anything," Collin said.

"Are you outlaws?" asked the boy.

"Sort of," Collin answered, holding up a hand to his companions, who were all reaching for weapons. "We'll leave right now, okay? Please don't tell anyone we were here."

The boy looked suspicious, but he lowered his makeshift weapon and offered Collin a hand instead.

"I won't tell them you were here. My master's cruel. He might hurt you."

Collin smiled. "Thank you. Here." He handed the boy the dagger he slipped out of his sandal straps. "Better than a hay fork if you run into trouble." He winked at the boy and motioned his companions that they should start toward the ladder.

They sneaked past him and down the ladder. "Thank you, sir. What do I do with this, though?"

Collin took the slender knife and slipped it gently into the boy's brown work boot. "Keep it here, so no one knows you've got it. If someone tries to hurt you, or you need to defend yourself for any reason, bend down like you're ducking a blow, pull it out and stab upwards. Practice a few times. You'll be a natural."

"I'm a *malderone*, sir. We aren't allowed weapons."

"It's a gift – just in case. I'm going to go now, with my friends. Don't forget." Collin put a finger to his lips.

The boy copied him and whispered, "I swear by Zeno I won't tell."

Collin ruffled the child's shining black hair and headed for the ladder.

"Hey, wait. Are you him?"

"Him?"

"The Borderling they keep talking about who wants to set the Riverfolk free? I heard Senator Byrd had him killed, but... you look like the posters."

Collin recovered from the shock as quickly as he could. "Um...I think I am."

The boy grinned. "I thought so."

Collin sighed. "I'm Collin. Nice to meet you."

The boy seemed giddy with delight. "I'm Grady. Thank you for...everything."

Collin lowered himself down to the ladder. "I haven't really done anything for you yet. But I promise you, I'm trying."

EIGHTEEN

THE SPEECH

"I'm starving," Jacque said as they trudged across yet another field. As if on cue, Collin's stomach rumbled loud enough to make Sacha's head swivel toward him.

"We're all hungry, Jacque," Sacha said with a grin. "We have to get ourselves as far from Collin's fan club as possible before we stop."

Collin rolled his eyes heavenward. "Please shut up."

"I feel so lucky to be in the presence of the great savior of the poor and oppressed," Sophie said with a gusty sigh.

"Again, shut up." Collin had come down the ladder and discovered all his friends had heard the conversation between him and the *malderone* boy. They'd taken every opportunity to bring it up that morning.

Sophie slipped her hand into his. "I was wondering, dearest Collin, when you're done eradicating evil here, could you possibly find it in yourself to save we poor Kiatri from the clutches of our enemies? I mean, that might be a bit harder to tackle. But truly, it's only ever bands of werewolves, Lightlings and rogue Fontre who plunder us. After taking on all Northern injustice, that should be nothing for you."

"Get off, Sophie," Collin grumbled, pulling his hand away.

"Sorry. Hope I didn't violate some trust thing between you and Elle," Sophie snickered. All three boys fell silent. Sophie looked at them. "Is there something I don't know?"

"Elle's done with me," Collin muttered.

Sophie looked surprised, then sad. "Sorry, I didn't know. Really, I wouldn't have teased about it."

He shook his head and smiled at her. "No problem. It's no big deal."

Sophie frowned and she cocked her head. "Right. No big deal. Only the love of your life who marched off to war with you. So, what lame excuse did she give? I assume it's another boy."

"No-one else that I know of. She's just not a member of my fan club."

Sophie looked at the other two boys, who looked uncomfortable. "He's too good for her," Jacque muttered.

"I'm not normal. And she really wanted normal." Collin glared at Jacque.

"He's making trouble to help the slaves in the North find freedom. It's nothing to do with anything else. No one's fault." Sacha shoved his hands in his pockets and walked on ahead.

Sophie put an arm around Collin's shoulders. He grimaced as her weight bore down on the raw skin of his brand. "You really are too good for her. I love her. You know that. But, in my opinion, normal is terribly overrated."

He sucked in a deep breath and nodded. "Thanks, Soph."

"You're welcome. Are you hurt? Why are you all clenched up?"

"I'm alright. They branded me and it's raw after wearing that stupid armor yesterday."

"They branded you?" Sophie sounded disgusted, but Collin had all the sympathy he wanted for one afternoon.

"It's nothing. A ritual they do. I'm sure they did Sacha and Jacque too."

Sacha nodded and pulled his shirt up off his back. There was an angry red circle below his left shoulder blade that matched the brand on Collin's breast.

Jacque shook his head. "They didn't brand me. I wasn't a high enough level for it."

"Good lord, what horrible people," Sophie breathed. "Let's stop here for a few minutes. I've got stuff in my bag that'll help."

Collin grinned. "Taking after your Uncle Hollis?"

"Take your shirt off, gladiator, and let's have a look."

"D'you really have to rub in the gladiator bit?" Collin peeled his tunic off, waiting to the last possible second to pull against the burn. Everyone let out a gasp when they saw it. Red streaks spread from the wound, which oozed yellowish fluid. Collin looked away. He wished he could cover it again and walk on. "It's not that bad. Chaffed from the armor."

"It stinks," Sophie choked. "That's infected, Collin. Sit down. You need to drink something."

"Could I eat something instead?"

"I have water here. No food left, sorry. I was coming into town. I figured I'd have time to refill my food stores, but then I saw the posters with the boy wonder pitted against the vicious Fontre warrior and decided I should probably head straight to the arena before you two ended up killing each other."

Collin's glance darted to Sacha. "I knew it was rigged."

"Yeah. I figured that too. Didn't know they were printing posters though."

"This'll sting. Hold still."

Sting wasn't the word for the pain that hit him. The medicine Sophie pressed into his wound hurt so deeply Collin had to clench his teeth to keep from screaming in her ear.

She cringed at the look on his face. "Sorry."

He looked at her through watery eyes and shook his head. "S'nothing," he managed with what little breath he had.

"Second thoughts, Soph. I think I'll pass on that," Sacha said, his face drained of blood.

"No, you won't, and I have something milder for yours. It's not infected like Collin's. Why didn't they put medicine on it?"

"Starklee didn't want to put anything too strong on it because if the skin completely heals, it won't leave the scarring they like."

Sophie shook her head, grabbed her satchel and went to treat Sacha's burn. Collin held the medicated rag against his wound and reminded himself it could be worse. They could both be dead.

THEY SLEPT that night with nothing in their stomachs but a few herbs from Sophie's pack steeped in water from a stream. All were thrilled to see the tree line diminishing and signs of a town coming into view.

"Let me go into town alone," Jacque offered. "I can get us some food without drawing much attention."

"We're staying together," Sacha said.

"But what if he's recognized? What if they have posters up here?"

"I'm hungry and we're going into town and getting a decent meal. If anyone tries to grab me or cause trouble, I'll murder them," Collin growled.

Sophie's eyes widened. "Well, there you have it then. The official word from the boy wonder."

"Will you knock off the boy wonder stuff?"

She giggled. "I don't know. It's so golden. It's hard to let go of material like that."

"Hey, I know this place." Jacque gave Collin an uneasy

glance. "This is Haggathin. If that doesn't ring a bell, maybe you remember an event known as Carnivalle?"

"No," Collin moaned. "I bet they hang posters of my face here, if they haven't already."

"If we get into town and there's posters, we'll leave. But I must eat something soon or I'm gonna' start shooting people, beginning with you idiots." Sophie fingered her bow for emphasis and the boys picked up the pace.

"There's a really good pub here, super famous. I bet it's discount rates the week before everything picks up for Carnivalle," Jacque said, his excitement building.

Collin grinned. He hadn't seen the lighter side of Jacque in a while.

"Well, only if it's really famous. I can't deal with lesser pubs in the same week as I rescue people from arenas," Sophie said.

"You know, you don't have to say every thought out loud," Sacha reminded her.

"Anyone got money?" Collin asked.

"I have a little," Sophie said. "I was saving it for a special occasion. I guess this'll have to do."

The town was already filling up with people buzzing with excitement about Carnivalle. Everywhere he looked, Collin saw half set up booths, giant wooden structures that would be rides in a couple of days. The air held a faint aroma of stale beer.

"Here it is," Jacque shouted. "Zeno, I never thought I'd see it in person. It looks exactly as it does in the pictures."

The pub didn't look like much from the outside, but the clapboard was painted bright red with a green door. The bright colors stood out against the sandstone structures surrounding it. Over the verdant door hung a sign, which read: "Silver K Public House."

Collin's mouth began watering the moment they stepped in. The smell of fried potatoes and meat grilling was enough to make his stomach roar.

They squeezed into a corner booth with two benches instead of chairs. After they'd placed their orders with the waitress, they got down to planning their escape.

"I say we go back to Lashai," Collin spoke in a low tone so they wouldn't be overheard.

"Right. I have twelve danari. Surely that's enough to get us all the way there without any trouble." Sophie's sarcasm was starting to rub Collin's nerves. "Except, I think I'm paying for this meal, so never mind. I'm skint."

"We managed to make it all the way to the Westerling Field with no money at all," he reminded her.

"You already had food, water and the blessings of all the Lightlings. Now we're working with our weapons and good looks. Between you and me, I feel that's kind of…"

"Never mind. You made your point. Please stop."

Sophie snapped her mouth shut. Collin wondered if she was deciding whether to shoot him. He drummed his fingers nervously on his knees under the table but didn't break eye contact. "Sorry. Sarcasm is an old, bad habit," she said quietly. "I think it might be easiest to find a place on the outskirts where we could blend in for a while and maybe let some of the heat on us evaporate."

Collin nodded. "Okay."

Jacque bit his lip. "News travels fast around here. Not sure how long we can hold them off."

"What about the creekstones? Do you know Elian's word? I can't ever remember it," Collin asked.

Sophie looked uncomfortable. "Do you really want to bother Elian with all this?"

"With us being imprisoned and possibly tortured and killed? Yeah, I think Elian may be the exact person to care about that."

"Who's being snotty now?" Sophie said. "Anyway, even if I manage to reach him, it'll take them days to get here. *Ellesair.*"

She had pulled the stone from her pocket and whispered in it despite her pessimism. "Trouble with Lightlings. Need Help."

Their food arrived at that moment and Collin was grateful for the distraction. Tempting as it was to sit and stare at the stone waiting for Elian's reply, he dug into a steak with a sauce on it that brought actual tears to Sacha's eyes.

"Good food," Sacha murmured with his mouth full. "It's been so long."

"It's been two weeks," Sophie said.

"Felt like months. This sauce. What is in this?" Sacha busied himself with tasting his food in tiny bites and rolling it around in his mouth to get the full flavor profile.

Jacque took a swig of the wine he'd ordered and grinned. "That feeling of ecstasy you're feeling right now..." He held up his wine glass and Sacha clinked a forkful of steak against it.

"Cheers, Jacque."

"Cheers to you, Sacha. Here's to not having to fight each other to the death."

Collin held up his water glass. "And cheers to Sophie for swooping in and saving the day at the last moment."

Sophie held up her own water. "I'll drink to that," she said, grinning.

A sudden commotion outside the window made all four turn. On a platform in the town square surrounded by half-constructed Carnivalle attractions a *malderone* girl stood. People gathered around the platform as the girl delivered what looked to be a passionate speech. Collin saw armed men weaving through the crowd, heading toward her.

"So...instead of the hiding-out plan, how do we feel about adding a little more heat?" he asked.

Sophie left money on the table and they exited the pub.

"This event brings in thousands of pounds of gold and silver for all these merchants, but do they pay their help? No! They bring slaves instead and make an even greater profit. They pillage the villages of peaceful people to capture more slaves to sell! This must end!" the girl was shouting to the crowd.

Some looked shocked by what she said. Some nodded back and forth to one another, considering her words. A few looked angry. The armed men had almost reached the platform.

Collin looked at his friends and knew they'd never reach the girl in time. "Hey!" he yelled at the top of his voice. The crowd turned toward him, including the men heading for the girl, and the girl herself. He raised a fist in the air and shouted, "Free the *malderones*! Start a revolution!"

The effect was immediate. The men frowned and started toward them, the girl on the platform forgotten.

Collin grinned. "That worked."

"Almost like magic," Sophie said dryly. She had an arrow pointed toward one of the men before he'd taken ten steps. The boys drew their swords and Sacha pulled the mace off his back. "Back down!" she shouted at the men. "I swear I'll shoot."

"You shoot a village guard, and there'll be consequences you don't want, little girl," boomed one of the men.

Collin closed his eyes and shook his head as Sophie released the string and the arrow shot into the man's thigh. The man screamed.

"You men," Sophie said. "Always thinking you know what girls want. Who's next?"

The guards hesitated for one moment and then moved toward them from all directions. Collin counted nine without the man who'd buckled to the ground.

"Good one, Soph. You might shoot a couple more to even the odds," Jacque suggested.

Sophie smiled the smile that always made Collin's heart rate triple. "As you wish," she said. She shot two more men in what looked like one motion, one in the arm the other above his right knee.

The uninjured guards charged. Collin stepped forward to

meet them. His sword felt weightless in his hand, an extension of his arm. It moved in a fluid motion and slashed one of the men across the chest before he had a chance to counter with his own blade.

It wasn't a deep cut, but the man's eyes went almost hysterical. He drove his blade toward Collin's. The Lightling's height made him slow and Collin dodged, gashing the man's arm.

More metal hit metal. The other guards had reached the companions. A shout of rage and pain rang in Collin's ears but he couldn't pause to see where it came from.

They fought until one guard lay bleeding out into the cobblestone street, one of Sophie's black-feathered arrows sticking from his chest. The others saw their fallen partner and backed away.

Sophie aimed an arrow at the closest one, a wild look in her eyes. "You're next," she growled at the man.

"N...no!" he screamed and turned to bolt. The others followed.

Collin approached Sophie, who had one eye shut, taking aim at their backs. "Don't, Soph, it's over," he said, completely winded.

"You're bleeding," said a quiet voice behind them.

Collin checked his side, which dripped blood from a sword slash he hadn't realized connected. He turned to the girl who had been speaking from the platform. "A flesh wound," he assured her.

The girl smiled. From under the bright orange scarf wrapped around her head, black curls stuck out in every direction. The girl's giant brown eyes sparkled like the gemstones around her neck. "Let's get you out of here. They'll be back with more."

NINETEEN
THE PLAN

The girl took Collin's hand and pulled him through the crowded street. Everyone watched them and words buzzed around him like a swarm of curious bees. No one approached them, however.

"This way," the girl said. She turned a corner and walked about halfway down another street lined with vendors beginning their set up. None of the men and women gave them a second glance. "My horse and cart are over there. Can you make it that far?"

Collin grinned. "Yeah, I think I could manage that." He knew his side was still bleeding. Blood seeped out between his fingers, but he barely felt the pain. He suspected this had to do with shock and blood loss.

"We're all fine, back here, by the way," he heard Jacque say. "I got a cut on my hand, but you don't need to hold it or anything."

"Aw, Jacque, I'll hold your hand if it makes you feel better," Sacha offered. Collin could hear the smile in his voice.

"Here," the girl pointed to a hay-filled cart pulled by a stallion who pawed the dirt impatiently. "It's alright, Bastian. We've got some company." She helped Collin into the cart. "You lie down there in the hay." She untied the horse from a post.

"Comfy?" Sophie asked from the other side of the tiny cart.

"Not really," he answered.

The cart began bumping its way down the busy, cobblestone street, and Collin started to feel his injury. He tried to sit up and tell the girl he'd walk to wherever it was they were headed, but as soon as he moved, his head spun. Afraid he might throw up, he lay back down and tried to relax for the journey.

When they'd passed through most of the town, the road turned from cobblestone to gravel, which did not improve Collin's comfort. He clenched his jaw and bore it until he felt the cart slowing down.

They parked under a canopy of trees and, when he pushed himself painfully up so he could see over the side, what he saw made him smile.

The girl had stopped in a dapplenut grove. Nestled in the middle of the tiny clearing was a stone house with a grassy roof that sloped almost to the ground. A furl of smoke twisted from the chimney.

The stallion whickered and stomped with delight as the *malderone* girl stroked his mane and spoke to him in a language Collin couldn't understand.

"How are you?" the girl asked, approaching the cart.

"Brilliant," Collin answered untruthfully. "I think the bleeding's stopped, but I may have dripped a bit into your hay. Sorry."

"Doesn't matter." The girl shrugged. "What's your name?"

Collin looked around at his companions, wondering if he should reveal his identity, knowing he was a wanted man. "Erm...Collin," he said. Surely this wasn't the sort of girl about to turn him in for anything. "Are you sure we should be here? It'll make trouble for you if those men come looking for us."

"They won't look for me here. They'll ransack my little flat in town again. This is my grandfather's house, but they don't know it. My name is Natalia since you didn't ask."

"Sorry, nice to meet you, Natalia. This is Jacque, Sophie and Sacha. We're kind of...between living arrangements at the moment. We certainly don't want to impose on your grandfather, though."

"Don't fret. All of you come in. You've all got things that need mending, it seems. Grandfather will be delighted to have you."

The girl's shiny black curls bobbed against her neck as she walked down the clover-lined path. A man, clearly not from the River, peered out a window. Collin squinted, trying to make out the man's race of origin.

"Tali!" shouted a man from inside. He threw open his door and the girl disappeared into his arms. When he saw the rest of them, the smile slipped away. "Who are you? Are you causing trouble for my girl?"

"The opposite, Pops. They got me out of a tight spot in town. I was about to be arrested." Natalia said this so blithely, Collin wondered if almost being arrested was a regular occurrence. Her grandfather sighed so deeply Collin heard it from several yards away.

"Alright, better come, in all of you. I've put supper on the stove, but I guess I'll need a bigger pot." He turned and walked back inside.

"He's from Lashai," Collin's realization came out as a whisper.

He took a step forward, but his head spun and his legs went wobbly. He stumbled, but Jacque caught him. "Easy there, Armrest. I've got you. Let's get you situated somewhere, shall we?"

They hobbled into the house. Jacque had to dip his head and shoulders to get through the arched doorway.

They came into a kitchen decorated with every color of the

rainbow. The walls were sky blue, but the cabinets were yellow, and there was a red hutch squeezed into the corner. The stove, upon which a small soup pot sat, was cheery orange and the teapot set to the side was purple. The whole place felt like a hug.

"Come in. I'm Hugo. There's a kettle on if you like tea. Sit him over there so we can patch him up," said their host. He waved toward a couch visible through another arched doorway leading to the next room.

Jacque ducked as he crossed the barrier between the kitchen and living room. "This place wasn't built for Lightlings, that's for sure," he said.

"I think Hugo's Lashain. His skin's too light for a Borderling, and too wrinkled for Kiatri," Collin whispered.

The couch was in a corner next to the fireplace. "Good lord, what a cheerful fire. I could sleep for hours here," Sacha said, stretching out on a large, braided rug with one arm under his head, the other over his eyes.

Natalia entered holding two steaming mugs of tea balanced on a tray filled with light brown biscuits. "These are grandfather's secret recipe, brown sugar cookies. I'll tell you the secret," she said, her voice dropping to a whisper. "Brown sugar."

Collin grinned and accepted a mug. He noticed her smile wasn't nearly so warm when she handed Jacque his mug.

"So, your name is Collin? I assume you came into town for Carnivalle," she chattered as she crossed the room and rummaged through an old dresser.

"Not exactly. We came to this town sort of by accident," Collin said.

"How do you come into a town like this by accident?" she asked, pulling out a wooden box.

Collin looked at Jacque. "We were escaping," Jacque answered. "They had us fighting in the arena as gladiators."

Natalia gave him a hard look. "A Lightling in the arena? I thought that was illegal."

Jacque shrugged. "I guess nothing is illegal if you say the wrong things to the wrong people."

"Your speech today was brilliant," Collin said.

She gave him the same look she had given Jacque. "What did you like about it?"

"It's brave for a *malderone* girl to speak out against the goings on at Carnivalle." Collin instantly realized he'd said something wrong. Natalia's lips pressed together and she lifted her chin.

"I'm not a *malderone* girl. I'm a freethinking person and I've a right to get up and say whatever I like."

"Of course you do," Collin said.

Her shoulders relaxed, but she still studied Collin's face as if she was trying to read something in his eyes. "So...a Borderling boy, a Lightling, a Kiatri girl and a Fontre come out of a pub and..."

"That sounds like the start of a terrible joke," Sophie interrupted, stepping into the room with her own mug of tea and dropping next to Sacha on the hearth rug.

Collin wasn't sure how Natalia would take Sophie, but she grinned, and he saw she had dimples in both cheeks. "All of this sounds like a rather bad joke. Who are you people?"

"We're everyone from everywhere," Sophie said. "And we'd like to help you if we can."

"How can you help me?"

"We're rather good with swords and things," Sacha said. He didn't take his arm off his eyes. "You're rather good with words. We can maybe help your words be heard by the people without you getting arrested."

The girl shrugged. "I've been arrested before." The blazing look in her eyes told Collin she was proud of this fact. "I want the *malderone* system to end."

"Us too," Collin said. "It's why they put us in the arena in the first place. Senator Byrd and I had a difference of opinion on the matter."

Natalia hissed at Senator Byrd's name and passed Collin another cookie.

Jacque kept his gaze on the fire. "There were several Lightlings in the arena. We weren't even rare enough to be put in real fights." It seemed strange to Collin this fact seemed to hurt Jacque's feelings.

"You were a rare enough Lightling to care about the fate of the *malderones*," Collin said.

Natalia glanced at Jacque again, her expression more intrigued than hostile. "Rare indeed. Thank you for that."

Jacque nodded his red head and smiled. "No problem."

"Medicine!" Natalia yelped, slapping the top of her wooden box. "I totally forgot why you're here. Collin, let's look at you first."

"I have some remedies in my bag too. He has one wound that's infected," Sophie said. She stood up and went back to the kitchen where she'd apparently dropped her satchel.

"Alright, let's get your tunic off first. You look like a little Lightling boy in this outfit. This stuff is magic, but it stings a bit at first." Natalia held up a small blue clay pot.

"Doesn't everything?" Collin said under his breath. He lifted his arm slowly as Natalia pushed his tunic up to examine the slash in his side.

"We should take it off completely. Is that alright?"

Collin nodded and lifted his other arm as well. Every wound on his body protested. He groaned through it. Natalia swept his tunic off in one motion. "Arms back down again. Sorry."

"No big deal," Collin muttered.

"Goodness. The cut really isn't terrible, but this...what happened?" She stared at the burn on his chest. It felt like the iron was being pressed against him afresh.

Collin looked at her. He wished he could tell her a brave tale of swordplay and danger. "They branded me." *Like an animal*, he added in his head.

Her giant brown eyes sparkling with unshed tears made him wish to sink into the couch. "I'm so sorry."

"It's really nothing. Sophie managed to rescue us before the worst could happen."

"What was the worst? Were they going to execute you?"

"No." Sacha finally sat up and stared into the fire. "They were going to make us execute each other."

"Have a cookie, my dear boy," Natalia's grandfather had come into the doorway. He handed a brown sugar biscuit to Sacha. "Dip it in the tea and you'll reach absolute Nirvana."

Sacha grinned and dipped his cookie in his tea. He took the savoring kind of bite that Collin had come to recognize very well in his friend. "Good lord, that's beautiful."

"Isn't it? I'm guessing you're all in need of a bit of good food and rest. Stay as long as you like. The soup's as good as the sweets."

Collin shook his head. "I don't think we'll have time for that. I guarantee there will be posters up tomorrow with our faces plastered on them. We've got to get out of here."

"Did you have a biscuit?" the old man asked.

"I did."

"Have another. They're good for calming useless anxiety."

"Urgency, not anxiety. We're looking for someone specific among the captives here. I promised someone I'd find her if I could. Lady Ella was helping me before. If I can get back to Halanah without getting arrested — if I could get an audience with her."

"You haven't had much news lately, have you?" asked Natalia.

"We've been in the arena for two weeks," Jacque said. "We haven't heard anything except which bloke we were fighting next."

202

"Lady Ella has resigned in disgrace. They said they found fearful substances at her house."

Collin snorted. "I'm sure they found stuff at her house. They don't like her because she's been speaking out against their new *Malderi* initiative."

Natalia's eyes went misty. "If only all that nonsense hadn't happened in Lashai, none of that violence would have happened to these innocent villages."

"Lashai? What have they got to do with this?" Sacha asked.

"You really don't hear anything do you? The uprising."

The group stared at her. Collin grabbed her hand as she was about to rub medicine on his wound. "Tell us about the uprising."

Natalia frowned. She'd realized something was wrong. "A group of rebels, a ragtag army from little towns on the Border, created a whole lot of trouble. I heard even the fairies were involved. They overthrew the Fontre and ran them out. Surely at least *you've* heard of this," she said to Sacha.

"Rumblings," Sacha replied quietly.

"I'm so sorry. Probably some of the people killed were your mates. What a waste. All for a girl who claimed she had Namarielle blood. And get this, the person who helped her with the whole ordeal…the *Genraal Majure's* own brother." She looked excited as she dropped this last bit of news, but as she watched for the shocked reactions that didn't come, her brows knit together.

"You don't say," Jacque said.

"I heard he's a terrible person. Killed all sorts of his own people."

Sophie grinned. "He has his moments."

"Wait. You know him?"

"Vaguely. He taught me how to keep sheep," Collin said. "And how to wield a sword."

Natalia frowned. "Well, he's made a right mess of foreign

trade. Lashai used to supply the traders with everything. Granite is ridiculously expensive now. There are no new shipments of workers from the kingdom. My grandfather needs a new kidney, and he can't get one anywhere."

She rubbed salve on his burn and Collin held his breath. The pain overwhelmed his interest in the conversation for a few moments.

"Sorry. I know it stings at first. It's meant to be soothing eventually." Natalia gave him a pained look and he tried to stop scowling in return.

"Can I ask you something? Where do you think the Fontre got all their granite and those people you called workers, but you know they're actually slaves."

The girl looked surprised that his voice had grown hostile. "Some are slaves, but some are sold as servants. They get compensation and everything. Surely you're on my side." Natalia turned to Sacha.

Sacha's face held its signature calm, and he took another sip of tea. "I feel you've been misinformed on many things. I fought with Elian if that's what you're wondering. I do not agree with the way the Fontre ran things. And Ffastian was a scumbag of the worst variety imaginable."

"Ffastian?" Natalia asked.

"The High King," Sophie said.

"I was never allowed to call him anything except High King."

"Right, neither was anyone else. As in, it was against the law to call him his actual name. I think that's a problem, but we'll leave it for now in light of other things." Collin pushed himself to sit up. The salve was working and the burning eased. "Here's some news you've missed from Lashai. The granite mines, run by the Fontre, were worked by punitive labor forces. That's why it was cheap. Every man and woman enslaved there was being punished by the Fontre for something, usually for speaking out against the Fontre's cruelty. They weren't fed enough to survive and worked to death."

Natalia's usually dark rosy face was draining of color. "What?"

"Collin," Jacque said quietly.

"So, second bit of news," Collin went on, because his fury burned brighter with every word. "Organ donors were unwilling participants. People were cut open and their organs taken without their consent, while they were still alive —another Fontre punishment."

"My goodness," Natalia gasped.

"Third…" he went on.

"Collin, enough. She gets it." Jacque was louder this time.

"Slavery should be illegal. It doesn't matter where the human flesh comes from, everyone has a right to be free. No one should be forced to work with no pay."

"I wasn't saying…"

"You were saying that. As long as it's not people you know and love, fine. Better them than you."

"I…"

But Collin couldn't bear to deal with whatever backlash resulted from this rant. He wrenched himself off the couch, and pushed past Jacque, who looked like he wanted to stop him. He stomped out the door and slammed it behind him.

TWENTY
THE MALDERI

Collin settled under the largest dapplenut tree. He picked up the nuts that had fallen, cracked them on a sharp stone he found embedded in the ground and ate them absentmindedly. His side was bleeding again, but he refused to look at the wound.

"Well done," Jacque's voice cut into his thoughts.

"Leave me alone, Jacque," he muttered. Jacque ignored him and lowered himself to the ground. He took the dapplenut Collin was hitting against the stone, cracked it himself and handed the meat to Collin.

"I really thought she was okay..."

"She is okay. She's been told all sorts of rubbish by blokes like Senator Byrd. You know not everything has to be a war, right? We beat the Fontre, and it feels like all you've done since is find new people to fight."

Collin felt fire igniting inside him. "Did I tell you what Ffastian was going to do to me at the end? Definitely would have done it if Elian and Hollis hadn't gotten there when they did."

"No. The only things I know about are the ones you scream in your sleep."

Collin glared at the dapplenuts Jacque kept putting in his hand. "He was going to dissect me alive. That was his last line of torture, after dosing me with that draught."

Jacque swallowed hard. "That's despicable. I'm sorry."

Collin looked away from him. He wished he hadn't said anything. "It's nothing for you to be sorry about. I'm letting you know why it winds me up so much. We spent two weeks of our lives as slaves. I'm all bashed up and almost had to slit my own throat to keep from killing one of my best friends. I'm certainly not getting excited about them spreading around the labor force, or whatever nonsense she said."

Jacque pulled his knees up and propped his chin on them. "She's working with the information she has. I've heard a lot of Lashai-bashing since I've been back. Everyone is blaming them for changing policies and making Northern life more difficult. If that's all you ever hear, and you don't have first-hand experience, it seeps in after a while. Unintended consequences."

"I didn't know they were down on Cassai and Elian. I don't know why I didn't figure. It's not like Lightlings are decent humans." Collin felt terrible the moment these words escaped him, but Jacque gave him a sad smile. "Jacque..."

"No. It isn't like that at all. It looks as if someone else wants to discuss this with you, though."

Collin followed Jacque's gaze to Natalia. She hesitated a little way from the tree. Collin looked back at Jacque. "How bad was it? On a scale of one to Colonel Hollis?" he asked.

Jacque laughed and slapped Collin's knee before pushing himself off the ground. "I'll let you kids talk, shall I?"

"Jacque," Collin said, putting a hand on his friend's leg so he'd stop. "I didn't mean what I said. A lot of Lightlings are wonderful people. You, chief among them."

"I knew what you meant. No worries, Armrest." Jacque nodded to Natalia before he walked back toward the house. Collin felt his stomach churn when she smiled back and the dimple on her left cheek showed. Her smile turned nervous as she approached the dapplenut trees.

"I didn't mean that the way it sounded," she blurted out as she approached.

Collin forced a smile and tried to relax. "It's fine. I'm a little touchy on the subject, if you couldn't tell. Sorry."

"May I sit?"

"Of course. It's your grandfather's house, you can do whatever you like," Collin replied.

"I mean, am I welcome to sit, or do you wish I'd leave?"

"I wish I could explain, and I'm happy to give you the chance as well. Fair enough?"

"Fair enough." She sat.

"You go first."

"I don't want anyone to be a slave. I know you guys broke away from something horrible, and they hurt you and threatened you. I know. But I've spent a lifetime with this garbage. My parents gave up everything. Worked like dogs, bought my freedom almost by illegal means. My grandfather helped them. Still, people think I'm a slave because of…" She paused and shut her mouth tight like she was holding in tears.

"Your skin color."

"And hair color, and eyes and everything. I'm from the River, so I must be enslaved. They're still trying to get me back into the *malderones*, but I have official documents that state I'm legally free. So, they can't touch me yet. But it feels like they'll never stop trying."

"So, when you said you wish they could spread the work force around-"

"I don't really wish that. I wish it wasn't always us who have to suffer."

"I was in the mountains before the fall term began. They've been raided twice since the Fontre were removed from the Inner

Kingdom, and I don't know how many times by the Fontre before the war. Everyone is suffering, Natalia."

"I know." Tears glistened in her eyes.

"The mines are a terrible place to be. Lightlings can deal with not having their pink granite columns for a while. The slaves from the Inner Kingdom were tortured and bred and used in experiments and then brought here when the Fontre had no further use for them. The organ trade is abominable. I understand you're concerned for your grandfather, but he needs to find a willing donor."

"He needs a kidney. Most Lightlings die of old age and their organs are destroyed by the time they do. Too much drinking and…and luxurious living. It's terrible for their bodies."

"So, the alternative is to find some poor bloke who can't fight back, tie him down and pull stuff out of him?"

She looked like she might throw up. "Of course not."

"That's what you were getting from the Fontre."

"I didn't know that."

"Well, now you know."

Natalia sat in silence for a while, picking at the shell of a dapplenut. Collin didn't say anything, but he took her hand and poured the nuts into it.

"I'm sorry I said that. It was a dreadful thing to say," she said.

"I'm sorry I snapped your head off instead of explaining. It's my fault," Collin replied.

She ate one of the nuts he'd given her and looked him over as she did. "What can we do for you, Collin of the Borderlands? You saved me from being taken by those men today. I'd like to help you."

"You nursed my burn wound. I guess we're even."

"Make it uneven then. Why did you come here?"

"I want to disrupt the slave auction at Carnivalle. I want to send a message to Senator Byrd to show him the anti-slavery movement is building. And I'm looking for a girl, as I said. Someone specific."

Natalia's dimple was showing again. "Brilliant. How on earth do you intend to do that?"

"Do they bring people in before the auction? Hold them somewhere or something?"

"Yes. They have a cave in that little mountain range out there." Natalia waved her hand in the direction of the distant mountains. "They collect people for a while before auction and take care of them according to how valuable they think they'll be."

"I want to set them free."

"That place will be swarming with security. Serious men. All this anti-slavery talk is giving Riverfolk ideas about escaping. It's making slavers nervous."

Collin grinned. "Let's make them really nervous then, shall we?"

Natalia's eyes widened a bit. "You are insane, Collin. I thought no one was a bigger nutter than I am about this stuff."

"I'm okay with that, Natalia."

"You are making me very happy right now. By the way, my friends call me Tali."

"Are we friends then?"

She stood on tiptoe and kissed his cheek. "I hope so."

"THIS IS TOO FOOLHARDY FOR WORDS." Natalia's grandfather huffed as he hobbled around the house grabbing things he thought the companions could use. "What else?"

"Thank you, Grandpa. Food and water for the journey is plenty," Natalia assured him. He shoved a bag of medical supplies into the already stuffed satchel.

"Know anyone else in town who might be sympathetic to the

cause?" Jacque asked. "You had a pretty good crowd gathered there."

She grinned. "If we had more time I might be able to rally some friends. We have a secret code we use when we need to meet."

"What's the code?" Jacque asked, pulling parchment from his bag like he was preparing to make a flier.

"We use *Kaelish*, the language of the Riverfolk. Lightlings think we're primitive, so they don't bother learning it. They make us learn and speak in the common tongue." Collin hoped she didn't mean this to sound like an accusation, but Natalia's tone was pregnant with disdain.

Jacque smiled graciously and put his pen away. "Right. Okay. I guess you should do the writing then."

"So we're clear, Jacque is for your freedom, and a lot of other Lightlings agree with him. He's already been practically disavowed from his family for trying to free their household slaves and risked his life to save two *malderone* girls before they were sold off to really terrible people," Collin said.

"And *you* just said you were fine if slaves came from other races, also known as the Kiatri, so you might want to tone down your righteous indignation," Sophie said. She'd stood in the corner with her arms crossed for so long Collin had forgotten she was there.

Natalia blushed. "I really didn't mean that. I'm so sorry."

Sophie nodded, but didn't offer reassuring words.

"Sophie means it's fine and she understands. She promises not to shoot you in the back while we're heading to free people." Sacha translated. Sophie grinned and still said nothing.

Natalia nodded to them both and took the parchment from Jacque. "I'll write something we can post up."

She worked silently for a while.

Collin looked at the others, ready to plan. "The stronghold where they hold the slaves is in the mountain range to the south. Tali said it's well guarded in case the slaves get any ideas."

"Tali?" Sophie repeated, giving Collin a look.

"Shut up, Soph."

"Fine, I didn't realize she was Tali now."

Collin glared at her. "Anyway, I want to go there tonight when it gets dark and explore the place."

"What do you think the odds are? One of us for every twenty? I'd love to take out twenty at once," said Sophie. Her eyes sparkled at the mere suggestion.

"You *have* taken out twenty at once," Jacque muttered. "Time for new goals."

"How many fighters do you think you can recruit?" Sacha asked Natalia.

"Maybe ten? I don't know. At different times there's more or less. Most of my people work, so they can't always come."

Sacha squinted at the poster. "Is that tomorrow night? You want to take the place tomorrow?"

"No, I'm asking them to a meeting tonight. Your *Kaelish* needs work," Natalia said.

"Sorry, my *Kaelish* instructors never taught me how to read the writing. Only how to speak it."

"You had education in *Kaelish*?" Natalia studied Sacha. "You're an interesting man."

Sacha wiggled his eyebrows. "You have no idea."

"When does the auction happen?" Collin asked, eager to get back on track.

"Three days."

"Will they move people before then?"

"Yes, they'll move them the night before. There's a preview for the more expensive ones." Natalia's tone dripped with contempt.

"I have an idea that may be simpler. We wait until they start to move them. It'll be easier to take a caravan on a road than a fortified mountain. We can disable carriages, break open cages, instead of breaking stone walls and dodging weapons." Collin looked around to see what his friends thought of this idea.

Sacha propped his chin on his hands on the table, staring into the middle of it, as though picturing the caravan and what they would have to do. Sophie was smiling again, drumming her fingers on the table. Jacque nodded.

"Good one, Armrest."

"We'll still be dodging weapons. The caravans will be guarded, but I agree it'll be easier. Why does he call you Armrest?" Natalia asked.

Jacque grinned and Collin rolled his eyes. Jacque rested his elbow on Collin's shoulder. "He's the perfect height."

"Which isn't to say that you should ever start to call me that."

"I think I'll call you that from now on," Natalia said.

"I think I'll have Sophie shoot me now."

Sophie winked and twirled an arrow between her fingers. "It would be my pleasure, Armrest."

TWENTY-ONE
THE ARMY

It took the rest of the day to make copies of the flyer Natalia had written. Collin tried to commit the words to memory as he wrote. He knew they were telling people to meet them at an already agreed location at midnight. His arm and chest throbbed by the time they'd finished.

"You need more medicine," Jacque said. Collin had broken out in a sweat, even though the evening was cool. "Your skin looks like paste."

"Thanks, Jacque. I'm sore from writing."

"Let's see it," Sophie said, pulling Collin's tunic up to his chest without preamble. She unwrapped the bandage they'd wound around it that afternoon. "Good lord, Collin. It's still angry red all around the initial burn."

Collin ground his teeth. Natalia was watching all this with too much interest for his taste. "Can we put my shirt back down, please?"

"Hold this up a minute. I'm going to put another layer of salve on and give you something for the pain." Sophie handed Collin the scrunched hem of his tunic and reached for her satchel.

"I'm fine," Collin said. "We dressed it."

Sophie was back and this time she came nose to nose with him. "It's already infected, you little idiot. And it's conveniently located right over your heart, so guess how long it'll take that infection to really make you miserable. Care to wager? No? Then shut your mouth and hold up your shirt."

Collin leaned away from her intensity, but she was already working over his chest, opening various pots of lotion and smearing them on.

"Take one of these." She handed him a tiny green pellet.

"What is it?" he asked. Her growl came from deep in her throat. "Okay, okay. Someone hand me that water please."

To Collin's great relief, they finished doctoring him and gathered things up for the trek into town.

They didn't take the horse and cart this time, but the trip was shorter than it seemed on the way there. They took the road at a jog and got into town as the lamplighters were going from street to street. Collin thought it was a pretty touch but didn't mention it. He shuddered to think what Sophie would do to him if he called something pretty.

"*Hushcel,*" Natalia muttered, glaring at the flickering lights. From the tone in her voice, Collin gathered this was a curse word in her native language. "I was hoping we would beat the light. Come on, let's head down the side roads. We'll hit as many spots as possible without being seen."

At her beckoning, they darted around the back of two buildings. She stopped halfway and pasted one of her flyers in a grimy window. She tapped twice on the window and meowed like a stray cat.

She kept moving without explanation, but as they rounded to the darkened street on the other side, Collin saw the window open, and a hand reach out and snatch the flyer before the window shut again.

It took them what felt like hours to get the leaflets distributed. Natalia kept up a pace that made Collin's legs ache. By the time they came to the crumbling stone stairwell which led to their meeting place, he felt he could drop right there and sleep until the next evening.

Natalia, using considerable force, yanked open the door and went inside. A man built like a werewolf stood on the other side of the door.

"Oy, who are all these blokes, Tali?" His voice boomed over the loud voices and reverberating music in the background.

"Friends of mine, Mace. They got me out of a tight spot today."

Mace nodded and gestured a beefy hand toward the lights and music. "Any friend of Tali's…" He let the sentence hang, but they took it as an invitation to enter.

"More coming through in a bit, 'kay? We're going to use the back room."

"I'll have it cleared for you," said the giant man.

They made their way down a dark, narrow hall and through a doorway curtained by hanging beads.

The ceilings were higher than Collin expected and lit with candles. A group of boys, who looked a few years younger than Collin, were set up on a tiny stage. Three sang and strummed stringed instruments, while one sat on a stool behind them pounding on barrels with animal skins stretched over them. Collin realized the beat they were keeping was a half beat off his own heartbeat.

It made his chest ache and his body want to dance.

He grinned.

It was fun.

Several young couples danced in the middle of the room, while others lined the walls, sitting on cushions and talking over the music. Colorful drinks were passed around and the entire room was hazy with smoke from pipes and cigars.

Natalia moved between tables and dancers to the rhythm of the music, occasionally stopping to speak in someone's ear as she passed. Collin looked over his shoulder at Sophie, who seemed to regard the entire scene as nothing short of a nightmare. His grin broadened. Her Uncle Hollis would have hated it as well.

The back room was quieter. Men of the same build as Mace were moving through it when they arrived, uprooting couples from couches and physically pushing people toward one of the two exits. "Get a move on, boys," growled a guard to a group of five boys in the corner. "This room is needed."

"But we've ordered another round," a boy complained.

"You can have your round in the main hall, now get out."

The boys shoved past Collin and his friends, grumbling about the service and saying they'd be speaking with their fathers about their treatment.

"Yeah, you tell your father that, kid. Tell 'im Raulf kicked you out, and tell your mother I'll meet her at the usual time and place tomorrow, eh? Save me a messenger."

Collin couldn't tell whether the boy turned crimson with rage or humiliation. Whichever it was, he left without another word.

"We'll get you kids situated here in the pit, shall we?" Raulf smiled at Natalia and Collin saw most of his teeth were either chipped or missing.

"Thanks, Raulf. I owe you," Natalia said, standing on tiptoe to kiss the man's stubbly cheek.

He patted her cheek. "You don't owe me nothing, girl. I'll get you a drink." He left.

Natalia beckoned to the group and they followed her into the center of the room, which was called a pit because the floor was three steps down in a large oval. There were pillows and cushions everywhere for people to settle on to, giving Collin the feeling of sitting in a giant circular couch.

"We'll wait a moment for the others. Anyone got a light?" Natalia asked, folding her legs up under her and taking her jacket off. She pulled a thin, white stick from her pocket and put it between her teeth.

"I do," Jacque offered. He dug through his pocket and pulled out a short gray rock and a metal square. When Jacque flicked them together, the end sparked and lit a tiny flame with which he ignited Natalia's stick.

"What are you doing?" Collin yelped as the stick started to smoke. "That's dangerous!"

"Haven't you ever seen someone smoke? This is a mini cig. Relax. It's supposed to be burning."

"Mini cig? Aren't those terrible for your health?" Collin asked.

Sacha put a hand on his shoulder. The squeeze that followed was friendly, with enough pressure for Collin to realize his error. "Yes, but so is starting revolutions, so we're probably not the people to be giving health advice, yeah?" he said. "I hope they have good food here."

Natalia didn't look at all put out by either comment. She grinned at Sacha. "They do. The food was the reason we started meeting here and, trust me, Raulf will make sure we get well taken care of."

Collin tried to recover. "Friend of yours?"

"Yes. He was my dad's buddy in the war."

"The war?" Collin asked.

"The Dukain War."

"Right," Collin nodded. He remembered that Laurelle and Marc's parents had fought in that war as well.

"Here they come." Natalia smiled.

"Food?" Sacha brightened.

Tali rolled her eyes. "Is that all you ever think about? People. Our army is arriving."

Collin looked at the door and saw two boys younger than him walk in, one with his arm over the other's shoulder. They wore tunics tucked into their pants with thick leather belts around their waists. Their shiny black hair stuck up in all directions and one had a ring in his lip. Both were laughing at something.

"Titus and Gus. They're really smart and fun, but they can get serious when you need them to." Natalia smiled at the two boys each kissed her on a cheek and settled onto the sunken couch.

"What's for food, Tali? I'm starving," said the one with the lip ring.

"Food's on the way, Gus. Did you see any others coming?"

"Oh yeah," said the other. He stretched his arms across the back of the cushions and stretched out his long legs. "They're trickling in from everywhere."

"Titus and Gus are both half-*malderone*, like me. They put up with a lot of rubbish about it too."

Collin looked at the boys again. Their skin was lighter than Tali's, but now she mentioned it, he saw the resemblance.

The room continued to fill with people and trays of food arrived that made Sacha's face glow. Fried potatoes with six different sauces to dip them in, soft pretzels that were bigger than Collin's hands, and trays of assorted cold meats and cheeses were spread out on the floor in the middle. Pitchers of iced juices and coffee were added, and they ate and talked and laughed until Collin was afraid he'd never get them to serious matters.

"Can we talk about why we're here?" he finally yelled over the din. No one noticed. "Everyone, can I speak to you a moment?"

"All of you—shut it!" Tali shouted.

Silence fell.

"Thanks, Tali. We called you here because we're heading out to do something dangerous and the more back-up we have, the better," Collin said.

Gus grinned at his brother. "We love all things dangerous. What are we setting on fire?"

"Do not let him set anything on fire," Titus warned.

"No, it's nothing like that. How many of you are any good in a fight?" Collin asked. Everyone raised their hands. He looked at Natalia, who shrugged and sipped her iced drink.

"We grew up fighting, Collin. They're not lying."

"Right, but fighting a bully and fighting armed men are two different things," Collin clarified.

"I'm pretty good in a fight," said Raulf, joining the group.

Collin raised his eyebrows. "I believe you," he told the massive man. "We want to destroy a caravan full of slavers. You up for it?"

Raulf grinned and winked at Natalia. "Yeah, I think I could manage."

"I know a really good spot for an ambush," Gus offered. "Lots of big rocks and trees to hide behind. Most of the road is too open, but this spot's perfect."

Collin nodded. "Good. They move in two days."

"Tomorrow night. They'll pull into town at sunup. If we want to head them off, it'll have to be in the middle of the night," Natalia said. "Like in a couple of hours."

TWENTY-TWO

THE CARAVAN

Collin knew he should feel tired. He hadn't slept well in days, and it would be hours before they could sleep again. The next time may be in a prison cell, he admitted to himself.

The group had scattered from the pub at 1:00 am and locals had gone back to their homes or hovels to collect weapons. Collin's group stuck together, walking down the dark path out of town and dodging a few curfew officers bunched together outside the pub.

When they felt safe on the road, Collin moved to walk between Tali and Jacque. "Where are their parents?" he muttered.

"What?" Jacque asked.

"Where are the parents of those kids we just talked into this fight?" asked Collin.

Natalia shrugged. "Some don't care what their kids do, some are working all the time, some don't know the kids sneak out."

"They could get killed," Collin said.

"Everybody dies eventually," Natalia replied.

"Hey!" Collin grabbed her arm, stopping the group in the

street. "They could get killed because of me. I can hardly shrug that off. This is serious. Those slavers are savages."

Natalia looked at her arm where Collin's hand rested. "I know how savage they are. I'm not taking their lives lightly. I'm saying they want their lives to matter. I can't advise them to sit at home and twiddle their thumbs while innocent people are being bought and sold. I thought that was the point."

"It is. Sorry," Collin dropped his hand. His brain buzzed with everything that had passed between them that day. "It was. I...I talked some kids into another war once, one never returned, and another is permanently crippled. Also, their parents care what they do. They can't not care if their kids are out there putting themselves in danger."

Natalia shook her head and walked again. "I know. I'm choosing not to dwell on it at the moment. Stop worrying about it. We need to be focused."

Sophie cast him a glance as they followed her. "Not a great moment for second guessing," she said.

"I'm not second guessing. I'm regretting. It's different," Collin muttered.

"This is the rendezvous spot," Jacque dropped back to join Collin and Sophie. "Looks like some of the group are already here."

The black silhouettes of the people they'd met earlier in the evening surrounded the boulder Natalia led them to. Collin recognized Titus and Gus where the two perched on the top, several feet over everyone's heads.

"We're the grown-ups now," Collin whispered to his companions. "They may be fighters, but we're soldiers. We get them home safe at all costs."

Sophie nodded. "Agreed. I'm going to scout out a spot to shoot from. Trust me, I'm watching out for them." Sophie adjusted her quiver straps.

"I trust you, Soph. Stay safe." Collin patted her arm before she melted into the darkness. It was odd for him to feel so adult and responsible. He didn't enjoy the feeling like he'd always imagined he would.

"There they are!" He heard Gus shout.

As they approached, he smiled at the boys, although it was too dark for them to see. "Everyone here?"

"Not yet, three more heading this way now," Titus called down.

"I think that's the lot, then," Tali said.

"I see a really big guy behind them, actually. I think it's Raulf."

"Oh no," Tali said. "He has kids. What is he thinking, coming to a thing like this?"

"He's here to break things," Collin assured her. "None of you get mixed up in the combat. We'll handle them."

"We can fight!" Gus protested.

"Wrestling your brother isn't fighting," Sacha snapped. "Leave the bloody stuff to us. We've done this before...a lot."

"We've fought peacekeepers for Tali before too," Titus added. "We're not totally useless."

"If you were useless, you wouldn't be here," Collin said. "I need you in your best capacity, which is disabling the caravan. But the slavers are bad. Very bad. They overpowered three of us without even trying. They'll make mincemeat out of you lot."

"We weren't armed at the time," Jacque clarified.

"Right. We weren't armed and we were surrounded by inno-cent bystanders. We weren't going to put them in danger. Remember, break wheels, cut harnesses, destroy whatever you want, but don't hurt the horses. They're our escape."

"Also, hurting horses is despicable," Sacha added.

Collin grinned. "Yes, it is. We don't injure innocent animals."

Natalia nodded and her friends followed her lead.

"Good. Find good hiding spots along the road. The Weaver

go with you all and keep you safe." Collin's palms felt slick as he delivered the words he thought Elian might say. He instantly wondered how this group of Lightlings would feel about his mentioning the Weaver, but they nodded solemnly and scattered into the darkness on either side of the road, finding places out of sight to wait for the caravan.

It took longer than Collin expected for them to arrive. Tali had curled up against him behind the boulder and fallen asleep. He smiled but felt wrong about her pressing against him. His chest ached as his thoughts wandered to Laurelle.

What would she say about him now? If she was frustrated at his petty attempts to rebel in the Elythium, he could only imagine the earful she'd give him if she saw him starting up a proper dissent against slave trafficking.

Feeble purple light was barely filtering through the morning clouds when Gus called out: "I see it! They're coming!"

"Get down. I don't want them to see us until we're right on top of them," Collin whispered loudly.

The two boys jumped from the boulder and landed on their feet inches from Tali's legs.

"The caravan is almost here," Collin whispered to her. He peeked around the giant rock and saw the others scurrying in the dawn light, finding spots to jump from.

Collin raised his hand for them to freeze. He could hear the wheels of the carriage crunching the rocks on the road. The air filled with dust.

"Now!" he shouted.

Collin grinned at the enthusiasm with which his new acquaintances burst from bushes and rocks. They crawled over the caravan like giant, destructive mice before the slavers realized they'd been set upon.

Collin drew his sword as a wide-set, heavily muscled man jumped down from the driver's seat.

"Oy! Get off, you street filth!" The man shrieked in a higher voice than Collin would have imagined. "Stop it!" The man drew a sword himself, but Collin was too quick. He'd slashed the man's arm before the sword could clear its sheath. The man shrieked again, turning toward Collin, his eyes wild with pain and shock.

Collin pressed his sword into the man's throat. "Give me your keys."

"No chance, boy."

"Very well," Collin cut his throat from one side to the other. The man gagged and Collin jumped away from the blood spurt. Collin took a deep breath and went to his knees beside the giant heap of jerking slaver bleeding out into the gravel road. "May your next life be better than this—it couldn't possibly be worse." He reached for the bunch of keys laced through the man's leather belt.

"Collin!" he heard Sacha yelp. His hand had closed around the enormous key ring, when he saw three men bearing down on him. He abandoned the keys and rolled away from a sword which slashed the space he'd just escaped.

"You killed him, you little insect! I'll squash you till your insides come out," screamed one of the men.

Collin jumped to his feet and lifted his sword again. His heart pounded and he assessed which man should be next. They all took a step toward him—he grinned. Jacque leaped from the other side of the carriage and toppled one.

Collin jumped toward a tall, weedy-looking man who'd frozen, stunned by Jacque's appearance. The man raised his sword against Collin's seconds before it ran him through. Metal clanged. Tali screamed from somewhere not far away. The strength behind Collin's blows doubled in his urgency to see what was wrong.

The man stepped back. "Stop! Wait. I surrender." His voice was nasally, and he wheezed as he tried to catch his breath. "Don' kill me, please."

"Drop your sword and get on your knees," Collin ordered.

The man complied, kneeling delicately on the sharp rocks. "Don't kill me, please. I have a family."

"Put your hands on your head and shut up." Collin kept his sword on the man but turned as the man's companion smashed into Collin's side.

"You're dead, you little whelp! You've no idea who you're robbing here," the man growled.

Collin lost his footing and fell beneath the weight of the larger man. His body pressed against the rocks, and he ground his teeth together to keep from crying out in pain. He tried to wriggle from under him, but the man shoved him back to the ground.

"Hope yer ready to go on to the afterlife, kid." The man's elbow grew heavier on Collin's neck, making it harder and harder to breathe. A cold, sharp blade touched his throat. Collin made one final attempt to pull away from the dagger.

"Get off him!" Sacha roared.

Collin heard a thud and a groan and the man rolled off him, the dagger clattering to the ground by Collin's face. He lay still for a moment, trying to catch his breath. He rolled to his back coughing as his lungs filled with dust.

In the scrabbly brush lining the road, Sacha grappled with Collin's attacker. Neither had weapons anymore and their faces were red with strain as they locked arms, each trying to force the other to the ground.

The weedy man had regained his sword and fought furiously with Jacque. Collin snatched his fallen sword and threw himself into the fray.

"Sacha, duck!" he yelled. Sacha broke the man's grasp and dropped as Collin thrust his sword into the man's chest. The man's eyes widened in death and his mouth gaped as if he wanted to say something, but instead his eyes turned glassy and he fell sideways, taking Collin's sword with him.

"You okay?" Collin took one breath to ask.

Sacha was bent double, pulling in as much air as he could. "Yeah, you?"

"Fine," Collin assured him. He grimaced as he pulled his sword from the man's chest. The sound of it scraping the man's breastbone made Collin shudder.

"Caught your breath?" Sacha asked, nodding toward the man Jacque was still fighting.

"Yeah," Collin responded, raising his sword again. With the three fighting together, it was over in seconds. The man went to his knees, his hands raised over his head for the second time. Collin brought the hilt of his sword down on the man's temple with a thud, and he dropped.

"D'you kill him?" Jacque asked, approaching the man and nudging him with his foot.

"I didn't do him any good," Collin answered. "Let's figure out what's going on with everyone else."

Sacha bent over to grab his mace, and Collin picked up the dagger which had almost ended his life.

"Thought I was a goner there for a second."

"I thought you were too. Lucky you have me, eh?" Sacha laughed, nudging Collin with his elbow.

"More than lucky," Collin answered.

The three rounded the corner and froze. Every one of the people they'd met in the pub the night before knelt in a circle, hands on top of their heads, surrounded by a dozen slavers. One held Tali against him, a sharp knife pressed against her cheek.

The man who held her grinned at Collin—his smile was missing teeth. "Hey Borderling. Come on over here, and let's talk."

TWENTY-THREE
THE SLAVER

Collin looked into the petrified faces of his new companions. "Let them go."

The slavers laughed, none louder than the one who held Natalia. The knife was pressed hard against her skin, and the man held her shoulders tightly. "I think there are friends of mine looking for you." The man's missing teeth made his esses hiss.

"Yes. I escaped from the arena a couple of days ago. They want me badly. If you let these kids go, I'll grant you the privilege of returning me." Collin's head was spinning, but he tried to look calm and undisturbed by the trickle of blood tracing down Tali's cheek.

"You'll grant me the privilege?" roared the slaver. The group laughed again. "Well, thankee kindly, yer High and Mightiness. How 'bout you step on up and join yer friends here before I carve my initials in this pretty little face?"

"Do it, Nephitsa! Ugly her up," jeered one of the slavers.

Collin raised his sword. "Carve anything in her face and I'll remove your hands for you. Here is my offer: if you let them go,

I'll come with you quietly. If you don't let them go, the three of us will fight you to the last man. If I don't kill you, I'll make you wish I had." He couldn't believe how steady he held his voice.

"You'll come quietly?" Nephitsa looked shocked, but Collin suspected it came more from surprise that Collin stood his ground than any real fear of Collin's threat. "Oy, Chester!" the man shouted into the night. "Chester, step out here and tell this kid off fer me, will ya?" The man stared intently beyond the boys. His forehead wrinkled. "Lowry? Mick?" No one answered.

"I'm afraid they've done all the talking they'll ever do in this life," Collin said, realizing the man was calling for the three men they'd killed. "Sorry about that. We didn't want to kill them."

The man's face turned puce, and Collin worried he'd pushed him too far. "Chester?" he bellowed.

"Let her go, and I'm yours to do with as you like. I'm sure you'd like to exact some revenge on your mate's killer." Collin lowered his sword.

"I'll kill you," the man's voice had turned to ice.

"Not from over there you won't."

The slaver slashed Natalia's face and threw her away from him. Her scream rang through Collin's ears. "No!" he roared and lunged at the large man, who was already charging toward him.

Collin's sword collided with Nephitsa's. The strength of the slaver's blows pushed Collin backward, but he managed to regain his footing. "That's my brother you slaughtered, boy," the man spat.

Collin was too busy blocking blows to respond. From the corner of his eye he saw Jacque and Sacha engaged with the other men in the group. Collin ducked again, trying to get a moment of rest between attacks. "Sorry if I don't have much sympathy for a man who traffics in humans," Collin growled when he'd gasped a few breaths.

"This is my job, boy," Nephitsa said. "I got kids to feed."

Exhaustion pressed into Collin's muscles and fear came with it. His arm grew heavier with each jarring blow, and it was harder to block the blows. Nephitsa noticed his waning strength. He twisted his sword so that Collin's weapon flew from his hand and landed on the ground a few feet away.

Nephitsa took a deep breath and shoved Collin into a carriage so hard he banged his head on the glass and it shattered behind him. Collin gasped for air. He drove one knee up as hard as he could between the larger man's legs.

Pain lanced across the slaver's face, but he didn't slacken his grip. "Yer dead, kid."

Collin glared at the man but said nothing. Nephitsa pulled the still bloody knife from his belt and laid it against Collin's jaw. Collin swallowed one last time. He didn't want to die this way. One moment he felt the cold blade cutting his neck, the next, darkness pressed over his face.

Collin pitched forward next to Jacque who grabbed him and kept him upright. "It's alright, Armrest. I've got you."

Collin nodded wordlessly and dove for his sword. The ground was strewn with bodies. Some still breathing, some twitching in ways that made Collin feel like vomiting.

"What the bloody devil is this?" he heard Nephitsa shriek from the carriage where his hands now grasped at nothing.

"How are you feeling, Jacque? Up for a fight? This guy's raring for one."

Jacque glared at the slaver in a way that made Collin uneasy. He'd never seen Jacque so dark. "I'm ready for a fight, alright."

Nephitsa turned and saw the younger men yards away from him. "I don't know how you did that, but you'll pay for it. I was gonna to make it quick, but not now."

Collin nodded and raised his sword. "I know, I know. I've heard it all before, trust me."

From the depths of Nephitsa's throat came a screech that sent a jolt through Collin's spine. He charged at them.

Jacque's sword swung in an arch so powerful and quick that Nephitsa's arm severed and rolled away from them. Fingers still gripped his sword. He screamed and pulled back, grasping at his stump with a look of terror and disbelief. Collin realized the pain hadn't registered yet. "You'll make him pay, will you? You great piece of scum! Come toward him again!" Jacque shouted at the bewildered slaver.

Collin swallowed. "Hey, Jacque, it's okay." Collin didn't dare approach or touch his friend in this state.

Nephitsa stumbled backward and fell. Collin realized later it was probably a normal fall, but at the time, it seemed he was moving in slow motion. There was so much blood. Too much pain. Collin stepped away., his whole body shaking out of control.

"Collin?" Jacque murmured. "Hey Collin, are you okay?"

Collin closed his eyes. He doubled over and put his hands on his knees.

"Hey, Sophie got them out! Look, Collin, the slaves, they're free." Jacque was beside him. He put a hand on Collin's back, and Collin managed to see, through the haze in his brain, the people streaming from carriages all the way down the line.

"It worked! We did it!" Sacha yelled.

"Jacque, I…I need…" Collin tried to make his tongue form the words. His vision filled with thousands of popping lights, and then everything went black.

SOMETHING cold and wet was laid across his forehead. Water dripped into his eyes. "Erg," Collin muttered, wiping at the drops that refused to leave him be.

"Hey, is he coming around?" Jacque sounded right next to him.

"Looks like the water either revived him or annoyed him to the point of reviving himself." Sophie was on his other side.

Collin pushed the rag off his forehead and opened his eyes. He started to sit up, but everything swirled so much that when Sophie's hand pushed him back down he didn't fight her.

"Easy there, hero. Let's take this a little at a time, shall we?"

"How many?" He pushed the question out, feeling pain in his head with each word.

"How many what?"

"Kids got killed?" Collin completed his thought.

No one answered and the silence stretched inside Collin like a long unspoken scream. "How many?" he asked, louder.

"Five," Sophie finally said.

"Five," Collin repeated. Tears leaked from his closed eyes and he felt them run down the side of his face and into his ears. "Crap."

"Yeah."

"Tali?"

"She's alright." Sophie's voice was quiet.

"Gus and Titus?"

"Titus is gone. Gus is...I would say he's okay, but..." Jacque answered this time.

"But Titus is gone, so he'll never be okay again." Collin finished for him.

Jacque sniffed. "Yeah."

"We shouldn't have let them come," Collin said. "Help me up. I think I'm okay."

Two sets of strong hands lifted him.

"He's awake? Is he okay?" Tali's voice sounded like music to Collin. The girl came into his line of sight with a bloody rag pressed to one side of her face.

"I'm alright," he muttered. "Pathetic enough to pass out as

soon as the battle ends." Collin glanced around him and saw a roaring campfire and realized they were well off the road and away from the destroyed caravan. Horses gathered in a clump neighed and pawed the ground a few yards from the fire.

Clusters of survivors were huddled close together for warmth and comfort. Gus sat alone, curled up, his head on his knees.

"You've got quite a bump on the back of your head. I'm pretty sure that's the culprit for your moment of weakness there," Sophie assured him.

His hand went to his head and he winced when his fingers found the spot. "Must've been Nephitsa throwing me against that carriage. I'm fine. Tali, what about you? Let me see."

Tali's chest rose in a sigh and she gingerly removed the rag from her face. "Not too bad. Not as bad as it could've been."

Collin ground his teeth at the sight of the clean slice from the apple of her cheek right through her dimple. "I'm sorry. I tried to talk him down." He cradled her uninjured cheek and looked into her dark eyes. They filled with unshed tears at his touch.

"He was about to have all those blokes break at least two bones apiece and pile us in a carriage to be sold for half the usual sum. You know what happens to injured slaves?" Her lips trembled.

Collin shook his head. "No, but I imagine it's awful."

"Yeah, awful is the word. If your little trio hadn't shown up, we'd be in bad shape now." Tears spilled and she pulled her face away, trying to hide them.

He lowered his hand. "I'm sorry about Titus," Collin said, barely managing to speak the boy's name.

Natalia replaced the rag on her face and walked to the fire. She sat next to Gus.

"Raulf's gone too," Sacha whispered.

Collin hung his head. "I was stupid to get them involved in

something this serious. We knew what this fight would be like. I knew they weren't ready for it."

Tali glared at them from her seat. "Stop. We got involved in this on our own. We were involved long before you showed up. It was always coming down to this and at least we got something accomplished. Look at all those slaves we set free."

Sacha handed Collin a water skin and settled down cross-legged beside him. "We have to leave."

Collin rubbed his temples. "Yeah. Does anyone know who was among the intended slaves? Did we free any Kiatri?"

Sophie shook her head, knowing what he wanted to know. "Josie's sister wasn't with them. I checked."

"They were a mix of Riverfolk and Kiatri and...and a few that've been..." Natalia couldn't finish. Tears choked her voice. She glanced around at the survivors and shuddered.

"That've been what?" Collin asked.

"They have a group of child slaves who are clearly a mix of races. Specially bred."

Collin cringed. "They're breeding humans? Like...?"

"Like the Fontre," Sophie said in a hoarse voice.

"Where?" Collin looked back at Natalia.

"The mountains. There's lots of room in those caves. There's a whole operation going on."

"That's despicable." Collin pressed his lips together, worried he might vomit.

"Yeah," Tali agreed.

"We need to find a spot to rest and lie low," Sacha said. "None of us has slept and we need better tools to stitch up our little group."

Tali looked down the road in the direction of the town. "We can't go back into town. They'll arrest us on sight. Or they'll get curious, come looking for their shipment and then all Sheol will break loose."

Collin's head ached with the thoughts swirling around. Out,

or in? "What if we don't hide? What if we seek? Make them hide."

Sophie leaned in close and pushed his head forward to examine his wound again. "You must've hit your head harder than I thought. You know there's only us, right? It's only the four of us here to fight..."

"Five," Tali snapped.

"Four who can fight and one who can give raging speeches," Sophie amended.

"Hey!"

"Excuse me." Sophie pushed herself up, and Collin recognizes the gesture. She was about to make her own raging speech.

"Soph, let her be."

"No. She needs some sisterly advice. You understand what happened to you and all your friends, right? You were rounded up like sheep, to be broken, tortured, used to whatever ends these spores of sub-humanity could dream up, and then killed. You are not a soldier. You have to stop."

Natalia's eyes narrowed.

"Hey." Collin pushed himself up, thankful his feet were solid enough to stand without swaying. "It's not because you aren't tough. No one is saying you're useless. We're only saying, in a fight you're in more danger than you need be."

The girl turned away from the group and walked toward the carriages. Collin felt his stomach drop as she left. What could he say to mend her feelings but convince her to stay behind?

"What exactly do you mean to try?" Jacque's question startled him from his musings.

"I mean, let's go to the mountain and destroy them, or go to Carnivalle and destroy them. One way or another..."

"Destroy them," Jacque repeated. Collin nodded. "The mountains sound strenuous. I prefer a party before I do any destroying," Jacque said.

Sacha grinned. "The food at Carnivalle is supposed to be amazing."

Sophie shook her head. "Are you all mental? That's still two days away. Where are we going to hide out until then?"

Collin squinted into the darkness. "Tali? Turns out we need you after all."

TWENTY-FOUR
CARNIVALLE

"W hy can't you make some normal friends? You know there are some kids who like to eat and sleep and go to the theater on a Sunday afternoon?" growled Natalia's grandfather as he gently mopped the blood around her wound.

"Normal is no fun, Pops. You know that."

"Keep your face still. I'm about to start stitching," he chided.

"I'm so sorry, sir. It was my fault," Collin said.

After they'd made the decision to stay, they released the horses and burned the carriages. Collin sent the rest of the young group home to their parents with strict instructions to lay low, say nothing about the night and avoid Carnivalle at all costs. He couldn't bear to have any more deaths on his conscience.

"It's true. It's his fault I'm not trussed up in the back of a carriage with two broken legs," Tali said.

Hugo flinched and the needle twitched between his crooked fingers. "Don't speak, girl," he repeated.

"Thank you for letting us stay. I promise, it'll only be a

couple more days. We'll pay you for the food we eat," Sophie said.

Hugo frowned. "Nonsense." Nothing more was said as he returned to his granddaughter's stitches. She jumped when the needle pierced her cheek. "There there, my girl. It'll be over soon if you can only stay still."

"Here," Collin shifted to the couch. "Lay her head here and I'll help hold her still." He put a pillow in his lap and Tali lowered her head onto it. He wrapped his hands around the sides of her head.

"Thank you, Collin," she murmured.

"Of course. Close your eyes and think of all the people you saved tonight," he said as her grandfather worked. "Think of all those children who are now free. You're their hero." Tears dripped into her hair and onto his fingers. "Somewhere out there, right now, there's a little girl who may grow up a fighter like you. Maybe she won't let a man touch her. Maybe she won't work for some cruel mistress who beats her. Because of you. The scar on your cheek will always tell her story. You are so brave."

Collin realized the tears on her face weren't all her own. Hugo's eyes reddened and fat tears dripped off his nose and onto her broken cheek. "I never met a boy like you, Collin. Who are you?"

Collin swallowed his own emotions. He concentrated on keeping Tali's face steady as the needle threaded across the slash again. "I'm nobody. Just a guy who's always causing trouble for everyone who meets him."

Hugo looked up from his needle. The intensity of his gaze pierced Collin through. "Don't lie, boy. I've met many everyday people in my years. Well-meaning folks who'd stick their neck out for you in a pinch, but no real mettle about them. You are extraordinary and don't you ever believe any different."

COLLIN BOUNCED on the balls of his feet. "I wish it was night already."

"We still don't have a solid plan, so don't wish that, please," Jacque said.

They were in the little stable that housed Natalia's horse, Bastian. Sophie perched on a stack of hay and Sacha paced the length of the stable so many times he'd worn a path through the scattered hay.

"Tali's staying here, right? We've settled that?" Sacha asked.

"Yes. It's only us tonight. She said the auction always starts with furniture and livestock. Slaves come last. So, a couple of us will create enough diversion to draw attention away from their holding cells and the other two beat the crap out of the guards and get the keys."

"I'll be the distraction," Sophie offered. She fiddled with the razor sharp tip of an arrow, pushing it in hard enough to prick her finger. She didn't react to this. "I'll shoot the auctioneer through the heart."

"Soph," Collin warned, "No killing unless we have to. I don't want to incite violence. I want the villagers to see what kind of people these are."

"The fact that they enslave people isn't enough information for them?" Sophie said. She wiped the blood from her finger on her tunic and pushed the arrow tip against her thumb.

"Will you stop that, please? My fingers hurt watching you," Jacque said.

"Sorry," she muttered. "I do it without realizing."

He grimaced and massaged his fingers. "How?"

"I'm hungry," Sacha said.

Collin laughed. "You're always hungry."

"I'm buying one of those fried meat stick things before all the fun begins."

"So, what's our diversion if we aren't killing people?" Sophie huffed.

"Set something on fire. There hasn't been proper rain here in weeks. It won't be hard to light something," Collin said.

"Wait, where are we starting this fire? I don't want to risk burning the restaurant down," Sacha said.

Collin rolled his eyes. "Only the fairgrounds. Light one of the rides up, preferably with no people near it."

"I'll beat guards up," Sophie volunteered.

Collin nodded. "I'm with you. Jacque and Sacha can handle the fire. Make it look like an accident and make sure you give yourselves time to escape."

"Why can't you help with the fire and give yourself a chance to escape? You and Sacha are the most recognizable fugitives among us. If someone important sees you before you see them, you're as good as dead. Or worse—a slave again," Sophie said.

Collin shook his head. "I have a weird thing about fire. I know it'll work but I...I don't think I can set it. Sorry. That's on them." He hated the sympathetic look Jacque threw him.

"That's alright, Armrest. We'll handle it. Where do we meet up after?"

"If we get out after we set people free, we'll come back here. Wait for us a few hours. If we don't turn up, don't forget Sophie's killing everyone she possibly can to get back to you," Collin said.

Sophie grinned. "Count on it."

THE FOUR COMPANIONS walked into town as the sky was turning deep red. "Blood red sky, that's appropriate," Sophie commented.

"Remember to blend in until we get into position," Collin muttered. "By blend in, I mean hide your bow and arrows."

"No. My bow and arrows stay put. I'm Kiatri and a target for these maniacs. I'm not walking in unarmed."

"It's alright, Carnivalle is a costumed event," Jacque said. "She won't really stand out."

Collin soon learned the truth of this. As they threaded into the press of people heading for the fairgrounds, they saw people dressed in every sort of costume imaginable. Everyone from little children to forty-year-old men swung fake swords, axes made from sticks and plaster, painted to look real but Collin could tell by the way they carried them that they weighed very little. His own sword slapped against his thigh, carefully hidden under his long coat.

"It smells like Havilah here," Sacha groaned. "Look what that couple has over there. How do I even describe that smell?"

"It's funnel cake," Jacque supplied. "They fry dough in a funnel motion and sprinkle it with powdered sugar."

Sacha's eyes lit up. "I'm getting one."

"Hey, Sacha, you let us know when you've had your fill of food, okay? We certainly don't want to start a fuss until you've tried all the local delicacies." Collin's tone was unmistakably sarcastic, but Sacha nodded soberly.

"I will. I'll start with the meat and work my way to the funnel cake."

They moved through the crowd, buying food and enjoying the spectacle of the fair for a while. They ate juicy sausages dipped in batter and fried. The funnel cake melted in their mouths. The spun sugar, called a candy cloud, was so disappointing Collin took one airy bite and handed the rest to Jacque.

The rides were architectural marvels the likes of which Collin could never have imagined. A gigantic wheel spun slowly, carrying people up on swinging seats toward the sky. It peaked high enough for them to see the entire town, and then turned back toward the ground.

A pirate ship full of benches swung back and forth like a

241

pendulum. Sophie managed to talk Collin into this one when they'd finished their battered sausage on a stick. He felt it trying to come back up after each swing.

A building three stories high had been erected since the group had been in town. It was called the fun house and Collin flatly refused to go inside. Sacha was glowing when they came out.

"So many mirrors. So much stuff swinging at you. Then at the end, there's this giant twisty slide you go down to come out. Totally brilliant, mate. You missed out."

Collin grinned. "I'm good. I'll take your word for it."

As the night wore on, the atmosphere subtly changed from family friendly, to drunk and bawdy. He saw fewer children as parents shuffled them off to the tent city or their homes in town.

Men laughed and sang songs with lyrics that made Collin want to launch at them.

Street performers wore fewer clothes, depending more heavily on shock to wow the gathering crowds than talent. A man stood in the town square dressed only in a vest and pants that ballooned out at his thighs. His body was covered in inked-on art and several parts of him that Collin didn't know could be pierced, were pierced. They followed the crowd, watching to see what the man would do.

Collin jumped when the man spit fire into the sky.

"What the devil?" Sophie yelped.

"He's a fire eater," Jacque explained, smiling from ear to ear. "It's so much fun to take you people new places."

"Shut up, Jacque." Collin punched his arm. "Hey, looks like the kids are pretty well cleared out. Let's get started."

The companions withdrew into a shadowy alley.

"I heard that drunk bloke say the auction would be starting in an hour," Jacque said.

Sacha, whose spirits had soared since he'd filled his stomach with every battered and fried food available, laughed. "Yeah, let's go set fire to stuff."

Collin felt the familiar feeling of dread that always accompanied going into battle settle in his stomach. He gripped their arms, not in the mood for levity. "The Weaver go with you and guard you from harm. We'll see you back at Hugo's. Start the fire well away from the tent city. There are a lot of families over there."

Sacha's grin faded. "Right. Sorry. You two be safe and do whatever it takes to come back, alright? If you don't return, we're coming after you."

"Don't come after us," Collin ordered. "And Jacque, don't use the ring and leave Sophie high and dry either. We'll get out safe together or not at all. Either way, at least none of us is alone."

Jacque nodded. "Okay."

"Promise me."

"I won't twist the ring."

"You'll leave Sophie alone if you do," Collin emphasized.

"I know. I promise." It was Jacque's turn to grab Collin's arm. "But come back, Armrest. You swear too."

Collin looked into his friend's green eyes. "I will. It'll be alright."

Sophie reached up and rested her elbow on Collin's shoulder. "Oh, Jacque, I'll bring your Armrest back to you. Don't you worry your pretty head about it."

"So, do we kiss now, or are we actually going to do this?" Sacha asked. Jacque sighed, bent over and kissed Sacha on the head.

"We can get going now if you want."

Sacha punched him as hard as he could in the ribs. "I want to switch partners."

Collin shook his head. "Alright Soph, let's give these two some privacy."

TWENTY-FIVE

THE HOLDING CELLS

Collin and Sophie no longer walked with the sea of humanity pushing toward the towering rides and attractions. They moved away from the performances and rides and ducked into the shadows beside the slave compound. Like the rest of the attractions, the compound had sprung into existence overnight.

There were booths scattered around a large wooden platform. People were already setting up the booths with scrolls and signage.

"What do their signs say? I can't read that," Sophie asked in a whisper.

"The booths surrounding the seats in a semi-circle are all currency exchange. They take Northling marques or Lashaian danarius. The ones closer to the platform are companies selling the *malderones*."

"Okay, smartie, what about that sign there? What language is that?"

"Feygöld. Yikes. Imagine being sold to a fairy."

"What do the fey want with *malderones*? They have magic."

Collin shrugged. "I think fey keep people as pets."

Sophie grimaced. "Gross."

"I'm guessing the slaves are kept out back. Let's circle the spot and see what we find."

They moved quickly and quietly. The amphitheater was filling with men and women exchanging money and saving space on the benches closest to the platform.

Collin and Sophie slipped behind the building, but couldn't get closer to the back because of a fence at least ten feet tall, each post topped with a spike meant to discourage climbing.

"Now what?" He groaned.

"I don't see any holding cells yet, do you? Let's keep circling. There must be an entrance and exit. How else would they get anyone in?" Sophie said.

The longer they worked their way around the fence the lower Collin's optimism sank. "This fence wasn't even here three days ago. How did they build at such lightning speed?" he demanded, kicking the offending structure. This didn't budge the fence, but it did make his foot ache.

"Settle down. A broken foot will do us no good. There! Look at all those guards. That's got to be the entrance. Why would they have so many people there?"

Several men with builds similar to Raulf's meandered around an iron gate as tall as the fence.

"So...we're fighting those guys?" Collin hissed.

"Hopefully, not."

As though on cue, Collin and Sophie heard screaming and saw people running away from something.

"Smell that?" Sophie asked with a grin. The air filled with smoke drifting to the sky and blacking out the stars. "Smells like a brilliant distraction."

"It's so close. What did they set on fire?" Collin coughed.

"The amphitheater!" Sophie shouted. "Good Lord. Those boys are perfect."

"Oy! What the devil's going on up there?" One of the gate

guards shouted. The other men's head swiveled toward the flames. They yelped, threw open the gate and bolted toward the back entrance of the theater with surprising speed for such large men.

"Well, that took care of that problem," Collin muttered.

The gate crashed closed again and two men looking on edge stayed to guard it.

"I think our reputation precedes us. They're afraid to leave anything unguarded." Sophie pulled an arrow from her quiver and unslung her bow.

"Wait, are you going to kill them?"

Sophie shot him a look that indicated he could be next. "In the mood for a bit of hand-to-hand combat?"

"No, I mean, definitely not. I've got my sword, though. We could fight them."

Even in the darkness, Collin could tell Sophie was rolling her eyes. "Well, pull out your sword, Collin the Bloodletter. Let's hope you don't have to use it."

The arrow made a humming sound as it flew toward the remaining guard on the left. It sank into his chest.

Collin thought the man might scream, but he pulled at the arrow without success, flailed a hand toward his mate and crashed to his knees. The second man realized what was happening one moment before an arrow was sticking out of his shoulder.

"Missed my mark," Sophie growled, nocking a new arrow in the bow. Before Collin could look at her and say it would surely kill him anyway, the second arrow pierced his Adam's apple.

Collin swallowed and touched his own throat. "Ouch."

"Come on," Sophie grabbed his shirt and pulled him beside her until he was moving quickly enough on his own.

They stepped over the dead guards and rattled the gate. "Surely one has a key," she said.

Sophie dropped next to the men and rifled through their

pockets until she located the keys. She tried five before one slipped in the lock and clicked. They stepped into a horseshoe shape of structures and looked everywhere trying to figure out where the slaves were being held.

"At least one of those stable-type buildings is a holding cell. All the guards looked this way when they saw the fire," Collin said. They darted to a hastily constructed building where two little boys were peering out between the boards.

"Hey, boys," Sophie said in an upbeat voice Collin had never heard her use.

"Oh no, they're here," one boy whimpered. His face disappeared into the darkness, sobbing quietly.

Collin frowned and looked over the building for an entrance. "Still have those keys? There's a hefty lock on that chain," he said. They moved to a door with a double chain and a locking mechanism that looked very advanced.

"Maybe this shiny one?" Sophie guessed, but the key didn't fit. They worked through several.

People were losing interest in the fire. Collin heard jumbled voices as the crowd dispersed.

"Hurry, Soph," Collin muttered.

"Ha!" Sophie said as a key finally fit and the chain thudded to the dirt at their feet.

Collin drew his sword and yanked open the door. They stepped into almost total darkness, but darkness that felt full. "Up you all get. We have to move quickly." As soon as he said this, a woman started crying. "No, we're here to help you escape. We're not with them."

"But we do have to move fast." Sophie's voice was full of urgency. "If you come with us, you may still be in danger, but if you stay here, you will surely be sold as *malderones.*"

A gangly boy stumbled into the slice of light that streamed through the doorway. "Who are you?" He approached Collin. The boy was no taller than Collin and his clothes were torn, and a purple and red bruise covered his left cheek. He'd put up a fight.

"I'm here to help you. Come on."

The boy bit his lip, looked over his shoulder into the blackness. "He ain't one of those guys. I can tell." He moved to stand next to Collin. "Come on. How could it be any worse?"

Two more shuffled closer.

"We're going. We're leaving the door open, and we're armed. If you come with us, we'll fight off your captors and do all that we can to get you free. Let's move." Sophie's arrow gleamed for one moment in the light of the torches surrounding the compound. She grabbed Collin's arm and they hurried out.

Four men returning from the fire were laughing at a story one was telling about singeing off his eyebrows. They made eye contact with Collin and Sophie and froze. They stared at the pair, bewildered.

"Oy, who are you?" said one of the men. "Who told you that you could unlock that door? It's restricted."

"Sorry about that. I think I may have also left it open," Sophie said in mock regret.

A few of the captives had ventured out, but they pulled back at the sight of the men.

"How did you...? Hey, Morris? Jinks?" one man screamed in the direction of the back gate.

"Were those blokes friends of yours?" Collin asked. "I'm afraid they've hopefully gone on to a better place, though I'd imagine the temperature is significantly higher in their new location."

The men looked confused.

"We sent them to their eternal reward. I wonder what that is for a person who traffics in people." Sophie aimed one of her arrows at the man who'd yelled for his companions. "If you're going, now's the time," she growled at the captives behind her.

Collin backed up to the door. "It's alright. We'll take care of these idiots. You get yourselves out the gate." He waved the timid captives into the street.

"Get back from there, boy!" screamed one of the guards.

Sophie let her arrow loose and nocked another before it hit its mark. It hit the man's chest. She aimed the next. "How much are they worth to you? Ready to join your friends in Sheol?" she shouted.

One man put his hands into the air. "I ain't armed. Don't shoot."

This reaction had a marked effect on the people who'd been huddling at the door.

"Let's go," whispered one of the women to two small boys. She grasped both close to her and darted behind Collin toward the gate.

"Help!" screamed one of the slavers. He turned, running toward the amphitheater. "We're under attack and they're freeing the merchandise!" In the next moment he dropped, a black-feathered arrow lodged between his shoulder blades. The man screamed again, so loudly that many of the escapees clapped hands over their ears as they bolted toward the gate. None spared the dying man a backward glance.

Collin watched the captives stream from the stable, surprised they'd fit so many in such a small space. They must have been crammed on top of each other. He wasn't counting, but he guessed well over sixty had already escaped. The boy with the bruised face came to stand beside Collin rather than run for the gate.

"Get going. This could get ugly," Collin muttered to the boy.

"I'm staying with you," the boy insisted.

Collin stared hard into the boy's muddy face. He saw his own obstinacy reflected in the boy's unflinching gaze. "Right. Okay. I'm Collin, by the way. Take this and shove it into whatever body part you can reach if it comes to it." Collin handed the boy a dagger.

"I'm Liam."

There was no more time for talk. The guard's cry had its intended effect. More guards streamed from the amphitheater toward the horseshoe of buildings.

"Liam, are there any other buildings full of people?" Collin asked over the growing uproar.

"There's some people in a cell next to the platform." Liam pointed and Collin's heart sank. There was no way to get to the other cell unless they killed the entire entourage of slave traders.

"Soph, we need to get out of here," he yelled to the girl, who was releasing arrows as quickly as she aimed them into the crowd.

"Too late for that. You two run. I'll hold them off."

"Are you mad?" Collin screamed as the men rushed toward them.

"Go!" Sophie screamed.

"No," Collin said, raising his sword.

"What the devil?" yelled a man, kneeling at the dead guard who'd screamed for them.

"D'you like the devil, then? I can arrange a meeting," Sophie called.

The man glared at her. He threw his arms out toward the other men. "Stop. She'll shoot me."

"Ah, one with brains. That hasn't come up before," Sophie jeered.

Dirt filled the air as the men skidded to halt a few yards from Sophie, Collin and Liam, who held up his dagger in a way that made Collin worry he'd never handled a weapon.

"Is that the brat you taught a lesson to, Bront?" asked a guard, leering at Liam.

"Aye, your girl's fine, by the way. I didn't do her no harm. In fact, she's better off now she knows what it's like to be with a real man."

Liam roared and charged toward the line of slavers.

"No!" screamed Collin, grabbing for him, but he didn't catch him in time. Collin didn't take a moment to think about the consequences. Didn't wonder if Sophie had a plan. He took off after the boy.

Liam reached the guards before Collin did. The men grabbed him. Liam flailed his arms wildly, the dagger shining in the torchlight as it flew through the air and landed harmlessly in the dirt.

"Where is she?" Liam struggled against the meaty arms holding him while another man lay into him with solid fists.

"Let him go!" Collin shouted.

Another man crumpled with an arrow in his stomach. Collin swung his sword at Liam's assailant. A spiked wooden club deflected his blow. Collin recovered from the tooth-jarring club and swung into the man's side when he raised his arms to bring the club down. He threw himself away from the man's girth.

"Break up this fight!" boomed a voice so loud Collin felt it through the crowd like a tremor.

Someone grabbed Collin from behind and his sword was wrenched from his grasp.

"What is the meaning of this? The auction needs to start!" The high, wheezing voice bored into Collin's ears before his arms were pinned behind him and he was turned to the hawkish face of Senator Byrd.

"My apologies, Your Grace. This unprofessional display is very out of the ordinary." The voice that had stopped his men brawling came from behind Collin. "I don't know who these children are or how they came upon weapons, but I guarantee it won't happen again."

The senator slunk forward with a delighted, hungry look on his face. "I know this boy. I...I last saw him in the arena. Perhaps a less glorified form of slavery suits you better, eh, Borderling? And who is your friend here?"

Collin felt a heavy hand on his head, forcing it toward a flurry of arms, arrows, and jet-black hair. They'd grabbed Sophie as well.

"Let her go and I'll come quietly," Collin said, wishing he could keep the despair from his voice.

The senator drew so close that Collin could've touched his nose to the man's breast buttons. The man's claws clutched Collin's chin and twisted his face up. "You'll come along quietly one way or the other, boy."

Collin spat on him. The man's pallid face turned puce. "I want this one. Put him with the elites," Senator Byrd ordered.

"As you say, my lord," said the man holding Collin.

Collin kicked the senator's shin as hard as he could. Senator Byrd gasped and bent double to grab his leg. "Let him taste your whip to bring him to compliance," he said in a strained falsetto.

"I'll comply if you set Sophie free. Otherwise, I will fight you to my dying breath," Collin promised.

"Maybe a double taste of that whip," Senator Byrd wheezed.

TWENTY-SIX

THE AUCTION

They dragged Collin into one of the stables and wrapped his arms around a post inside. One guard pulled a whip from his belt, while the other held Collin's wrists in one of his enormous hands.

Collin didn't make a sound when the whip lashed across his back. He hadn't been stripped, so it took a while for the pain to register. When the whip crossed his permanent stripes, Collin ground his teeth together to keep silent.

"Why don't he cry out? You ain't hittin' him hard enough."

"I'm cutting in as hard as I can. He's stubborn." The other guard gasped, out of breath.

"We hafta hurry, though. The auction's startin' in a minute."

"Fine." The whipping stopped. "Let's get him to holding. That's the best I can do."

Collin took a deep breath, wishing the burn would quit when the whip did.

"Alright. That's good, boy. You learned your lesson?"

Collin glared at the pair.

"He's a right mule, he is. Look at 'im scowlin' you down."

They pushed him out of the stable and down the dirt courtyard to another building. Collin's heart pounded. He felt a brief flare of hope. Perhaps he was going to find Miriam at last. She was Kiatri and, if she looked like Josie, surely she'd be set aside for a noble.

"Keep him bound and guarded until he's up for sell," Collin's guard barked at the man pacing in front of the other barn.

"Sale," Collin corrected because he couldn't help it.

"Wha's that, boy?" asked the man.

"Until I'm up for sale—not sell. You are selling me, so I'm for sale," Collin explained.

The man's mouth drooped in confusion. He thrust Collin down a narrow path lined with stalls; at least ten people were crammed in each.

"I don' know what he's on about. But either way, watch him."

"Got it. He won't give me trouble. Will you, kid?" A shorter, stocky guard gripped Collin's arm to get his attention.

"Wouldn't dream of it," Collin said.

"Senator Byrd wants him, so he's to stay here till he's collected at the end. Got it?"

A stall unlocked and Collin was thrust in. This stall wasn't crowded, but every person in it was bound with their hands behind their backs. Most were injured, telling Collin this was the spot for those who gave them trouble. One was crumpled on the floor, his face drawn in agony.

"See tha' guy there?" asked the stocky guard. "He put up a fight. I broke his leg. Know what he's good for now, boy? Eh?"

Collin frowned and didn't move as his hands were tied behind him with a splintering rope. Even if Collin didn't twist them at all, his wrists would be chaffed within moments.

He stumbled forward when he was finally released. He caught his feet before he pitched into the hay littering the floor. It smelled like manure.

The stall gate clattered shut and the stocky guard marched back to the barn entrance.

"Y'okay, kid?" asked a man sitting in one corner, hunched uncomfortably in his bonds.

Collin sighed and looked around at his fellow captives. There were two other men besides the one with a broken leg and the hunched man who'd checked on him. One very young woman huddled against the farthest wall, as far as possible from them all.

"Fine. Anyone not tied up?"

"Nope, this ain't the place for bein' untied," said the man. "I'm Hermann. What's yer name?"

"Collin." He couldn't keep his eyes off the woman. "Are you hurt?" he asked her.

Her eyes filled with tears—her face was already red with them. She shook her head and pressed harder into the wall behind her.

"Sorry." The word was so inadequate and idiotic for what the girl seemed to have suffered, Collin instantly wished he hadn't said it.

They heard a scuffle behind them and the man who'd muscled Collin in dragged someone else toward their cell. He heard a sharp blow and a pitiful yelp. The gate opened and Liam was thrown into the hay at Collin's feet, his arms already tied.

"All of you, shut up!" roared the slaver before he slammed the gate closed again.

"Liam," cried the girl in the back.

"Della," Liam moaned. "Are you alright?"

The girl threw herself to the boy's side. She sobbed into his shoulder. Liam pulled himself up to sit, the girl still pressed into his shoulder. "I'm sorry they got you. I'm so, so sorry. I ...tried to stop them b...but ..." Apparently Liam could think of no further explanation. He broke off, took a shuddering breath and looked at the ceiling.

Della didn't answer and the two shuffled away to huddle as closely as possible against a wall. Collin felt ill.

"There's got to be something," he muttered to himself. He circled the stall taking in as much information as he could in the darkness.

"The stall's solid, boy. They've been at this awhile," Hermann said.

"This stall wasn't even here three days ago. There's a weakness somewhere," Collin argued.

"None that I can find."

Collin stopped pacing and looked at Hermann. He appeared to be about forty. Broad shouldered and strong as an ox by the look of him. "How did they take you?"

"Drugged me in the night and took me to a fortress in the mountains. I never seen them before then. I'm a farmer."

"A farmer?"

"They don't much care who they nab anymore, as long as it ain't someone important enough to be connected. Slaves are hard to come by now."

"Do you have a family?"

"A wife and a baby. I don't have a clue what happened to 'em. For a few weeks, I fought and screamed and tried to get someone to tell me what I'd done. Where my Sadie and Nania were. Nothing. I got nothing but more bruises for my ranting. For all I know, they're in a stall here somewhere, about to be sold like animals…same as me."

Collin shook his head in frustration. He heard noises outside that sounded like people assembling. A single voice rang out over the crowd, exciting them about what was coming next.

"Are we first to be sold? Is that why we're in this stall?"

Hermann shrugged. "We're elites, actually. I heard I've already been sold to a senator from another province. I won't ever see my Sadie again."

Collin sighed. He looked at Liam and Della, who stared

vacantly into the darkness. "I wish we could get her freed at the very least," he whispered.

Hermann nodded. "She's been put through a worse ordeal than any of us. I couldn't get them to leave her be. I tried hard."

Collin nodded. The gate rattled again, and he resisted the urge to lunge at whoever was coming in. The ropes were too tight to do anything except get himself injured.

"Get on yer feet," the guard growled at Della.

"Hey, halfwit. Leave her alone," Collin said.

The man turned slowly toward Collin's corner as though he could hardly believe a captive had dared insult him. "Alright, boy, perhaps you'd rather I take you first? We can stop off in the middle somewhere and have a chat."

"That would be lovely. I'd enjoy a good chat," Collin replied. He closed his eyes and made a snap decision. As the guard advanced on him, he worked his wrists enough to twist the ring on his finger.

Jacque appeared between him and the guard. The guard yelped and jumped back. Jacque turned around, squinting, made eye contact with Collin, and winked. "Hey, Armrest, fancy meeting you here."

The guard recovered himself and bolted from the cell screaming for help.

"Quick, Jacque, do you still have your sword?" Collin asked.

Jacque nodded. "Who first?"

"The girl."

"Hang on a moment." Jacque pulled both a fey blade and his sword from his belt. He turned Collin around. In the next moment Collin felt the rough ropes break free. He turned toward Jacque, who handed him the fey weapon. "Happy hunting."

Collin darted across the cell to Liam and Della. "Up you get, both of you." He pulled Della up and cut her ropes as she stared in confusion. "It's alright. You're going to be alright. Liam, you're free. Get her out." Collin pulled the dagger from his boot and held it out to Liam. "Thrust it in wherever you can, as hard as you can. Don't hesitate. They won't."

Liam nodded. He grabbed Della's arm to lead her out. "What's going on, Liam? Who's that Lightling boy? Where did he come from?"

"Doesn't matter. We're escaping." The two slipped through the gate and disappeared into the darkness.

Collin cut Hermann free next, while Jacque worked on the other men's bonds. Hermann had breathed a sigh of relief and turned to look at Collin when the guard returned with five others as burly as he.

"What the devil's this? All of you on the ground, now, before I end you right here."

"End us, then," Collin growled, brandishing his glowing blade.

He and Jacque stood side by side at the gate of their stall, giving room to only one assailant at a time. Collin slashed the first guard's gut, and as he fell, Jacque finished him.

Collin ducked the sword of the next and Jacque decapitated him. The other guards backed away as their companion's head rolled toward them. One of them bolted. The others gathered their courage and took one last stand against the two soldiers.

The guards were both dead in the next minute.

Collin swallowed and avoided looking at the severed head in the narrow hall. "Don't look down, get yourselves out," he warned the unarmed men.

"Here, take a weapon with you. All of you." Jacque stripped the guards and handed swords to the men they'd freed.

Hermann came to stand beside Collin. "I'm staying with you. Possibly I'll find my wife and girl in this labyrinth of Hades."

Collin shook his head. "You should run while you can. You're no good to anyone captive and sold into some other province."

Hermann didn't budge. "I'll fight by your side, boy. I never did see the likes of you, and I may never again. But if I can't help them, I can at least help you."

"Do you know what to do with that sword?" Collin asked, trying to hide how much the man's speech moved him.

Hermann slashed the air in front of him with impressive style. "I do."

Jacque exited the stall, propping up the man with the broken leg.

"You should leave me. I can't fight. I ain't no good to you," the man muttered, his voice full of pain.

Jacque looked at Collin. "What can we do?"

"We can't leave him. They'll torture him to death if we do. Get him to the woods outside the compound and come back. We'll collect him when this is all over and get him back to his people."

Jacque nodded. "Twist your ring in half an hour. I'll have him to safety by then, hopefully."

"Agreed."

They all walked together to the barn's exit and Jacque helped the injured man hobble toward the back gate. Collin was surprised no guards stood outside, but he assumed more were coming.

"What now?" asked Hermann.

Collin looked at the rear of the giant platform they'd erected to sell their human merchandise. "We look for more people to free."

Hermann nodded and clapped Collin on the shoulder. "I like you, boy. You are truly extraordinary."

TWENTY-SEVEN
THE BLAZE

Collin and Hermann ran around the back of the platform. As ornate and glittering as the front was, the back was in perfect contrast. Bare logs and branches wove together to bear the weight of the wooden planks and beautiful façade.

"We could burn it," Hermann suggested.

"If we do, we could kill a lot of innocent people being driven to the top like cattle."

Hermann chewed his bottom lip and nodded. "Good point."

"There's a holding pen over to the right where they bring people for sale, and there's another on the left for the sold ones. Let's take the one on the right first." Collin moved stealthily toward the large pen, made only of rough-hewn logs.

Two men guarded the back entrance. They held their swords at the ready but clearly hadn't seen Collin and Hermann lurking in the shadows. The guards cast nervous glances back and forth and jumped at the lightest sound. Collin grinned at their stance. He bent to pick up a rock.

He threw it as hard as possible in the opposite direction to their approach, causing both guards to whip around. "Oy, what was that?" one exclaimed.

"That boy and his friends, maybe. It came from behind that tree." The other pointed away from the men who crept up behind them.

"Boo," Collin said before slicing the first man's throat.

"They're here! Help! They've got us!" screamed the other as Hermann drove his sword into the guard's lower back. Hermann withdrew his weapon and the wounded man dropped to the ground, writhing and gasping for help.

Collin kicked the back gate down. "Run!" He shouted through the confused crowd. "Fight if you have to, but get out of here." He handed the fallen guard's sword to a woman who shuffled from the pen clutching a little girl to her side. "Use this if you have to. Hit them as hard as you can."

The woman took the sword, her eyes blazing. "I will. Thank you so much."

Collin nodded. "Go."

People streamed from the back of the pen and ran into the darkness. There were yelps of surprise in the distance, where Collin assumed other guards were trying to manage the rapidly decaying situation.

"What the devil is going on here?" screeched someone from the top of the platform.

The auctioneer poked his face over the banister and screamed. "They're getting away!"

More guards appeared, but not as many as Collin expected. A tiny ball of hope glowed in his chest. Maybe they were running out of reinforcements.

"Can I burn it down now?" Hermann asked hopefully. He held a blazing torch under the spot where the auctioneer had appeared.

Collin craned his neck to see if anyone was still on top who might be a slave. "I think you're clear. Burn it."

Hermann's smile glowed as he touched the flame to the dry wood. "For you, Borderling!" he shouted with a grin.

Collin nodded his appreciation as the last man escaped the pen. "What are you doing next?" the man asked, out of breath. He kicked the dead guard over and pulled a short blade from his belt.

"I'm heading to the other side. They'll be trying to get their purchases away before they realize an emancipation is happening."

The man nodded and tucked the blade into his belt. "Lead the way."

Collin started running, ducking as pieces of the blazing platform fell. "I'm Collin, by the way," he yelled as he ran.

"Christoff. Thanks for saving my neck," answered the man.

Hermann joined them as they bolted to the other side.

The opposite side was in chaos. Large, burly men swung their beefy fists at the captives who'd caught on to the shift in power and were fighting and clawing to escape. A human wall pressed against the pen, some trying to escape captivity, others seeing the fire edging nearer, pushed to get free of the blaze.

"Get them rounded up. Get them out of that pen or they'll be worthless!" The auctioneer screamed at the giant guards. "Don't let them escape! That one's sold to Senator Elseworth. She'll have our necks if she doesn't get her due!"

Collin ignored the chaos and scanned the pen for weaknesses. There was no back gate on this side. The logs of the pen were stacked and held together on each side with tall posts stuck in the ground. The fence was only as tall as Collin, but solid. "If we get the posts down, the fence will fall," Collin said to Hermann and Christoff. The three men heaved a post, which barely budged.

"They're in deep," Hermann said in a strained voice.

"Try again on three," Collin said. Each man took hold and

Collin counted them down. Two more pulls and the post pulled free.

Logs tumbled to the ground and the men grabbed them and pulled them down so people could exit. "This way!" Collin shouted to the slaves. "You can get out through here."

"Stop them!" screeched a voice that turned Collin's blood cold. Senator Byrd had joined the madness. "They're escaping out the back!"

Collin caught sight of him through the boards. The senator's face was the color of old grapes, screwed up in rage. "Sorry about the mess." Collin called out, doffing an imaginary hat to the Senator.

"Get that wretched Borderling!" Byrd screamed, jabbing his finger toward Collin. Every vein in the man's neck strained as he bellowed.

Collin backed away from the flood of humanity escaping their captors' grasp. The guards who'd been cuffing people back into the pen and grasping at fallen logs, trying to restore the cage, dropped what they were doing and stumbled over wood and people to get to Collin.

"Ain't it him making all this ruckus?" yelped one guard. He waved a long arm toward the general melee.

"Yes. Ignore the rest and get that boy. He's mine!" the senator squealed.

Collin backed up another step and raised his sword. His pulse pounded in his neck. He felt a surge of excitement. If everyone came for him, the others could be free.

"Let him be," shouted Hermann. The man stepped in front of Collin. Christoff pressed his shoulder against Hermann's.

"You'll have to get through us," he said.

Most people had claimed their freedom and dissolved into the woods.

"You two get out of here. I'll fight them off as long as possible. Get those people through the woods and see they get to safety," Collin said to his would-be saviors.

"No," Hermann responded without turning away from the guards bearing down on them.

"Get yourselves and those people out!" Collin yelled making them both turn in surprise. "I'm a soldier. I'll fight them. You get out free or it's all for nothing."

The first guard rushed Hermann, but Collin ran forward and thrust his sword through the man's chest. He felt his blade slip between the man's ribs.

As the guard fell heavily to the left, Collin pulled his sword out. "Go," he repeated to his new friends. "They need leadership, or they'll get nabbed again. Keep to the woods, as far from main roads as possible."

Hermann finally nodded. "You're a good man, Collin of the Borderlands."

He grabbed Christoff and the two melted into the darkness with the rest.

Collin saw the senator making his way over the broken fence. The other guard had halted when Collin killed the first and stood as far from the Borderling as he could without being near the burning platform.

Collin took one look at the petrified guard and the mottled fury of Senator Byrd.

He raised his sword.

"Where is Miriam?" he muttered, and he twisted his silver ring.

TWENTY-EIGHT
THE TRAINER

J acque appeared at Collin's side. Senator Byrd's visage drained from splotchy crimson to pale puce. "What devil's trickery is this?" he wheezed.

"Hey, Jacque," Collin said.

"Hey, Armrest."

"Are they alright?"

"There's an enormous group helping them out now. Two big blokes showed up who seem fairly competent. Friends of yours?"

Collin nodded and turned back to Byrd. "I'll go with you quietly. We won't kill your last guard." He nodded to the guard. "I want to know where she is."

"Are you still on about that stupid Kiatri whelp?" Byrd snarled.

"Fine. We'll kill you both," Collin took a step toward the guard, who stepped back and tripped over one of the fallen logs. Jacque clapped a hand over his mouth to suppress a laugh.

"You get that swine and I'll take care of this one," Collin said, pointing his sword casually toward Byrd.

"Put the swords away, before you do something you regret," Senator Byrd said in a tone that made Collin pause. "There's someone here who wishes to speak with you."

Collin felt a sense of foreboding even more acute than usual at the tone in the senator's voice. The senator did not move toward him to force him along. He turned and started walking as though perfectly confident the younger men would follow.

"I'm not going anywhere with you. Who wants to see me?"

"It isn't so much they want to see you, as you will certainly want to see what became of them."

Collin swallowed hard. He felt very small all the sudden. There were lots of people he'd encountered since coming here whose well-being the senator could destroy. He held his sword up and followed the senator at a jog to keep up with the man's long strides.

He felt Jacque behind him and knew the Lightling hadn't put away his weapon either.

Senator Byrd led them to a large well-lit tent full of people dressed in velvet and lacy ruffles, and other nonsense Collin wouldn't have been caught dead in. "What's with your race and ridiculous clothes?" he muttered to Jacque.

"I like that doublet, though." Jacque's eyes glittered as he pointed out a man in a purple velvet jacket. "I think I'll ask who his textile vendor is."

"Jacque," Collin said, calling his friend back to the reality of their situation.

"Right. Later then."

"In here." Senator Byrd pulled back a flap which led to a small, darker room. Collin saw coats and wraps hanging from hooks and stands that lined the canvas walls. He hesitated and Byrd grinned and crooked a long finger at him. "Come along, boy. Don't be shy."

As he stepped through the opening he saw in the flickering

light of a lantern two figures, one very tall and lanky, one very small next to him. "Starklee?"

His arena trainer wouldn't make eye contact with him. He stared at the floor. The tiny figure beside him made Collin want to scream, Amatha. Her face was bruised, and one eye swollen almost shut. He had no idea the state of the rest of her body, but he could make a good guess.

Collin turned his sword to the senator. "You scumbag. What did you do to her?"

The senator feigned astonishment. "I? I did nothing to her, dear boy. It was you who set this whole distasteful business in motion. Starklee lied for you, he let you go. He owed me a debt he still has yet to pay."

"What debt? He worked for you for years." Jacque shot Collin a look. Collin tried to swallow the enormous lump in his throat.

"You. Your blood. He owed you to me. If you surrender now, his debt is paid and he's free to go. If you don't –" The senator's snakelike face split in a smile. "We'll find someone else's blood to cover it." He looked at Amatha.

Collin took a step toward the man. The tip of his sword touched Senator Byrd's abdomen. "I can think of someone's blood to cover it."

Byrd's eyes flicked to Starklee. The trainer reached Collin in one stride. Collin felt the man's powerful arms around him, trapping him, forcing his sword from his grasp. Collin struggled to break free but knew it was useless. There was no move he could make that Starklee wouldn't anticipate.

He heard scuffling at the door and stopped struggling long enough to see Jacque and Byrd grappling with each other. Byrd was no match for the younger, stronger soldier and Jacque had him pressed against the wall in seconds. His muscular forearm bearing down on the senator's windpipe.

"Don't Jacque," Starklee warned in his usual calm voice. He sounded deeply saddened. "Let him go, or I'll kill Collin."

Jacque's face was almost as red as the senator's and beads of sweat dripped from his eyelashes. "You'll kill an innocent man for this worm?" he demanded. He released Byrd's neck but didn't free him.

"I will. That man is my only chance of freedom. Let him go now or watch your friend die."

"No!" Amatha burst into sobs. "Please don't. He's so kind, sir. Please sir, let him go. He's such a kind man." Collin felt her tugs on Starklee's arm.

"Get off me, girl," Starklee said in a strained voice.

"Sir," Collin murmured. "We can set you free. Truly free. You can come with us and live in Lashai happily. The Namarielle are good, just rulers. They can get you out of this mess if you want it."

"I – I can't." The trainer's voice broke.

The senator's smug expression made Collin snap. He felt Starklee's grasp falter and wrenched himself free, dropping to the floor to escape his trainer's long reach. He reached for his sword.

"Guards," cried the senator.

"Don't," shouted Collin rolling back to his feet. "Unless you wish to die. Just don't."

"Break the girl's neck, Starklee. Let's make our point, shall we?"

Collin looked at Starklee. His long face was as battered as Amatha's and two of the fingers on his right hand were bandaged together. Amatha backed away from him, her face still damp with tears. Her whole body trembled.

"Amatha," Collin said. "Move over here. Get behind me." As he said it, he knew it was impossible. She would have to cross right in front of Starklee to get to me. The man would stop her.

"What are you waiting for? Kill her, you fool!" screeched Byrd. Jacque punched him in the stomach.

Starklee looked at Collin. "Are you sure they'll take me into Lashai? If I leave, I never want to come back here. And Amatha. They'll take her too?"

"You'll never have to come back. They'll keep you both safe."

Starklee knelt and reached out to Amatha. She came to him, wrapped her tiny arms around him and sobbed into his neck. He hugged her and spoke in a low, soothing voice. "It's alright, Ama. I'll keep you safe, dear girl."

"Weird your guards never showed up," Jacque quipped turning back to Senator Byrd. "Maybe they're occupied with, I don't know, the escape of every single slave you were going to auction off."

Collin tapped Starklee and jerked his head toward the door. "Get her out of here. We're right behind you."

Starklee stood. "The Weaver bless you, Collin," he said to Collin's surprise.

"You follow the Weaver?"

"Not well, but yes."

"Can we finish this later? I'm seriously fighting the urge to end this idiot. The sooner we go, the better for everyone involved." Jacque kept his sword fixed on Byrd until everyone had shuffled past him and exited.

Collin paused; his blade joined Jacque's pointing at Byrd. "Where is Miriam? Tell us now, or I'll slit you straight up the middle. Of all the ways to go, that's not a pleasant one."

"She is with Lady Ella."

Collin looked at Jacque. "No, she isn't. Tell us the truth."

Byrd tried to seem unconcerned with the sword at his belly, but his glance kept dropping to it. "I swear. Miriam was part of a settlement for the Lady's silence. Hard to push through legislation to do away with slaves when you own them yourself."

Collin lowered his sword at last. "Fine. We'll look there. If she isn't, we're coming for you."

"I'll hold him here. Bring me along once you've reached the road," Jacque said.

Collin nodded and left without another word.

TWENTY-NINE
THE LAST

Collin squinted down the darkened road and spotted the silhouettes of a small group of people in the distance. He drew his sword. "Are you friend or foe?" he called.

"It depends. Did you bring anything to eat? I'm starving," shouted Sophie.

Collin sheathed his sword and twisted his ring. Jacque appeared at his side. "Ah! You called me in the nick of time. Forget stabbing. I was about to wring his head off."

Collin grinned. "They're just down the road."

"There's more than I expected. Who's that with them?" Jacque asked.

"I don't know. I hope no captives stayed behind."

They approached and saw Sacha and Sophie, safe and sound. Starklee and Amatha huddled to the side looking like they didn't belong.

Collin paused. Next to Sophie stood Hollis: arms crossed over his chest, feet wide apart, the look on his face annoyed, crossed with murderous.

"Good evening gentlemen," he said.

Collin felt like he was shrinking with each word. It occurred to him that he'd broken dozens of laws and killed people that Hollis would've disapproved of killing. And those kids. He was responsible for Titus dying. Tali's beautiful face was scarred forever because of him. "I can explain."

"Can you? Interesting."

"I'm sorry."

Hollis seemed to thaw slightly. "We found Miriam."

Collin gasped in shock. "Is she alright?"

"She is. She was treated quite well. You'll never guess who had her," said Hollis as though they were having a regular catch up.

Collin took a deep breath. "Lady Ella?"

Hollis nodded. "Lady Ella. How did you know?"

"Threatened to gut Senator Byrd if he didn't tell me. How did *you* know?"

"I'm a grown up. I used words," Hollis growled. Collin looked skeptical. "Fine. I threatened to bring the wrath of the Namarielle down on the Head of Senate if they didn't tell me."

Collin nodded. "That sounds more believable. Sorry about – everything. I was trying to help, but ends don't justify means."

Hollis gave him a look he could only interpret as understanding: the kind of look Julius might give him. "You've done alright, Collin."

"I've killed a lot of people," Collin muttered. "I also got a few good ones killed."

Hollis glanced at Sophie. "So I've heard. And I'm glad it still makes you sorry." Collin thought he saw a ghost of a smile on the older man's face. "I hear they tried to make you a gladiator."

"I was rubbish as a gladiator."

"Not from the information I obtained." This time Hollis looked at Starklee, who inclined his head slightly.

Collin let his face crack into a grin. He looked at the floor and steadied himself. "Is Miriam going back home?"

"She is."

The boy nodded. "Good. Am I going home?"

Hollis raised an eyebrow. "You can go home at some point. Elian wants you in Lashai first."

Jacque frowned. "He didn't mean for people to get hurt."

"It's fine Jacque. Does Elian know what I did?"

Hollis raised an eyebrow at Jacque then nodded. "He knows a little. I didn't know the extent until I arrived in the North. Sophie kept me posted. I believe Elian has a job for you. Miriam's dying to meet you. And there are the others who wish to see you as well."

"The others?"

Instead of clearing Collin's confusion, Hollis turned and began walking.

"Are we walking to Lashai?" Sophie asked. Hollis shot her a look and she threw her hands up defensively. "Not that I'm complaining. I like walking," she hastened to add.

HOLLIS HAD carriages waiting at the edge of town.

"Oh, thank the Weaver. My feet are so tired," Sophie said only loud enough for Collin to hear. He grinned.

"You're riding in this one, at least for the night," Hollis informed him, opening the door of the first carriage. "The rest of you go to the next." Hollis pointed to a much larger carriage behind them.

"Yes sir," Collin said, climbing into the dark, cramped space. He was greeted by a pair of arms wrapping around his torso.

"Thank you!" cried the hugger in an unsteady female voice.

"Er... you're welcome?"

"I'm Miriam, sir. They said you were responsible for getting me back to the mountains. They – they said you brought Josie home!" Miriam burst into tears. Collin patted her back as she cried into his tunic.

"Josie is home safe and very worried about you. She'll be so happy to see you," Collin said.

She finally released him and sat on the bench. "Please sit and be comfortable, sir."

"Please call me Collin. I'm thrilled to meet you, Miriam. Gosh, you look like Josie." Collin managed to squeeze himself onto the bench and when he looked across to the other, he felt a wave of relief wash over him unlike any he'd felt since coming to the North.

Two girls sat in the semi-darkness, but their wide smiles were just visible. Brenna giggled and elbowed Ayla. "Hello Collin."

"Thank the Weaver, you're both safe."

"Our family's village was plundered before we arrived. We hid there for a while, hoping maybe the bad people wouldn't come back," Brenna explained. "For a few days, it was quiet, then –" Her voice choked off and she couldn't continue.

Ayla put her arm around Brenna. "Then Senator Byrd's men came. They knew our aunt lived there and figured we'd seek shelter with her."

"Senator Byrd is as horrible as they say. He was going to keep both of us. When he left, he left his large man in charge of keeping us. Then a man came with bow and arrows and said he'd kill the large man. He released us. The man with the arrows isn't as frightening as he seems at first though. He's kind."

Collin couldn't help but smile at this. "He can be. Are you heading to Lashai with us?"

"I'm going home. They're coming with you," said Miriam. "Hollis says this carriage will go to the mountains when we get to the River Kai."

THE COMPANIONS SPENT an enjoyable week traveling back to Lashai in relative comfort. Breaking away from Miriam at the river was hard. Collin felt like his last connection to Josie was leaving with her. She cried when she hugged him and thanked him over and over for tearing apart the North Country to find her.

Hollis and Starklee spent long hours in discussion of the politics of their situation. It reminded Collin of the argument he'd overheard with Senator Byrd. He wondered if he should mention it to Hollis. It had sounded like they were speaking about Lashai. He never had a moment alone with the Kiatri, however, and he decided the news would keep until he could tell Elian as well.

The younger group chattered nonstop about their adventures. Recapping and explaining parts the others hadn't been involved in, then enjoying the retelling of the more thrilling escapades.

They entered Lashai through the North Gate, which Collin liked as much as the first time he'd seen it. The lesser used gate of Lashai was overgrown with vines and some of the stones of the archway were chipped, but rather than looking neglected or forgotten, it seemed hidden and sacred.

The closer they drew to the Great Castle, the more his stomach knotted. Hollis gave him little information about Elian's reaction to Collin's time in the North Land, and his anxiety grew up to the moment they entered the Great Castle.

"Jacque, you and Collin will share a room on the second floor in the north corridor. Take your things up and get settled in. The king wants to speak to Collin first. I'm sure he'll send for you all later."

"I'm going in now," Sacha announced and disappeared through the doors to the sitting room without further comment.

Collin's shock was reflected in Sophie's expression. "What on earth?" she gasped.

"Sacha's his brother. Give them a moment and we'll follow. Sophie, not you."

"I'm family too!" Sophie burst out.

"It won't take but a moment. We'll call for you," Hollis said softly.

"What do you think Elian will do to me?" Collin asked as he rocked back and forth on his heels.

Hollis shrugged. "He didn't say. Your rampage through the North cost him dearly. I'm sure he'll work out an equitable consequence."

Collin was glad for a reason to pace and stretch his legs. Several days journey sitting in a carriage had left him restless and aching to move. Hollis offered no ease for his conscience. Collin was almost relieved Elian was seeing him tonight. At least he could get the worst over quickly.

"Collin!" Cassai's voice felt like balm to all his sore places. She beamed from the tall door to the sitting room.

"Hey, Cassai," he said with a grin. She flew into his arms and he hugged her tightly. He hadn't realized how tall he'd grown until she was swallowed in his embrace.

"Look at you. What did they feed you at that Elythium? You've grown six inches at least."

Collin pulled away to look at her as well. Her usually unruly hair shone in soft curls around her face and down her back. A circlet of gold sat on top of her head.

She glowed like a fairy light. "I am so glad to see you all in one piece. We got so many angry reports from the Light Ones, I feared they'd reduce you to ash before we could get you out."

Collin laughed and scooped her into his arms again. "You know me. Always making new friends in high places."

"Hello, Collin." Elian's voice sounded soft and welcoming.

Collin gave Cassai a final squeeze and straightened. "Hello,

Elian," he said to the Fontre who seemed to take up the entire doorway. "Er – your Majesty?"

Elian rolled his eyes. "Just Elian. How are you, my friend?"

"A little sore from the journey. But good. Alive."

Elian's smile grew. "Alive is good. We are so happy to see you. Come in, please. There's so much to talk about. Where's Jacque?"

Hollis shrugged. "I told him he needed to wait. He gets a little riled up about Collin. I thought you'd like to speak with Collin alone first."

Elian smiled at Sophie from the other side of the door. "We'll be right back," he promised.

She huffed and crossed her arms.

Hollis followed the group into the large, comfortable sitting room. Collin felt a pang as he looked around this room. In his last memory of this place, Devilan had lain on a couch bleeding to death. The room had been rearranged since then. That couch was nowhere in sight. Sacha lounged on an overstuffed sofa in front of the fireplace, the baby they'd carried and protected through the war was now a chubby toddler. She sat on Sacha's stomach, giggling and playing with a wooden ball. He grinned and wiggled his fingers at Collin when he entered.

"Hey Anaya," Collin said. The toddler squealed and whipped her head toward the sound of Collin's voice. A halo of curls bounced on top of her head as she laughed and clapped her hands.

"Naomi," Sacha reminded him.

"Right," Collin remembered they'd met the baby's mother and learned her real name after the war. At the sound of Collin's voice, Naomi's head whipped toward him.

Elian broke into his thoughts, wrapping him in a tight hug, which Collin returned. "I'm sorry, Elian."

Elian pulled away and gripped Collin's shoulders. "Good lord, how you've grown. Why are you sorry?"

"I...people got hurt. I caused a lot of trouble and expense. I thought I was doing the right thing, but it ended up...I just..."

"Upset the established order?"

Collin nodded. He wished Elian would release him. The man's intense blue eyes were difficult to look into.

"You did that once before as well. It must be habit forming." Elian didn't look upset. "We're working on the situation in the North. It's complicated, but because of you, possibly not as much as before."

"What did I do?"

"You've exposed the people of the North lands to the ugliness that permeates their way of life. Because of what you did, Lady Ella has been restored to the Senate and the good graces of the people. More and more contact her every day demanding answers to the institution of human trafficking."

Collin's mouth gaped. "Are you serious?"

"Slavery is far from over, but I'm quite serious. Several Elythium Omiliti have resigned in protest at new legislation intended to emancipate the *malderones*."

"But Lady Ella had them herself. She had Miriam all along."

"Miriam was being used as a pawn in Senator Byrd's political game. Lady Ella took Miriam as a parting gift to stay in her home and keep quiet about her thoughts on the new deal with the Kiatri. Byrd thought he'd be able to use Miriam against Lady Ella at some point. How could she protest when she herself owned a member of the Ageless Race?"

Collin's stomach roiled. "I hate him."

"He's deeply unlikeable," Elian said, grinning. "Come, sit and tell us all about what happened to you."

Collin related the adventures of him and his companions since they came to the North. Elian, Cassai and Hollis listened silently to his tale, reacting to the scary and sad bits exactly as he hoped they would. When he finished, he sat back on the deep cushions and breathed. It was good to get the whole story out at once.

"I'm proud of you," Elian said.

Collin's eyes welled with tears and his chest ached. "You are? Wow."

"I've always been proud of you."

Collin nodded and tried to fight back his emotions. "Thank you, Elian. Um…Hollis said you had a job for me?"

Elian looked like Collin had interrupted a deep thought. "I do if you're up for it. Not really a job, but another journey. Sophie is off on some sort of quest to the South."

"The South?"

Elian and Hollis exchanged a look Collin didn't understand. "To Dukai," Elian clarified.

"But…isn't Dukai a wasteland?"

Hollis wiped his hand down his face, clearly agitated. "She claims it's not. He told her there's colonies there."

"He?" Collin asked.

"Malcolm," Elian and Hollis grumbled in unison.

Collin's eyebrows shot up. He looked at Sacha, who was taking the ball from Naomi when she tried to chew on it, looking supremely unconcerned. Cassai smirked.

"What are you asking me to do?" Collin's hands clenched in fists he didn't mean to make.

Elian looked at Hollis, who leaned forward like he was making Collin a deal. "Go with her and keep her out of trouble," Hollis said.

"Me? Keep Sophie out of trouble? Are you mad?" Collin yelped.

"Keep Mal off her," Elian reworded.

Collin shook his head at them and scooted farther down the couch in his discomfort. "No. I'm not messing with Sophie and Mal. No way. Mal's the worst."

Sacha chuckled. "Also, it's her life and none of your business." He handed the ball back to Naomi and missed the glare Elian shot him.

"Of course, it's her life."

"Kiatri cannot involve themselves with mortals of natural lifespans," Hollis growled at Sacha.

"Ha! 'Mortals of natural life spans?'" Sacha sneered. "I suppose she should take up with a fairy then, eh?"

Collin's eyes widened at Sacha's nerve. Hollis jumped to his feet, both fists clenched at his sides. "Listen to me, boy. I can easily rip you limb from limb, or worse, I'll go to the kitchen and break your favorite spatula." He delivered this threat with a perfectly straight face, but Collin had to work hard not to laugh and risk getting himself killed.

Sacha shifted Naomi to the floor and rose, still calm. "You should let her be. She has centuries to be sad and broody. And if you touch my spatula, your lifespan won't be worth the paper it's written on."

Hollis glowered, but Elian stood as well and put a hand on the Kiatri's shoulder. "Let him be, Hollis. Collin, will you at least consider the trip?"

Collin stood and shoved his hands into his pockets. Sacha's calmness in the face of Hollis' rage had given him courage. "I'll go with her if she wants. But her love life is off limits. If she's fool enough to fall for a guy like Mal, it's none of my business, or yours."

"I told you we should have had him flogged," Hollis muttered to Elian.

Elian sighed and shook his head. "I've seen him flogged before. It's considerably less satisfying than you'd think."

Collin frowned. "Really? Exactly how satisfying did you think it would be?"

Sophie burst into the room at that moment holding a piece of parchment. "Hey, Collin, the post beat us here. You've got a letter from some bloke named Hermann."

Collin perked up. "What's he say?"

"'Dear Borderling, Found them. Thanks again.' I assume you know what that means?" Sophie asked.

Collin whooped and surprised her with a hug. "Yes! Thank the Weaver. At least something worked out. He was one of the men we freed at the auction. He's got his wife and daughter back."

Sophie laughed at his unexpected affection. "Great. You can let me go now."

"Sorry. Hey, Soph. I hear you're going on a trek. Want some company?" Collin asked, still unable to contain his glee at the happy news.

Sophie gave him a searching look, then glanced suspiciously from Hollis to Elian. "Why?"

Collin resisted the urge to look at the men for help. Instead, he stuffed his hands in his pockets and shrugged. "Just for fun."

Her smile made him wonder if she truly believed this. "Of course. I thought you'd never ask."

He grinned. "Good. Now let's see if there's anything to eat in this dump. I'm starving."

Sacha laughed and tucked a giggling Naomi under his arm like a sack of potatoes. "Oh, there is. I have it on good authority Da's been cooking all week."

Sophie flipped her long, black hair over her shoulder and left the room without another word.

Collin took a deep breath as Elian approached him. The larger man patted him on the shoulder. "Very smooth, Collin."

"If you really thought she wouldn't figure out your game, you don't know her at all."

The End

PRONUNCIATION GUIDE

Character Guide

Namarielle (Nuh-MAR-ee-ell)
   Cassai (Kuh-SY)

Fontre (Fahn-TRAY)
   Elian (El-ee-uhn)
   Kirkus (Kirk – US)
   Sacha (Sah – SHU)
   Devilan (Dev – LAN)
   Mattius (Matt – EE – us)
   Ffastian (Fast-CHE-an)
   Madeline (MAD – uh – line)

Fairy
   Theoris (Thee-OR-is)
   Lily (Lil-ee)
   Goliard (GO-lee-yard)
   Dahlia (Dah – lee – yah)

Light Ones

    Jacque (JAH-k)

    Nihl (Nile)

    Laurelle (Lau- ELLE)

    Marcole (MARK – ole)

Kiatri (Kee-AH-tree)

    Hollis (HOL – is)

    Sophie (SOF – ee)

    AJ (AJ)

    Alex (AL – ex)

    Lukkas (Loo – KUS)

ACKNOWLEDGMENTS

As we writers always say, books don't happen with just one small person in a room with a window and desk. That's the way they start, but they end up being a collaboration of lots of people's thoughts, encouragement and love.

Thank you to my husband who views writing as actual work and makes sure there is space in my life to do it. I love you so much. And thank you to my kids who also pretend that my writing is deeply important. You are all my favorites. Forever.

To my Marble Falls family and friends, the biggest thanks in the world for reading my books, hyping my books, supporting my books and all around, being amazing about them.

To Julia, my favorite editor in the world, we've been together a while now, friend. You are still just as wonderful as before.

To Tricia Anson, my proofreader who keeps me from looking dumb in front of my friends, thanks so much! You have things the hardest.

JOIN THE FIGHT

Slavery is more prevalent now than it's ever been. Join the fight to end it by visiting the following websites and of course, if you see something, say something:

National human trafficking hotline: 1 (888) 373-7888
    Humantraffickinghotline.org

Antislavery.org
    Enditmovement.com
    Endslaverynow.org
    Fairworldproject.org
    Fiercefreedom.org
    Foodnavigator.com
    Slavefreechocolate.org
    Thegoodtrade.com
    21 Wilberforce